BURN
FOR ME

SARA CATE

Editing: Briggs Consulting and Rebecca's Fairest Reviews

Proofreading: Rumi Khan

Cover model: Cole S.

Photographer: Wander Aguiar

Caution

This is a dark, bully romance with explicit content that may be triggering to some readers, including dub-con, abuse, mention of suicide, human trafficking, and murder. Cullen Ayers is covered in red flags, and I do not in any way condone his behavior. He comes from a dark place, and in many ways represents the loss, rage, and helpless grief that so many of us experience. It doesn't excuse the awful ways he treats people, but the bigger the bully, the better the redemption.

For Rachel
For being the best.

Prologue
Everly

Eight years ago

My hands are shaking in my lap. This is it. After months of research, and my life being turned upside down, I'm finally sitting here in the courtroom, my parents and friends behind me, waiting to watch the judge sentence the monster I helped put behind bars.

This all started out as a graduate project. As part of my internship at the *Florence Times*, I had to write an investigative piece on a local, someone from our city. I had no idea what I would find when I started digging into what I thought was only a little under the table tax fraud at the Ayers' hotel chain.

What I actually uncovered was a major human-trafficking operation that spanned the globe. George Ayers was responsible for kidnapping, displacing, and harboring thousands of underage women. And he made millions off it. Once the FBI took the case after only a couple months, it was out of my hands, but as far as the world saw it, I was the one who brought this giant down. A real-life David and Goliath.

My best friend, Thomas, is sitting next to me, grasping my hands to hide the way they are trembling. I don't know why I'm nervous. I'm not afraid of George Ayers, but something just isn't settling right. I feel a strange sense of guilt, although I know that's insane. I've done nothing wrong. In fact, I've done everything *right,* and yet, there's a dense weight on my heart, as if *I'm* the one on trial.

The courtroom doors suddenly open and a man in black ushers in a red-faced Mrs. Ayers. Bombshell blonde and about twenty-years younger than her husband, Valerie Ayers looks the part of a woman grieving the loss of her fortune far more than the loss of her husband, which is clearly shown in the way she clutches the pearls around her neck as she takes her seat.

Like a shadow, her ten-year-old son trails in with an almost smug grin. There's something about that boy that sends chills down my spine. Throughout this entire case, and even before, he has appeared so incredibly confident and haughty, as if he somehow believed his father would win this case. By his expression alone, you can just tell Cullen Ayers believes he is superior to everyone. Maybe it's those blue eyes beneath those dark brows and the jet-black hair that appears all wrong to me, but he just unsettles me.

As he sits next to his mother on the opposite side of the aisle from me, I can't help but glance his way every few moments. It's not lost on me how every time I look at them, the foreboding sense of guilt aches a little sharper.

The voice in my head tells me they are not innocent in this. I refuse to believe she had no idea what was going on. With their mansion and their money, they have reaped the benefits from the suffering of thousands. They don't deserve the clothes on their backs, and I hope they suffer once that man is in prison. I realize he's only ten and had absolutely no way of abetting in this crime, but there is just something about him that tells me he is just as evil as his father. I know it's an awful thing to think, but that boy has spent his entire life knowing no hardship, no struggle, no pain.

I want Valerie and her son to know pain now.

Just then, Cullen's ghostly blue eyes travel my way, and I freeze. It hits me at this moment that I'm not just bringing down George, but I'm bringing down Cullen too. He's an heir to the throne of a monster, and if things hadn't changed, he would be the next George Ayers, victimizing innocent people for his own personal gain. There is something sinister in his eyes, and I can't take that away, but I can strip him of his power, which is what I'm doing today.

I know Cullen Ayers hates me, judging by the look in his eyes, but I don't blame him. I've taken everything from him, and I regret nothing.

Chapter 1
Everly

A HORDE of students start filing into their seats about five minutes before the actual start of class. My hands are shaking as I open my laptop, trying to appear as natural as possible, even though I could literally throw up at any moment. In my smooth black dress, belted at the waist, and covered with a rich green cardigan, I attempt to look the professor-type.

This is my first class at Florence University, and with all of those faces peering down at me from the ten rows in the lecture hall, I'm starting to rethink this decision. I needed a fresh start, something other than a writing job at another publication. Instead of trying to constantly live up to the peak of my journalism career, I figured teaching at the local college would be the change I desperately needed.

After the big Ayers case, I thought my career would soar in journalism. Instead, it would seem the peak was behind me, and I was on a downhill slope. I spent the next eight years trying to attain that career high again only to fall flat on my face. Nothing ever compared, so my life became an endless cycle of seeking perfection only to find disappointment.

So, I took the professor job, a decision my parents who are both teachers were ecstatic about. But I can't seem to shake the feeling that this career move was my way of accepting defeat.

My phone buzzes in my bag, and I quickly take a peek, seeing a message pop up from my dating app.

Devon: See you tonight!

Another wave of dread crashes over me. Why I chose the first day of class as the same day to have a first date, with a guy I have very lukewarm feelings about, I have no idea. Oh well, I'll deal with that later. There's still a chance this entire day could be a major win instead of a complete disaster—although I'm not holding my breath.

The seats fill up fast, and I make myself look busy by scanning through my updated roster list again. Last I checked, there was only one empty spot in my Journalism 101 class. But as I hit refresh again, I notice the number goes from 199 to 200 students. Looks like we had a late registration. I feel a sense of pride at having my first class fill up so quickly.

Running through the list of names again, a familiar one catches my attention. It's a new name, definitely wasn't on the roster when I checked it last night.

Ayers.

A chill runs down my spine. I'd know that name anywhere. Eight years ago, my first investigative article, a thesis for my master's program, made headlines. My discovery for that piece contributed to a major federal investigation against George Ayers, a multi-millionaire hotel chain owner, who was convicted of running an underground, black-market, human-trafficking scheme.

It was huge news at the time. Not only did it launch a federal investigation, but it put my name on the map as far as up-and-comers in the industry were concerned—a high I've been chasing ever since.

Of course, I would have an Ayers in my first journalism class.

My curiosity gets the better of me and has me clicking on the name, just as class is supposed to begin. I wonder if I would recognize this specific Ayers or if there is any family connection. They were local to the area, so it wouldn't be that surprising.

And at first, I assume it's a distant cousin or something.

Ayers, Cullen.

It seems like time stops altogether as my eyes remain fixated on that name. Suddenly, blood rushes to the skin of my cheeks and my heart runs wildly in my chest, until all I can hear, aside from the white noise chatter of the two hundred students around me, is the acceleration of my breath.

The memory comes crashing to the forefront of my mind—a young boy with sable black hair, tan skin, and haunting crystal blue eyes staring viciously at me in the courtroom as his father is carted away in handcuffs, after being sentenced to thirty years in a federal prison. Cullen was only...what, ten at the time?

Still staring at the screen, I feel the eyes of the crowd of students waiting for me to begin class, and suddenly I've lost all train of thought, all power to think of anything other than the fact that in this very classroom my past is colliding with my present.

Is Cullen here? Is he looking at me right now? Does he remember me?

It must be a coincidence. I guess he would be college-aged now, but in my mind, he's still just a little kid. Most people have forgotten about that case by now. News dies as quickly as it arrives. And the whole point of taking this job was to move on from the past, but how can I move on when it's sitting right here in my journalism class?

When I finally gather the courage to look up, I'm overwhelmed by the number of faces peering down at me. Sure, a lot of them are still glued to their phones or laptops, but about half of them seem to be waiting for me to start class. I scan the crowd for a moment, looking for his face, but none of them stand out. Eight years have gone by, and I assume he's gone through puberty since I've seen him last, so there's a chance I wouldn't recognize him at all.

Knowing that I need to start class, I clear my throat and force a smile on my face. I lean back against my desk and say as clearly as I can, "Good morning, and welcome to Journalism 101. My name is Everly West, and I will be your instructor this semester. You can call me Miss West."

The mic attached to the neckline of my dress picks up my voice, carrying it through the room. It also picks up the shake and erratic cadence of my breath, so everyone is keenly aware of how nervous I am. Perfect.

Moving around to the other side of my desk, I click the button on my computer that brings up the presentation, mirrored on the wall behind me for the class to see.

I quickly go through the whole class portal and the syllabus, trying hard not to bore them to death, but it's not easy. This stuff isn't exactly riveting. All the while, I keep my eyes on the crowd, waiting to find those familiar blue orbs I remember from eight years ago.

For the most part, my nerves soon subside, and I fall into an easy rhythm. A few students ask questions, there's a little back and forth banter, and I even manage to crack a couple small jokes that have most of them chuckling. So far, it's not terrible.

As I scroll through the PowerPoint presentation of what I've accomplished as a journalist, and what is expected of them in my course, my heart practically stops in my chest as the slide freezes on a photo of me holding the paper with the headline I wrote when I was just twenty-four: "Ayers Under Investigation for Trafficking Scandal, Faces Thirty Years."

And right under the headline is a photo of him in handcuffs, while his family looks on in horror. I swallow the bundle of nerves that has manifested like concrete in my throat as I try to find the guts to keep talking.

"This was a photo taken with my first big article in the *Florence Times*," I manage to stammer. "Being an investigative journalist is about more than just writing the story. You have to...find the story, and sometimes finding the story means uncovering secrets and crimes no one ever knew were even committed."

"What a hero," a dark voice mutters from the crowd. My eyes dart up to the rows of students, searching for the speaker, but there is no sign of where it came from. But that was him. It had to be, even though I still don't see him, scanning each head for that mop of pitch-black hair.

I could respond to the remark, but I really don't want to get into that argument here in front of everyone. So instead, I choose to ignore it.

After taking a deep breath, I continue, "You will be required in this course to write your own piece of investigative journalism after doing research and compiling it into an expository article. This will be in place of the final exam at the end of the semester. The rubric can be found in your syllabus."

I hate how uncertain I sound. One kid has me completely unsettled. I feel the need to defend myself and my job, especially to my students—some of whom could actually be journalists someday. I was just doing my job. It's not like I was the one committing the crime, so I'm not going to feel bad about it. Even though I still sort of do.

After the quick mental pep talk, I square my shoulders and finish my first lecture, without another ominous remark from the crowd. Before I know it, class time is up, and I dismiss them with their first assignment.

The room erupts in noise as all two hundred college students begin filing out of the lecture hall. With my back to the seats, I busy myself for the next few moments with making notes on my computer. After about ten minutes, I glance back and see one student's still sitting in the corner of the top row. It's a male with bleach-blond hair.

"I'll be closing up the room in a moment," I announce casually, spinning around to face him. At first, I thought he was asleep, but then I notice he's just staring down at his phone. There is no backpack or laptop on his desk.

His head snaps up in my direction, and he's so far away I can't quite make out his face yet, but as he stands and walks slowly down the stairs toward me, my heart nearly stops in my chest.

Those baby blue eyes under dark brows make it hard to breathe.

It's him.

He reaches the bottom of the stairs, standing just a few feet away from me in complete silence, so all I hear is the distant chatter of the crowd outside the room.

"Can I help you with something?" I say, keeping the tremor out of my voice. I'm just going to pretend I don't know who he is. Maybe he'll do the same, and we can both get through this semester unscathed and without any awkward confrontations.

It's clear why I didn't recognize him. For one, he's not ten years old anymore. He's tall with a lean frame, sculpted shoulders, and thick forearms. His once black hair is bleached to a stark white with dark roots, and there is a piercing on his lower lip and right brow. It's a far cry from the rich, preppy schoolboy I saw all those years ago.

That little boy is now a man, and he's standing just in front of me, feeling like less than a stranger, but far from a friend.

Part of me wonders if I should say something about the case or his father or the giant fucking elephant in the room, but I don't. I can't. What could I possibly say to him now?

Oh hey, I remember you. I put your father away for your entire life. How's your mom? Oh yeah, I forgot—she over-dosed on pain meds less than a year after that court case we were both at. So...how've ya been?

Hard pass on that conversation.

I keep waiting for him to say something, but he doesn't. He stalks toward me without a word and no sign of stopping until he's finally crowding me, and I'm forced to move away from him. I stumble backward until I'm pinned between him and my desk, having to rear my head back to see the cocky expression on his face. I'm rendered speechless. Alarms are going off in my head. Should I alert security? Is this going to be an issue? Would he *hurt* me?

"What are you doing?" I whisper, once he's standing so close that I can feel his breath on my face.

I'm about to die. My brain registers the danger, and my mouth goes dry. Then, because he's standing so close, I can smell the clean aroma of the soap he used this morning. I also notice how long his lashes are and the perfect contrast of his lips against his warm, sun-kissed skin.

Jesus, Everly. He's eighteen. What the fuck is wrong with you?

Right as I'm about to say something, he leans closer, stealing every thought from my head. Oh fuck, is he about to...*kiss me?*

But he doesn't. Instead, his eyes glare intensely into mine, and he squints ever so slightly. I hear something land against the desk behind me. He just dropped something there without me noticing, but he's still so close I can't even turn around to see what it is.

As he finally pulls away, leaving me gasping for breath, he shoots me a sinister smile and winks. Then, without a word, he turns away and walks out the door. My gaze follows him in his tight black jeans and black T-shirt that hugs the muscles around his shoulders. I can't seem to move, so I stand there for a long time, just waiting for my heart to calm to a normal rhythm.

What the fuck just happened?

Turning around, I see what he left on my desk. It's an orange pill bottle.

What the...

Picking it up, my blood runs cold when I read the name on the label.

Valerie Ayers

The prescription is for Oxy, and I immediately drop the bottle on the floor as I read it. The Ayers family was in the paper twice that year. The first time for George going to prison and the second was for his wife, thirty-three-year-old Valerie, overdosing on her pain medication and dying in her sleep where her only son found her the next morning.

The doctors ruled it an accidental death, but the

community knew the truth. After the family lost their business, their wealth, their reputation, and their inheritance, she quickly became addicted to pills and killed herself, just days before they were supposed to be evicted from their million-dollar home.

I never blamed myself for what happened to George, but reading about Valerie's death shook me. It was hard not to feel responsible for it. I never really thought much about Cullen.

But I guess he was thinking about me.

Chapter 2
Cullen

Fuck, the restaurant is dead tonight. Wednesday nights are usually pretty lame anyway. Everyone is still trying to be responsible and eat at home. No one goes on dates on Wednesdays either. I only have two tables, both families, and they're both lingering on their phones with their to-go boxes getting colder by the minute. They'll probably tip like shit, too.

It doesn't help that I'm in a sour mood tonight after my first day at Florence U. Today took an unexpected turn for sure. It all started at eight a.m. when my advisor informed me that I was missing a critical writing block in my schedule, a block I needed to fill if I wanted to keep my stupid fucking scholarship. So there I was, bright and early in her office, scrambling for anything that would fit. I had no idea Everly West would be teaching a class, but lucky me. The second I saw her name on the screen, I had to do some shuffling in my schedule to fit her class in, because I mean...how could I miss that? It was a fucking sign.

It's been eight years since that woman fucked up my life, and I never really considered myself much of a revenge kind of guy, but then I saw her standing up at the front of that lecture hall. With her perfect little cardigan and her prissy-bitch attitude, I hated her instantly. I haven't been planning revenge on Everly West—fuck, before today, I couldn't have cared less about her. But I've never forgotten her face in the courtroom, looking smug as fuck like she had accomplished something. She was so damn proud of herself. There wasn't an ounce of remorse on her face for what she did to my family, stripping away everything in my life until I was left with literally nothing.

The pill bottle was a last-minute decision. I had just enough time before class to run back to my dorm and get it. And honestly, up until the moment I dropped it on her desk, I didn't know what I had planned. I imagined an argument, maybe a pity party I would throw to make her feel like shit. I wanted *something* on me that I could show her to make it all real for her. Like if she saw the pill bottle my mother used to end her own miserable existence, she would finally understand what she did.

It was a touch dramatic. I know.

But tormenting her on her first day wouldn't have been complete without a little present. It wasn't a death threat or anything, but fuck, I hope she takes it that way.

It's her fault my life is a shitshow now.

If only that stupid scholarship covered all of my other living expenses, so I didn't have to wait tables like a fucking tool bag just to pay the bills. If there was any other job I could do with flexible hours and a decent pay, I would.

At least this job gets me laid more than most. Customers, waitresses. Fuck, I got a quick BJ from the wine distributer last month. It sure helps take the edge off, and I guess that's not a perk I'd be getting if I was flipping burgers or driving a garbage truck.

What would dear old Dad think of me now?

Not that I give a shit. I wrote that asshole off years ago, when he fucked this whole family and left my mother a penniless mess.

Standing by the soda fountain, I'm watching the door, hoping Gina puts the next group in my section, so I stand a chance of actually making it worth even coming in tonight, when a familiar face walks through the door.

You've got to be fucking kidding me.

A certain petite brunette steps through the door and right up to the hostess stand with an uncomfortable smile on her face. Behind her, a man with brown hair, a high forehead, and glasses walks in, placing a hand on her shoulder just as he holds up two fingers at Gina. She grabs the menus and I say a little prayer.

Please don't put them in my section.

Sure as shit, she walks right over to the booth by the window, and I grimace. What the fuck are the odds she would come into my restaurant tonight? She probably told her ugly boyfriend all about the pills and the nightmare student in her class. Now I have no choice but to walk over there and greet them. Shit is about to get real awkward.

As much as I would love to cause a scene just to humiliate her, I cannot afford to lose this job. Gina smiles at me as she walks back to the hostess stand. The little bitch thinks she's doing me a favor.

I watch discreetly from a distance as Everly and her date browse their menus, and I catch the way he looks over the top of his as if he's sizing her up. She sends him a polite but unnatural smile.

Holy shit, they're on a first date. I can spot a seasoned couple over a first date any day of the week. It's one of the easier skills I've learned as a waiter at an Italian restaurant.

Established couples spend less time actually talking to each other and more time on their phones. First dates sneak looks at each other when they think the other person isn't looking, and there's a *lot* of awkward silence.

These two are definitely on their first date.

Taking a deep breath, I make my way over to the table. The dude looks up first, giving me a wry smile, probably a little freaked out by my appearance: tattoos up my neck, piercings on my face, and unnatural white hair. But I don't give a shit about what he thinks. That's why I did it in the first place. To make guys like my asshole father uncomfortable.

It's her I'm looking at anyway. I don't want to miss the expression on her face when she sees me, and fuck is it worth it. She's too busy browsing the wine list when I lean over her shoulder, getting as close as possible as I whisper, "Anything catching your eye?"

She jolts with a gasp and finally does look up at me. Her eyes widen as she stares. There's a flinch in her posture, and she leans back like I'm going to hit her or something. Then, she glances around, probably hoping I actually work here and I'm not just randomly showing up to torment her.

On the outside, I'm keeping my professional, polite face on, but inside, I'm dying laughing. A minute ago, I dreaded having her in my section, but now as I watch her squirm with nervousness, I'm delighted. This is so damn perfect.

"Good evening. Welcome to Valentino's. What can I get for you to drink tonight?" I ask with a big fake smile plastered on my face.

"Um..." Everly stutters, unable to take her eyes off me. Then she suddenly realizes she's supposed to be acting natural and she looks at her date. "Want to share a bottle of red?"

"I don't drink," he replies in a nasally tone.

Everly's nostrils flare as she forces a smile. "That's okay. I'll have a glass of red, then."

"Sure thing. Can I see your ID, please?" I ask.

She swallows, clearly uncomfortable as she pulls out her license. I love carding people, and policy says we have to card everyone, but it just makes me laugh how I'm not even old enough to drink (legally) and I'm making them prove to me they are. It's even funnier because I know for a fact Everly is over twenty-one. If I had to do the math, based on the fact that she was a senior in college eight years ago, I'd guess she's about thirty-two now.

And she's not bad-looking for a woman in her thirties. I don't age discriminate—I've been with ladies her age. And if she wasn't such a heinous bitch, I'd probably hit that.

Taking her card, I smirk at the picture, and not because it's ugly. She's actually kind of cute in her washed-out DMV mugshot with her blunt brown bangs and shoulder-length hair, but I smirk because I know she's hating every second of this. Then, I take a quick look at her address, and I don't even know why.

541 Sycamore St.

Of course she lives on Sycamore. I can just imagine the street, with those quaint renovated craftsman-style homes in a totally hipster part of town, where the food trucks park and the rich assholes walk their Goldendoodles. I hope she enjoys it, while I'm scraping by, living on leftovers from the restaurant and ramen noodles in my shoebox dorm room I have to share with two other guys.

Next, I peek at her birthdate. Doing the math quickly in my head, I mentally pat myself on the back. I hit the nail on the head—she's thirty-two.

"Everything all right?" the guy asks when I get lost staring at her driver's license for a moment too long.

"Yep, sorry." I hand her back her card, letting my gaze linger on her face for a moment. *I know where you live now.* It's like she can read my mind because her expression is laced with fear, and I love it.

It's not like I'm going to fucking hurt her. I'm not a psychopath, but it feels like the universe just keeps dropping me these little gifts. It might be fun to tease her a little bit. I'd like to make her hate my fucking guts, and that thought really gets me excited.

After getting their drink orders, I watch them from the bar as she tries to act normal through their awkward conversation. Fuck, I'm never dating. It looks terrible.

Gina steps up next to me while I'm waiting for the bartender to pour the red wine. "Cullen, are you coming to my place tonight? A few other servers are stopping by after work. We got the good stuff from last weekend."

By good stuff, I know she is referring to the Blue Dream we smoked over the weekend, and I admit, it was a fucking dream, but I can't afford that shit anymore. I didn't eat on Sunday because I spent my last dime on that. If she didn't have a boyfriend, I'd offer her sex in return, but I don't need to get into it with him.

"Nah, I'm good. Thanks, though."

"You sure?" she asks, leaning forward a little and shooting me a wink. I hate how she flirts with me—but only at work. It's so fucking obvious.

"Go home to your boyfriend, Gina," I reply as I take the wine and walk toward the table.

The rest of their dinner is uneventful, and I love watching her chew the inside of her lip as she pokes around her pasta dish, like I planted a bug or a piece of glass in it. I didn't do shit to her food. I'm not fucking twelve.

And their date looks like torture, anyway. Every time I pass, he's talking about himself, and she's struggling to appear interested. If he gets in her pants tonight, it would be a fucking miracle, because she looks like an ice princess sitting across from him.

To pass the time, I imagine ways I could make Everly's life hell, and it surprises me how good it feels. I have every intention of staying in her class, and I wasn't planning on being very nice to her to begin with, but now I feel like this is a sign that I need to do more. It feels downright diabolical when I think about it, but diabolical feels *good*.

Sure, I could let it all go, water under the bridge and all that, but there is something about this woman that entices me to torture her. She looks like the kind of person who considers herself tough and independent, and it makes me want to ruffle her feathers even more. Fuck, I think I'm almost turned on by the mere idea of her torment.

I end up bringing her two more glasses of wine, which he pays for in the end, and I notice the look of disapproval on his face when she asks for the last one. Can't say I blame her there. I'd need to be drunk to get through a night with him too.

As they get up to leave, I watch from across the restaurant as she follows him to the door. She manages one quick glance in my direction before leaving, and I send her a sly wink and a mischievous smile. It's at that moment that I realize I hate her more than I've hated anyone. Old feelings of childlike anger surge through me as if I've spent the last eight years of my life with this dormant resentment waiting to be reawakened. The only difference between the way I feel now and the way I felt at ten is that I used to hate her for what she did to my family—but now, as I watch her sulk out the door in misery, I realize I hate her for how pathetic she is.

The woman in that courtroom all those years ago had fire and passion in her expression. She despised my father and took pride in being a part of his downfall. She was a spitfire, full of angst and hate. But now, this woman I've seen twice today, is just...sad. And I want to hurt her even more for that.

Once she's gone, I feel almost bored. Hating Everly West was something fun to do. Even though I didn't really do anything to her, at least it was nice to have somewhere to focus my energy.

The idea is more and more enticing as I think about it. I'm going to make Everly West's life hell, and I am going to love every fucking minute of it.

Chapter 3
Everly

I CAN'T GET out of my car. It's Friday, which means my Journalism 101 students meet today. Which, of course, also means I have to face Cullen Ayers again.

I haven't seen him since he waited on my date and me Wednesday night, which had to have been one of the world's worst first dates. Okay, maybe not the world's worst, but it was definitely a waste of a good evening. Devon, the software engineer from Vermont, spent the majority of our date talking about himself. He had terrible breath, bad manners, and tried to correct my *accurate* grammar. At the end of the evening, he drove me home and actually reached across the center console to grab my leg when he thought he deserved a kiss. I told him to fuck off and walked away. On any other day, I might have actually kept my cool and wished him a good night instead, but he caught me on a very bad day.

I hate dating. I was never the kind of woman to care about attention from guys. I had a career and goals, and like everything else in my life, I was too focused on perfection, and no one ever measured up. Now that I'm in my thirties and the clock could not be ticking any louder, I find myself dating out of my comfort zone, letting them get away with stuff I never would have stood for ten years ago, and I'm starting to feel almost desperate.

Most of my college friends married young. They have kids and big houses, and while I've been focusing on my career, every other woman in America has been snatching up all the marriage material. God, listen to how lame I sound now.

Is that even what I want, though? To settle down with a guy like Devon and live the suburban life? At first glance, no.

But the nights do get lonely. It's been a long ten years, and I miss the excitement that my early twenties held. Which is how I ended up on the Mates app, fishing through a long line of mediocre hand-me-down potential husbands.

Maybe I'll take a break from dating for the time being. I have enough to focus on with three courses to teach and twenty students to counsel. Not to mention, a certain little white-haired problem who seems to pop up everywhere I turn.

Fifteen minutes before class, I finally tear myself out of my car and head into the English building. The lecture hall is usually locked when I arrive; I have a key to open it, but after making a turn down the hallway, I notice it already is.

Am I late? It should be nothing, but I have a sudden instinctual feeling that it's *not* nothing. What if I walk through those doors and Cullen is already there waiting for me? What if he wants to get me alone? Whether he wants to hurt me physically or corner me into an uncomfortable conversation, I dread both. Either way, it would be torture.

Passing the doors into the lecture hall, I breathe a sigh of relief when I notice my best friend standing at the front of the room. He's leaning against the table with his feet crossed at the ankles.

"Jesus, Thomas. You scared the shit out of me."

He glances up at me, looking confused. "How did I scare you? I'm just standing here."

I roll my eyes and drop my bag on the table. "Long story. Don't worry about it. What are you doing here?"

"Hank let me in. I thought I'd come see how it's going. Ready to return to the *Times* yet?" Hank is Thomas's ex, and the person who ultimately got me this job, although Thomas takes credit for it. We went to college together and got our first jobs at the paper together, too. We've been inseparable for a whole decade and have a lot in common, including our preference for men, which is the only reason I haven't coerced him into marrying me. Not that I still haven't tried.

"I'm thinking about it." I groan, while firing up my computer and connecting it to the system.

He bolts upright and glares at me with concern. "Babe, I was just playing around. Do you really not like it? What happened?"

"Nothing. It's just different, that's all." I haven't told Thomas about Cullen yet. He would worry too much because that's what Thomas does best. My parents moved across the country, and I'm an only child, so Thomas has really become the only important person in my life, and he takes his job as my protector very seriously. "I'm not coming back to the paper. Not yet at least."

"You know we'd take you back in a heartbeat."

"I know."

It's silent for a moment and I've only relaxed a little with Thomas around. I keep my eyes on the door in case Cullen wants to make an appearance. I don't think

Thomas would recognize him, but I don't want to take that chance.

Just then, students start filing in, and I glare at my friend, waiting for him to leave.

"All right, professor," he says astutely, standing up and straightening his tie. "I guess I will leave you to it." Thomas loves an audience. Too bad, the students who walked in aren't even paying any attention to him.

"Are you coming over for dinner tonight?" I ask, as he pockets his phone.

Baring his teeth, he tilts his head back and forth as if he's contemplating his answer. "I sort of had plans to go out tonight."

"Oh yeah, with who?"

"I don't know yet," he replies in a whisper, so no one hears him. That's another thing Thomas and I have in common. We're both painfully single. "I guess I'll find out at the bar," he adds.

As he leans in to say goodbye, I spot a familiar face over his shoulder. At that very moment, my best friend plants a chaste kiss on my cheek as he always does, but it does not go unnoticed. My insides start to boil with humiliation, my eyes following Cullen to his seat at the back of the room. Thomas leaves, not noticing anything, but I almost wish he'd come back now.

For the most part, Cullen behaves himself during class, but his presence still manages to distress me. He doesn't take notes or pull out a laptop. He just watches me the entire time with harrowing, intense eyes.

There's only one moment during class discussion when I let my guard down and he finds a way to torment me. The students have started a debate on the merit of tabloids in the industry of journalism, and I am impressed with their discussion. A couple of the girls in the front are arguing with a pretentious boy down their row. I am eating up their enthusiasm with a proud grin on my face, as if a good student debate is a sign I'm doing my job well, when I glance up and see Cullen laughing. He's mocking me.

Don't let him get to you. That's what he wants.

"As long as people are buying them then they obviously have something people want," one girl argues.

"Sleazy grocery store tabloids shouldn't be considered journalism. Whether people buy them or not," the boy quips back with a smug expression.

"Isn't all journalism sleazy?" Cullen's ominous voice suggests from the back of the room. The students in the front hush immediately. The girls glance up toward me, appraising my reaction, while the boy along with the one hundred and ninety-nine other occupants turn their heads in Cullen's direction.

He's trying to get under your skin. Don't give him the benefit of looking bothered.

My little internal pep talk barely helps, but I square my shoulders and peer up at him curiously. "What makes you say that?"

He shifts in his seat, giving me a playful grin that says he's actually looking forward to having a tit-for-tat with me. "Well, you pry into other people's business. You air out dirty laundry, spinning the story whatever way *you* want to, and then you call yourselves heroes for it."

My blood boils under my skin. "You see no merit in informing the public? Especially when some *heinous* crime has been committed."

To the rest of the class, we're having a very nonspecific debate, but to Cullen and me, it's about so much more. It feels surreal discussing this at all, and from a professional standpoint, I really shouldn't even be entertaining the idea. I should have him removed as a conflict of interest, but how could I resist this? He clearly harbors resentment toward me, like he's still the angry little boy he was eight years ago. It seems he hasn't grown up at all.

"No," he says matter-of-factly, straightening his spine and leaning forward with a stern expression. "I don't see any merit in being a cunt."

There is a collective gasp as the students in the room react to his insult, but I'm too stunned to move. The girls are looking at me again, waiting for me to do something, probably wondering if I should. They want to know if fighting with him is worthwhile, or if I should roll over and let it go because it's not worth the trouble to step into the ring with him if I'm only going to lose.

He wants to make you uncomfortable. Don't let him win.

"Well," I say, leveling his glare with my own, "I'd rather be a cunt than a coward."

The room doesn't move. You could hear a pin drop with how still everyone is. And after a moment, the corner of his lip twitches. But he doesn't respond.

Glancing down at my watch, I notice that class ends in five minutes and I still have so much more to tell them. Dropping our conversation, I round my desk and ease right into an announcement about their homework. The tension quickly deflates as the students start putting their things away. Some hang on to my every word, jotting down notes about the reading and the short writing assignment. The rest know they will be able to find it in the student portal and don't bother giving it another moment of their attention.

Cullen doesn't move, naturally.

After the class files out the door, without their usual chatter and smiles, I wait for him to approach me again. Standing behind my desk this time to put a literal barrier between us, I watch him stagger behind the rest of the students. He's still appraising me, a glimmer of approval on his face, when he pauses by my desk again.

"I think I'm going to like this class," he says, shining those pearly white teeth at me.

"Then you should watch your mouth or I'll have you removed."

"No, you won't."

Why is he doing this? What could he possibly be getting out of taunting me and making my life hell? I'm just his teacher. Doesn't he have a real life to worry about, sports and girls and whatever eighteen-year-old boys are focused on? Why on earth is he even giving me the time of day, especially if I don't give him the satisfaction of letting it bother me?

"Have a good weekend, Mr. Ayers."

His smile falters, the brightness in his eyes dimming with speculation as he squints at me. It was a subtle jab, calling him by his last name, the name he shares with the man currently in prison, the criminal that connects us. But it wasn't too subtle, because he felt it.

With that dark expression on his face, no longer playful and flirty, he turns and walks out of the room.

We are on the brink of something—I can feel it. It's either going to fizzle and go away or it's going to get a lot worse, and I have a feeling that if Cullen is anywhere as stubborn as me, it's going to be the latter.

Chapter 4
Everly

THANK GOD IT'S FRIDAY. With my first week at Florence U complete, I finally pack up my stuff and lock my office door. It's past five, and I really could have left an hour ago, but it's a Friday night, and aside from stopping at the market for wine and cheese for dinner, I have absolutely no plans.

I haven't bothered to even open the dating app since my disaster date with Devon. I'm perfectly content being alone, if others like him are my options.

Walking out to my car across the lot, I notice there is a crowd of male students in very short shorts and loose-fitting muscle shirts, walking to the rugby field behind campus. Averting my eyes as they pass, I try my hardest not to check out my scantily clad students, but it's not easy. They're all adults, right?

Fuck, what is wrong with me?

I need to get laid. That's what.

That's when I spot him. He's bringing up the rear, and instead of wearing the same white tank the other guys are wearing, Cullen Ayers is walking past me without a shirt on at all. I notice his tattoos start at his neck and drape all the way down his chest and into his black shorts. He's not completely covered in ink. They are sporadic, like an unfinished mural, but holy hell is it distracting. Any chance of me looking away now is long gone.

Cullen may be a pain in my ass, but I'd be blind if I didn't acknowledge how stunning he is. Everything about him is contrary—white hair, dark eyes, pink lips, tan skin. It makes it literally difficult not to stare.

Our eyes lock, and my mouth goes dry. Suddenly he stops and shouts something to his teammates who continue on without him. Then, he turns and walks in my direction.

Fuck, fuck, fuck.

God, I don't want this confrontation right now. I really don't need another reminder that he hates me or that I'm responsible for his mother's death. Didn't he give me enough shit during class?

Suddenly he's standing right in front of me. Still shirtless.

"Cullen, how can I help you?" I struggle to maintain a professional demeanor, as if I'm any teacher and he's any student. But trying to act like his professor is laughable. I sound ridiculous.

"Cut the bullshit, Miss West."

My eyes widen and I force myself to swallow.

"What do you want then?" I snap, as he said, cutting the bullshit.

At my question, he laughs. It's deep and sarcastic, chilling me to the bone. "What I want, you can't give me."

"Why don't you get back to your practice?"

He stares at me for a moment, sizing me up, as if he's deciding his next move. "I bet you want to just avoid this confrontation, right? Pretend you and I don't know each other. Pretend we have no history, and you didn't royally fuck up my entire life? Is that what you want, Miss West?"

"Perhaps you should request a transfer. This is a conflict of interest."

Again, he laughs, this time shining those pearly white teeth that send chills up my spine. Then, he bites his bottom lip, and my breath hitches. "This isn't a conflict at all, but it is interesting, isn't it?"

He's unhinged, and it scares the shit out of me. I don't scare easily. I've spent enough time working around men who thought intimidation was an acceptable tactic for dealing with headstrong female coworkers, so if this kid thinks he's going to push me around, he's going to be surprised to find I don't bend easily.

"Get to your practice, Mr. Ayers. Come Monday, you'll find a new schedule of classes."

When I try to maneuver around him, he steps in my way, glaring down at me and pulling his lip ring between his teeth. It's downright impossible not to gaze at it.

"You won't do that," he mumbles, trying to intimidate me again like he did after class.

"Trust me. I will." Again, when I try to step around him, he stops me.

This time, he leans closer, so close I smell the mint of his gum as he whispers, "Life has gotten a little boring, hasn't it? Your job was boring, so you picked a new one. Going home alone on a Friday night is boring. Now you're eye-fucking a bunch of college students because I'm guessing your Wednesday night date was too boring to put out, wasn't he?"

I gasp, wrinkling my forehead at him. "Cullen—"

"You won't change my classes because seeing me again is the most excitement you've had in...what, eight years?"

Hatred seeps through every word he utters, and I feel it in his gaze on me too. I hate that he's right. I am bored. Life is so mundane now, I almost enjoy the way seeing him again makes me feel, remembering the excitement of my past life when I was somebody, someone who accomplished something, someone people listened to and cared about. Now...I am nothing. And Cullen's challenge is the most I've felt from another person in almost a decade, so yeah, he's right. I probably won't change him out of my class because then my life would go back to nothingness.

"Ayers! You comin'?" one of his teammates shouts across the lot, and I suddenly clear my throat, moving away, so we don't look so suspicious standing this close to each other.

With one last menacing chuckle, Cullen turns and walks away, jogging across to the rugby field, and I can't help but look up and gaze at his back, the muscles rippling in the sunlight as he runs.

Standing alone near my car, I try to let my heartbeat regulate in his absence, but I am too shaken up. I don't want to get in my car now. I have no desire to go home alone and be pathetic and dull anymore, because that little asshole was right. I am fucking bored.

The shouting from the field draws my curiosity, so I pass my car and head that way. It's much like a soccer field with bleachers on each side and a long grass pitch the guys huddle in formation on. Once I get to the bleachers, I lean against the metal braces and cross my arms as I watch them.

There are a couple dozen guys warming up and running drills on the grass. Two coaches talk on the sidelines, and it's nearly impossible to miss Cullen with his tan skin, tattoos, and bleach-blond hair.

I don't know why, but I stand there and watch them practice. It just seems like the best way to spend my Friday evening, and there's nothing weird about a new professor showing interest in the college's rugby team. It's not until about forty minutes into the scrimmage on the field that Cullen catches me watching.

Instead of smiling, he looks momentarily caught off guard, and I love the way he takes a double glance. I've surprised him, and at this moment, it gives me the upper hand. It means nothing, really, but I enjoy the way it feels, to be the one infiltrating his life. As his teacher, I can't sabotage him the way he's sabotaging me. As much as I would love to humiliate him in front of his teammates, make him mess up, lose his scrimmage, throw off his game and really get under his skin, I can't. This is my job, and I'm a professional. Still, the look in his eyes as he glares at me from across the field says that just my being here is enough.

Then, maybe I'm imagining things, but he seems to put a little more into his practice. He runs at full speed toward his opponent, catching him at the same time another player does, and with more aggression than is probably necessary, they take him to the ground. The coach doesn't say anything about it until he does it again, tackling harder and putting all of his energy into every little thing he does.

"I love the spirit, Ayers. Keep it up!" his coach bellows from the sidelines as a couple of guys smack him on the ass and back. Cullen looks proud of himself.

Is he trying to show me how tough he is? More than likely he's just proving that I can't throw him off, but I let my mind dwell on the idea that he's showing off for me. It's ridiculous, but I get a little lost in the fantasy.

On the other side of the stands, there is a group of girls all ogling Cullen as he jogs by, and I notice the way he throws a quick smile at them. The blonde girl waves, and it deflates all of the air in my lungs. What am I even doing here? I feel like a complete creep even watching him, but just then, his eyes find me, and I stare as his tongue slips out, licking his bottom lip, the glint of metal showing, and I pause.

Sweat cascades down his rippled abs and his shorts hang a little lower than his tan line, showing off a pale strip of skin just above his ass, and I can't tear my eyes away as he runs back into the scrimmage.

Cullen maneuvers around the field with ease, and I find myself wondering how long he's been playing. Was this what he did in high school? Who comes to his games since his parents aren't around anymore? Does he have a girlfriend?

Then my filthy mind just careens down a film reel of images, picturing the way his body would move during sex. I imagine him being as cocky and arrogant in bed as he is during my class, taking and teasing and punishing. My body reacts to the mental image, warming my belly and dampening between my legs.

This is so fucking inappropriate.

He *is* eighteen, I remind myself.

Yeah, and I'm a grown-ass woman in my thirties who shouldn't be gawking at a teenage boy like a fucking cougar.

Suddenly I feel a different set of eyes on me, and it yanks me right out of my demented daydream. Cullen's coach smiles up at me while sending me a quick wave. I delicately wave back, half-expecting him to come over and talk to me. His smile tells me that he's not suspicious of my being here, watching sweaty college boys roll around in the mud, which is good I guess because even I'm starting to get a little creeped out by my behavior.

Instead of coming over to me, the coach directs his attention back to the field and calls the players to huddle on the field. It gives me a moment to check him out. He's not a bad-looking man, probably a few years older than me, but he reminds me very much of the duds I've been meeting on my dating app, which means it's a good time to get out of here.

Just as I turn back toward my car, ready to call it a night, thinking about the Merlot dinner I have planned, I hear someone call my name.

"Miss West, right?"

Spinning around, I smile politely, while grimacing on the inside, as the coach chases after me. So much for that swift escape. "Yes," I reply sweetly, "but please call me Everly."

"Coach Prescott, but call me Eric," he says as he puts out a hand for me to shake. "So, you like rugby?"

Nope, just tormenting my student-slash-enemy.

"I love it," I reply, which is a bald-faced lie.

"Well, I hope you come to our first game tomorrow. It's against Kings College at one. First game of the season, and I think you'll be impressed with the team this year. They're coming out strong."

My eyes dance over to the players behind him, and I catch the way Cullen is watching us, his brow pinched together skeptically. He looks...bothered.

Then it occurs to me—he doesn't like me talking to his coach. For all he knows, I could be reporting his behavior in class today. He has no way of really knowing, and as immature as this is, Cullen was an asshole to me today, so he deserves this. I decide at this very moment that appearing chummy with his coach is about the meanest thing I can do to him right now, so I'm going to do it.

You want to call me a cunt in front of my class, Cullen, then I'll be a cunt.

I plaster a bright smile on my face, knowing he sees it. "I would love to. Thank you for the invite!"

Eric smiles back at me, a small blush rising to his cheeks. "It's nice to see the new instructors showing interest in our sports program." His gaze drifts down to my lips, so I casually bite the bottom one between my teeth and fiddle with the necklace hanging from my neck.

Fuck, I am flirting so much right now, but by the looks of it, the coach is into it. Seeing him up close, I'm starting to realize he's definitely about ten years older than me, with thinning blond hair and wrinkles around his eyes. I'm not afraid to admit that I'd probably still take him home for at least a night if he didn't turn out to be such a dud during a date. He's got a nice enough body, broad shoulders, and thick arms, and let's face it—beggars can't really be choosers at this point. Can't be any worse than Devon.

"I'm looking forward to it," I reply, smiling a little brighter, knowing it's creating dimples in my cheeks.

"You know...the coaches and staff sometimes go out after the games. You should definitely come."

Reaching out, I place a soft hand against his forearm. "That's so sweet of you. I might take you up on that."

Cullen's intense glare bores into me from far behind Coach Prescott. I could let this go, call it a night and head to my car, but where is the fun in that? He *literally* called me a cunt in front of the entire class today.

I glance around skeptically before leaning in toward Eric. "I hope you don't mind me asking, but I'm curious. Do you ever have any problems with the blond one?"

He glances back, clearly looking at Cullen. "Ayers?" he asks, turning back toward me. "That kid has fire. Great player. Why? Is he giving you trouble?"

"We had a rough interaction in my class today. I don't think he respects his female teachers, if I'm being honest."

Eric's forehead wrinkles, a look of sudden anger forming on his face. The power I feel is intoxicating.

"You don't need to do anything about it," I add, touching his arm again. "I was curious if it was just me or if other teachers had a hard time with him. Great for a rugby game, bad for classroom manners."

"If he gives you any more trouble, let me know. Ayers is on a scholarship, and if he can't behave himself, he'll get kicked off the team and lose it."

My heart plummets into my stomach. He's on a rugby scholarship? Fuck. What have I done? I just wanted the coach to give him a little grief about his behavior, not potentially ruin his scholarship and get him kicked out of college.

And yes, his behavior today was on him, but I can't be the source of more Ayers' problems. I really can't. Plus, the thought of Cullen losing his scholarship actually makes my chest ache a little for reasons I don't understand. I should want him gone but I just don't have it in me to ruin his life any further.

He's still glaring at me from the bleachers, and I suddenly don't want to torment him anymore. Now, I just want to go home.

"Really, it wasn't a big deal. Don't worry about it. I'm sure it's nothing," I say as I start backing away toward my car.

"Okay," Eric says with a little uncertainty in his tone. "If you have any more problems, please let me know." God, he said that too loudly. Cullen definitely heard that. *Shit. Shit. Shit.*

"I can't wait for the game tomorrow! Thanks again for the invite," I call back, quickly changing the subject.

"See you then," Eric replies before turning back to the players. A knot of anxiety forms in my stomach because no matter how much I tell myself to stop worrying about him and the consequences of his actions, it doesn't go away. I just couldn't leave it alone, could I?

Once I reach my car, I notice something hanging from the driver's side mirror, and I freeze. My heart nearly plummets to the concrete parking lot floor when I recognize the pearl necklace.

Glancing back at the field, I notice neither Cullen nor the coach are looking my way. As I take the necklace off the mirror, I feel my hands start to tremble, adding to my already present guilt. It doesn't take a genius to figure out who left this here.

Nearly every photo ever taken of Valerie Ayers had one thing in common—her signature pearls. Cullen left this for me, whether as a threat or a reminder, I have no idea.

This whole week, I saw Cullen's behavior as a game, his way of teasing me for the part I played in his past. But after the pill bottle and now this...it's clear Cullen is not just messing with me. It's all so much more serious for him than I realized, and he's doing this to threaten and scare me. I hate to admit it's working, but it is.

And I may have just made things even worse.

Chapter 5
Cullen

COACH PRESCOTT IS SUCH AN ASSHOLE. It's his fault she's sitting in the stands on the Florence side. She did just about everything other than flash her pussy at him yesterday after practice. Makes me fucking sick.

Then she had to go run her mouth because that's what she does best. She thinks she's so fucking high and mighty, playing by the rules—her rules. Now I think it's time we play by *my* rules.

Prescott cornered me in the locker room this morning. "You giving the teachers a hard time, Ayers?" He tried to look so fucking tough too.

"No, Coach."

"Hot, young teacher shows up on campus and you think you have the right to fuck with her? You'll get your ass kicked off the team for that shit, so keep it in your pants, kid."

I scoff, shoving my bag in the locker. He doesn't bother saying another word as he storms off to the field, where the rest of the players have already congregated. I don't know what she told him, but he thinks I'm trying to fuck her. If he only knew I'd rather hold her head under water for a little while instead. I want to see what color she would turn if I held my fingers around her throat a little too tight. This has absolutely nothing to do with sex.

But I mean...it's not like I'd turn down the opportunity to make her scream. I bet she mewls like a kitten. She probably likes it vanilla and sweet. I wouldn't put it past her to make me sign a waiver beforehand, just so everyone is clear it's consensual.

God, now that I think about it, I'd love to see her lips around my cock and tears running down her face. I'd fuck her face so hard she'd never be able to run that filthy mouth of hers again.

That's the image I take with me out on the pitch, and the first thing I think about when I spot those dark brown eyes fixed on me through the whole game. I was supposed to be getting into her head, and now she's in mine. It doesn't hurt too much because we're in the lead, and I'm making passes better and faster than normal.

Every time I catch Coach Prescott glancing her way, I grind my molars. I don't need him getting involved in this. It's going to be hard as fuck to make her life hell if she's banging my coach the whole time. My scholarship rides on this team and my ability to play, so talk about a conflict of interest.

That's probably what she wants. If she's nailing Prescott, then she has me by the balls. I can't do shit to her without him finding out. If there's anything this bitch loves, it's fucking over my life.

We end up beating Kings College with a wide lead, and it should put me in a good mood, but it doesn't. Especially when she doesn't leave with the crowd after the game. She lingers, hanging out near the parking lot, watching us, and

Coach notices. When he makes his way over, I catch the way she smiles at him, pressing her tits up and clenching her thighs together.

As I pass them, I take her attention with me. Then I remember the little present I left for her yesterday. I nearly forgot about the necklace, since I dropped it there before class. It probably explains why there's a little more remorse on her face today. She isn't wearing the same self-assured expression she had on yesterday.

"Hey, Ayers. Do you need a ride home?" Coach asks, and my nostrils flare as I try to keep walking.

"No thanks, Coach." *Asshole*. He just basically announced how I can't even afford a car. I have to take the fucking bus everywhere, including home from this game, which means I have to sit at the bus stop for everyone to see. It's humiliating, and he just made the one person whose pity I don't want aware of it.

As I walk toward the road, I hear them exchange numbers, and I let out a groan. Just fucking great. Hopefully it'll be busy at the restaurant tonight and I can make enough to pay my phone bill, eat, *and* buy some of the good shit Gina was trying to sell. No one deserves to get stoned more than me.

On the way to the bus stop, I spot her car near the back of the lot. It's a white SUV, tall enough to hide my frame as I make the last-minute decision to lean against the driver's side door. I'm not done with Everly West today. I haven't gotten my fill of her suffering yet.

I wait for her by her car, hidden from view, without a plan or any clue what I'm going to say or do.

While I bide my time, I think about how I almost took a scholarship across the state, and I'm wondering now why I didn't. Because I can't seem to move on with my life, apparently. I should be taking every fucking opportunity to get out of Florence, but something is holding me back. Thank God no one seems to remember my dad anymore, but there are the rare occurrences when someone stares at me a moment too long, like they recognize me, or they flinch when they hear my name. I was just a kid—I wasn't the one in the news. But it seems that even changing my appearance doesn't help much.

Even more reason to get the fuck out of this town, but I can't. I'm just...stuck.

Suddenly the locks on her SUV click, and her shoes against the pavement warn me she's approaching. When she turns the corner, around the back of her SUV, she lets out a clipped yell.

"Oh my God, Cullen! You scared the shit out of me." She claps her hand against her chest before glancing around nervously.

"I need a ride home," I mumble, looking at her with a scowl on my face. "Or do you have plans to fuck my coach today? He's married, you know."

She does a double take, looking back toward him and then at me. "Drive you home? I'm not driving you anywhere."

"Yes, you are," I say, pulling open the door before she can stop me.

"Excuse me," she snaps, keeping her voice down. I notice the way she *doesn't* go running to Coach for help. Instead, she whispers like she's trying to keep me a secret. "Cullen...I'm serious. Get out of my car."

It's too late. I've already tossed my gym bag in the back seat. Then, I open her driver's side door, waiting for her to get in.

She stares at me for a moment, deliberating what she

should do. She could fight me on this, yell for help, and make a big fuss about it. But she doesn't. Instead, she tosses her purse in the car and moves to climb in. "You have a lot of fucking nerve, you know that?"

I smile as I slam her door shut. Moving around to the passenger side, I climb in next to her. She's rifling through her bag for something and a moment later, my mother's pearl necklace lands in my lap with a hard slap.

"What, you don't like it?" I tease.

"Do you think this is funny?" she asks through clenched teeth.

"I'd love to see you with a pearl necklace." I twirl it on my finger, thinking about what Coach said this morning about keeping it in my pants. That image of her gagging on my cock flashes through my mind again.

"I should report you." She doesn't say it very loudly, almost as if she's not one hundred percent serious. And she either doesn't pick up on my innuendo or she's ignoring it. Does she think about me painting her chest with my cum? Does it turn her on?

Glancing over at her, I notice the way she forces a swallow, pressing the start button on her car and skimming her eyes over the parking lot to make sure no one sees us together. I love this power I hold over her. The power to make her feel uncomfortable and to make her want it.

I drink in the sight of her as she pulls out of her parking spot, driving toward the road. In a tight pair of yoga pants and a loose-fitting top, I have to admit she has a great body, regardless of the fact that she's fourteen years older than me. Almost makes her old enough to be my mother, which is a sick thought, but also kind of hot.

It's a little weird being alone with her in her car. We

don't actually know each other, but it feels like we do, or like we *should*. The hatred between us feels almost intimate.

"Is he really married?" she asks, as we reach the traffic light.

"Yep. His wife's a nurse."

She cringes, keeping her eyes on the road. "Listen, Cullen. No more shit like this," she says, pulling the pill bottle out of her purse and chucking it at me. "You've made your point. Now, you have to drop it."

"Why did you come to the game today?" I ask, changing the subject.

She looks almost surprised by my question. "Because I like rugby and the coach invited me."

"Sure," I reply with sarcasm.

"Listen, Cullen. You need to just let it go now. If I get any more shit like this, I'm going to take it to the administration."

Her words seep into my pores like poison. She's threatening me, and the hatred toward her boils under my skin. All she sees are rules and facts, not people and lives and shit that I fucking care about. I keep quiet in my seat for the rest of the drive, stewing and just thinking about how I need to *let it go*.

She doesn't fucking get it.

When we pull onto campus, stopping in front of the dorms, I don't move.

"Do we have an understanding?" she says, like she's the one in control here. Like she has any say over what I do. I almost get out of the car and drop it—but I don't.

Instead, I snap.

I've never been violent with a woman before, and I've never really wanted to, but Everly West represents everything terrible in my life. She is my downfall, the stain on my history, and I won't sit here and listen to her tell me what I will and will not be doing, so as I spin toward her, I snatch her face in my hands and pull her close, only inches away. I realize I'm squeezing her jaw too hard, but I don't care. In fact, I like the way she whimpers in my grip.

"Listen here, you fucking bitch. This is the only understanding we have. You ruined my life eight years ago, and you've been able to live in peace since then. Do you know what I've been doing? Burying my mother after I found her fucking corpse in her bed when I was only ten, living with an asshole of an uncle who spent his weekends beating the shit out of me when he was drunk, and scraping by just enough to stay alive. The only thing that got me through was rugby, and it's the only reason I'm here at Florence U, so you're not going to fuck my coach or come to any more of my games."

"Cullen," she gasps. Behind the tears brewing in her eyes, there is pure terror. "Stop. Please." God, I love the way she begs.

"You think the necklace and pain pills were bad, Miss West? I only did that to remind you of the lives you ruined because you had to be so fucking righteous. That was nothing—*nothing* compared to what I'm capable of. I could have let it go, but then you go and threaten me again. You think you're in control, but you have no fucking idea the nightmare I'm about to bring into your life."

She cries out again, a deliciously strangled sound that feels like a shot of adrenaline to my bloodstream. She's struggling against my hold, so I use my other hand to grasp the back of her neck and pull her closer. Her erratic breaths are warm on my face. And for no other reason than she just has me unhinged as hell, I open my mouth and lick her from her lips up to her eyes, catching her salty tears on my tongue. She squeals in disgust, her claws biting into my arm as she tries to get away, but it's no use. I'm too strong and I have too much adrenaline coursing through my veins to be overpowered.

It occurs to me at that moment how much *more* I want to do with this new burst of energy—sick, twisted things I've never really thought about wanting before, and that thought has my cock getting surprisingly hard in my shorts.

"You belong to me now, Miss West. And if you even think about calling the police on me or telling Coach or the administration, you might as well slit your own throat because I won't let you sleep a wink without wishing for death. Do we have an understanding?" I snap, my tone laced with hatred as I grit out each word.

A tear slips down her trembling cheek. I force two fingers in her mouth, making her gag as I reach the back of her tongue. Her jaw pops open, and I act on impulse, spitting into her open mouth. She gags more, the pitiful sound of it making my dick twitch.

Our eyes meet for a moment, and there is no more smug indignation in her eyes, just fear. Something passes between us. It's subtle, and maybe I'm seeing something that's not there, but it looks like fire in her eyes, like maybe I love this and she doesn't hate it as much as she should. With her tear-soaked eyes still on mine, I force her mouth shut.

"Swallow."

She whimpers again and does what she's told.

"Good girl." Then I wipe her tears with my thumb before shoving her away from me. Her mess of hair is covering her face as she cowers in her seat.

"Have a good weekend," I grind out through tight lips as I slip out of her car. My skin is buzzing and my mind is racing. I should feel bad for that shit. It was too much, and there's a good chance I'm royally fucked. The cops will be banging down my door in less than an hour, but I couldn't give a shit right now because that felt...good.

As I reach my room, I pace the floor, feeling like a bomb about to go off. It's a weird mix of guilt and hatred swirling inside me, and I actually consider just bolting or apologizing or *something,* but then I remember I didn't do shit wrong when my life fell to pieces. It all came down because of two people: my father and her. When that asshole gets out of prison in roughly twenty years, I'll be waiting for him. But for now, Everly gets me all to herself.

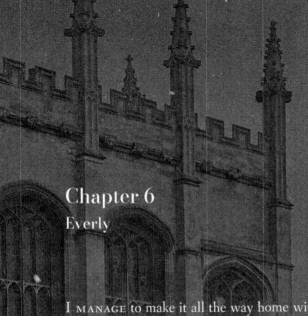

Chapter 6
Everly

I MANAGE to make it all the way home without crying, but once I step foot in my shower, I lose it. The entire drive my mind was just blank, trying to avoid even the slightest thought regarding what just happened. As soon as the water hits me, I feel his brutal grip on my face and warm spit on my tongue.

It was degrading. Humiliating. And he did it to intimidate me. He's getting what he wants, and that's what has me crying in earnest now. I can't keep fighting him. I don't stand a chance against him, so I have to back down.

If I go to the administration, it will be like the trial all over again, and I believe what he said—he would make my life hell. What could he possibly have to lose at that point?

So no, I won't tell on him this time. I'll just keep my mouth shut, endure whatever the fuck he has in store for me and then when this semester is over, he will be out of my life and I'll have paid my dues to Cullen Ayers.

I will finally be free.

My thoughts trail as I climb out of the shower, drying my hair in front of the large bathroom mirror. Cullen scared me today, but it wasn't just the way he grabbed me that shook me to my core. It was something else. There was something between us in that moment, and I know he felt it too—fear, anger, pain. As if years and years of it being buried and ignored have finally come to an end, and we're finishing a fight we started almost a decade ago.

There was fire there. I saw a passion in his eyes that seemed almost familiar. It was the same intense emotion I feel, and I know Cullen Ayers is the last person on earth I should try to relate to right now, but maybe that's why he and I have so much conflict—we're the same on the inside.

Cullen made it clear he wants me to pay for what happened to his family, but there's more to it than that. He thinks what I did was wrong, although that's ridiculous. I'm not going to take the blame for the hand he's been dealt in life. That's not on me, but I think I finally understand that he's going to make me pay for it anyway. Because it's not about revenge for him. It's about control.

I can't decide if that's better or worse.

Slipping into a pair of comfy PJs, I try to focus on anything other than Cullen, but he's clouded my brain. I'm still a little shaken up, but I don't think I could possibly focus on anything else. I need to understand more. And thinking about him has me thinking about that case and my journal article.

So, I crack open a bottle of desperately needed wine and sit down at my laptop, pulling up the drive with every-thing from that year. All the research and data is still there. I haven't looked through this stuff in a few years, but there were still so many loose ends I was never able to tie up after the arrest was made. Once the FBI had what they wanted, they lost interest in the case entirely. Never mind the missing person cases still unsolved or the other crimes

George Ayers probably committed. So many of his employees were undocumented trafficking victims, immigrants, and those in poverty who were just happy to have a job and a place to live they didn't care that they had to forfeit their passport and freedom to get it. It was heartbreaking to see, but when I went back through the case a couple years later, I was so devastated to see that many of the displaced people had never been reunited with their families or returned home. Most of them ended up in worse situations or, at the very least, very similar ones, working in terrible conditions for minimal pay or, at the very worst, deported back home with no money or security to live.

Flipping through the cases again has me feeling worse, like nothing I did really mattered. Yeah, George Ayers ended up in prison, but did the problem really go away? Not at all. Which means...Cullen's grief is for nothing. All of this, everything I did, would have been for nothing.

I find myself stopping on pictures of him and his family from about fifteen years ago. Most of my research was from his childhood and before. So, I have pictures on my hard drive of a tiny Cullen with dark hair and big round eyes. His mother was so fair, blonde-haired and blue-eyed. He must have really favored his dad, although she was beautiful. I can see why he dyes his hair. With those bleached locks, he almost looks like her now.

As I scroll back through the case files, I realize there aren't many pictures of him with his mother. She was there, but he was usually in the arms of his nanny, a young woman who looks no older than sixteen. I remember starting the case file on her, too, but gave up when I realized a few years back that any record of her existence disappeared, just like the rest of them. There's no telling what happened to these victims after the case, and that sense of helplessness only makes me angrier.

I am completely lost in the old research and pictures of tiny Cullen, when a harsh tap on the door makes me scream. My body freezes, my mind racing, trying to remember if I invited anyone over. Glancing at the clock, I notice that it's well past ten.

"Miss West..." a familiar voice calls through the door.

My blood goes cold, making me instantly dizzy with shock, and I can't think straight. This can't be happening. Cullen Ayers can't possibly be standing outside my door.

What does he want? Is he finally here to hurt me? Or just terrorize me again like he did in the car? Is this part of the *nightmare* he mentioned bringing into my life? Should I call the police?

Questions sprint through my mind, but they all go unanswered because I have no clue why Cullen is here, but there is only one way to find out. I jump up from the couch and rush to the door. Peeping through the window, I see him standing under the porch light in a black pair of tight jeans and a white V-neck shirt. There are two necklaces hanging from his neck, and I hate myself for how I peer at him. After how he treated me today, grabbing me the way he did, I should *not* be even entertaining the idea of opening that door for him. I *should* be calling the police instead of letting a teenager intimidate me. I have absolutely *no* reason to believe he wouldn't hurt me—physically, emotionally, sexually.

So why am I reaching for the doorknob?

"I knew you'd be awake," he says with a sly smile, leaning up against the small window next to the door. "I'm not going to hurt you. Just let me in."

"Go home, Cullen," I call through the wood.

"The bus doesn't come back this way for another forty-five minutes. You're not going to leave me sitting out here alone, are you?"

"And why the fuck would I let you in?" I reply, faking far more confidence than I have. The subtle shake in my voice gives me away, though.

"Because you want to."

"No, I don't." There's that shake again. This time I really sound like I'm about to cry—because I am.

He leans against my door, his face so close to the peep-hole, I can peek through and make out the length of his dark lashes against his skin.

"I just want to talk."

My eyes slowly close as I rest my forehead against the door.

Make it stop. Please, just make it stop.

I have to force out a shaky breath. If I'm going to call the police, I should really do it now. It doesn't need to end in him getting arrested. They could just calmly guide him off my property and maybe even give him a ride home.

Who the fuck are you kidding, Everly?

One look at him and they would probably cuff him on sight. I can't call the police and I can't ignore him. The longer I leave him on my doorstep, the worse he's going to make things. So maybe I can let him talk for the next forty-five minutes and then he can go home.

What is wrong with me? Is it guilt or curiosity that has me reaching for the door handle yet again? Why am I welcoming chaos into my life?

Because, I remind myself, what Cullen said earlier was true. I am bored. Bored with my life in general. Bored and lonely.

Against my better judgment, I turn the knob on the

front door and slowly let it open. My body blocks the narrow entrance, although I doubt that would stop him.

"What are you doing here?" I ask.

He bites his lip with a devious smile, and I get a rush of chills.

He leans in, resting a hand on the door frame above my head. "Don't you remember our conversation in the car? You're not getting rid of me, Miss West."

"It's late, Cullen. You should really go home."

"Let me in. I just want to talk."

"After how you treated me in the car? Are you insane? Go home."

There's a flinch in his expression, a crack in his armor, and it makes me wonder if there is any guilt or shame in his head right now. A true sociopath wouldn't show a flicker of remorse after what he did today, but I refuse to believe that's the case with Cullen.

When he reaches a hand toward my face, I wince, jerking my head backward. But his touch is tender this time, running the back of his hand against my jaw.

"I promise not to hurt you again, although correct me if I'm wrong, but I almost got the sense today that you like it a little rough, don't you, Miss West?"

"You're wrong."

"I thought at first you'd be some high and mighty priss who likes things the soft and easy way, but there was fight in you today. I like that. I hope you do fight me. It won't make things easier for you, but it will make things more fun."

I should slam the door in his face and end this right now. He wants to hurt me—he's literally saying that—but it also feels like he's...flirting with me. It's just another form of his bullying, I know that. This eighteen-year-old rugby player is not interested in me, but I bet he would love to watch me fawn over him, make me believe he wants me just to use it against me. It would be humiliating.

He stares down at me with a glimmer of mischief in his eye, and because the rational thoughts in my brain are not making a difference on my nervous system, a spark of excitement courses through every vein in my body.

"Can I come in?"

"Why would I let you in if you hate me so much?"

His face falls, sincerity coloring his features. "That's exactly why you should let me in."

"So you can push me around some more? It doesn't make any sense."

"I already told you I won't hurt you again," he replies with puppy dog eyes. "Please."

"No," I say as confidently as I can, but he replies with a sinister laugh. With that, he reaches a hand out, pressing firmly on the door until it opens far enough for him to squeeze his body through. He's pressed against me, toe-to-toe, and my heart races so fast in my chest I can feel it pulse in every limb of my body, but I don't budge.

Then his rough hands are on my waist and I'm being shoved into my own house. I try to put up a fight, but it's pointless. He's a brick wall, and I'm suddenly pressed against the hard muscles of his pecs and abs under his white shirt. I catch the familiar scent of the restaurant I was at just three days ago, and I realize he must have come from work.

"Cullen, I said no!" I shriek. Once we're inside, he shuts the door behind us and waltzes in like he owns the place.

"And I told you I like it when you fight back. I figured that's what you were doing."

"It's not a joke, Cullen. I'm your teacher, not your friend."

"Oh, you're definitely not my fucking friend." He's

inspecting my house, every photo and book and pillow on my couch. "We can talk about my grades if you want, Miss West," he says with a laugh.

Forcing myself to swallow, I glare at him. "All right, fine. This is about the case, so let's get it all out now. You can't keep blaming me for what happened to your family, Cullen."

"Who should I blame then? If someone single-handedly dismantled your whole life, who would you blame?"

"Start with your father—the actual criminal," I reply, letting my words pass by my mouth without any filter at all.

"Oh, I hate him too, but he's out of my reach right now. You're not." He passes the living room, heading into the kitchen. Cullen looks so out of place in my home, and it feels like such a violation with him touching everything I own.

"Nice place," he mutters, and I suddenly become aware of the wine and half-eaten cheese tray sitting out on my kitchen table. He apparently notices it, too, because he takes the glass and swallows it down before I can stop him.

"Come on! You're not old enough to drink. I can go to jail for that."

He doesn't respond, but he grabs a cracker from the tray and scoops up a slice of brie before piling it into his mouth. "What? I'm hungry."

A twinge of guilt works its way into my brain as I remember something he said today in the car—he has to scrape by just to stay alive. How bad has Cullen's life been since that day? Last I saw him, he still had a silver spoon in his mouth, but I have no clue what he's gone through since.

I stand there and watch him devour half the food in my kitchen, taking an apple from the pile and shoving it into his pocket before opening my fridge to snatch up a single serving of Greek yogurt. I can't bring myself to stop him.

Why didn't I check up on him? Why, when I was following up on all of those missing person cases, did I not follow up on the boy who was orphaned when he was ten? If I had done any digging on his uncle, would I have known he was an abusive drug addict and alcoholic? Could I have saved him?

When the news came out a few years ago that Frank Gilmore, brother to the late Valerie Ayers, had been arrested for driving under the influence and in possession of narcotics, I didn't think anything of it. No one did. By that point, the Ayers case was old news, and no one cared about the family anymore. Not like anything they did at that point would be surprising.

But I should have known there was a teenage boy in Frank's house. I should have known to search that news article for any mention of the child under his care, but the story never mentioned Cullen, and I never looked.

"What do you want from me, Cullen?" I ask, feeling a little defeated.

He grabs the wine off the table and finishes another glass. "Don't you think it's a little too late for you to offer me anything?"

"Then why are you here? What am I supposed to do now to make it right?"

He scoffs. "You can't make it right, Everly. None of you can. Not you, not my dad, not my uncle. No one can bring my mom back or go back in time and give a shit about the little kid who got royally fucked by every adult in his life."

It stabs me like a knife, but I fight back. "Is risking your scholarship and your education really worth getting back at me for doing my job? Is this the kind of man you want to be?" I'm speaking to him like an authority figure, like his teacher, and it just feels wrong. I may be fourteen years older than him, but in every other aspect, he holds the control. It makes me feel so small in his presence.

There's a drawn-out silence between us. He sets the glass down, and a cold chill works its way up my spine because I know I've triggered something. As he steps toward me, I back away until I hit the wall. He reaches out and touches my face, letting his finger drift down my cheek, along my jawline, until he's pinching my chin between his thumb and fingers. It's not as harsh as in the car, but it scares me all the same.

The blue and white flecks in his eyes shine like shards of broken glass in the bright lights of my kitchen. I keep waiting for someone to snap me out of this dream because I can't seem to move away or stop him as he leans toward me. I let out a yelp as his other hand scoops me by my waist and pulls me against his body.

With my eyes squeezed closed, I press my hands to his chest, but I don't fight him nearly as much as I should.

"What kind of man do you think I am, Miss West?" he whispers darkly with his mouth close to my face.

"Cullen, stop," I reply—a little too weakly, if I'm being honest.

"Answer the question." The hand around my waist squeezes harder.

"I don't know," I stammer. My brain isn't firing on all cylinders. It's like I'm short-circuiting from the intensity of his nearness. It's too much. My mind is confused, but not as much as my body, which has suddenly stopped pushing away from him.

"Yes, you do. What kind of man am I?" He shakes me harshly, and my eyes pop open to stare back into his, and I scramble for an answer. What does he want me to say? What if I answer wrong? What is Cullen Ayers capable of?

"You're—you're the kind of man who..." Something in his eyes gives the answer away as I see what I saw today in the car. He's not cruel or manipulative—he's lonely. He's passionate and maybe that passion looks a little bit like anger, but something in me recognizes that in him.

"...who likes control," I finish. There's absolutely no reaction in his expression to my answer.

"I do like control," he says in a cool, flat tone.

His mouth lands harshly on my lips. I'm too stunned to move. My hands are pressed against his chest, but not with enough force to actually push him off of me. In the recesses of my mind, I know if I really want him off, I can get away, but I don't. I just let him kiss me.

His tongue slides between my lips, diving into my mouth like he owns me, and I guess at this point, he does. The metal on his tongue surprises me for a moment as it slides against mine. He lets out a low growl when the hand around my waist squeezes me closer, practically fusing my body with his.

His hips rock against my body, and I curve into his arms, like putty in his hands. Warmth radiates from my belly, and a tiny high-pitched moan rattles through me.

Somewhere in the back of my mind, the naive part of me actually thinks *maybe this won't be so bad. Maybe I had nothing to worry about at all.* I mean, yes, this is highly unethical, but the kiss has tilted my world off its axis.

Still, I push against him, but only until he sucks my lip between his teeth, biting with just enough force to feel good and bad at the same time. My brain ceases to think or fight it because I know this is the best kiss I've had in a long, long time—maybe ever.

As he finally starts to separate our mouths, leaving us both breathless, I see something out of the corner of my eye, and I glance that way just in time to see his phone extended in his hand, the selfie camera open and his thumb over the white circle, already snapping pictures I can spot in the camera roll along the bottom.

"Say cheese," he mumbles against my cheek.

He hits it one more time, getting a shot of me with red lips and a look of horror on my face. Suddenly, waking from my daze, I lunge for the phone, but he's too quick, holding it out of my reach. A cruel laugh slips through his lips as he scrolls through the pics he just took.

"You asshole," I bark at him.

His hand is still around my waist, holding me to his body. "You were right, Miss West. I do like control, and these will give me all the control I need."

"Delete them, Cullen. You kissed me by force. I should have you arrested." I'm rambling, still trying to think clearly after that kiss that has my brain feeling foggy.

His expression darkens as he glares down at me. "You know what? I think we can do better." Then in a rush, he pockets his phone and hoists me up into his arms. Unlike the kiss, I fight back. My hands beat into his chest and panic seizes up my torso when I realize he's taking me to the couch.

"What are you doing?" I manage to gasp before I'm thrown onto the cushions of my couch. As I stare up at Cullen in horror, it chills me to the bone to see the life gone from his eyes. He straddles my waist and takes my wrists in his hands, pinning them above my head.

"I need a little more leverage on you than just some kissing photos." His hand grasps the bottom of my shirt, and panic locks my heart in a vise grip as he tears it up, exposing my bare breasts underneath. All I can manage is a strangled gasp. It feels like I can't breathe. All I can do is struggle, trying to maneuver my way out from underneath him, but it's such a waste of energy. Working around my wrists in his hands, he pulls my shirt clean off, tossing it on the floor and leaving me naked from the waist up.

"Not bad," he says, staring down at me. Bile rises in my throat and tears stream from my eyes down into my hair, but he doesn't care. He pulls out his phone and aims it at me.

I struggle harder.

"Cullen, stop!" I scream, my voice shaking as I fight back.

"Hold still." His fingers bite into my wrists and my legs flail uselessly. I refuse to lie still. I cannot let myself submit to his control. Rage courses through my veins when he brushes my wet hair out of my face.

He's getting frustrated with me—I can tell. So it's no surprise when he leans down and mumbles coldly in my face. "If you don't cooperate, you can only expect it to get worse, so if you want to get rid of me, Everly, you better fucking hold still and smile for the camera."

I want to vomit. I could scream and cry and tear his hair out with how much anger I feel, but I know what he's saying is true. If I want it to be over, I have to let him have what he wants. He can have his picture, but he's not getting a fucking smile.

When he feels me relax under him, he brushes my hair away again. I don't look at the camera, but I settle my gaze somewhere else, unable to brush the indignation off my face. I hear his camera snap a few pictures from various angles and distances.

"Thank you. Now was that so hard?" He puts his phone back in his pocket, but he doesn't let go of me. Instead, he pinches my right nipple between his fingers and my back levitates off the couch. His touch on such an intimate spot makes my insides turn and my mind go blank. A minute ago he was kissing me, and it was nice, but how did it get like this? Why is he so intent on making me suffer?

He kneads my breast in his hand, and it's all wrong. I can't even muster the courage to tell him to stop at this point. My body is lost in confusion, wanting this to feel good when it feels so, so bad.

I should be relieved when he lets go of my hands and bounds off me, parading through my home. I'm left tear-soaked and full of venom as I fish my shirt from the floor and quietly put it back on. I use it to wipe the tears and sweat from my face.

"Where is your phone?" he asks, scanning my living room.

"What? Why?" I ask, my brain still in an adrenaline fog. He passes my desk where the laptop screen is black, but I feel a sudden jolt of fear that he will wake it up and see his photos plastered all over my screen—photos of him as a small child.

He quickly spots my phone on the desk and snatches it up without touching my laptop. I breathe a small sigh of relief until I see him swiping the phone screen and holding it toward me before I can even react. It opens immediately with the face scan, and he starts going through it. I jump up in a rush to claw at him or try to get it back; he doesn't even react.

"What are you doing, Cullen?" I yell.

"Just making sure I can keep track of you while I'm not around." He says it so calmly it makes my skin crawl.

"What does that mean? Why?"

Looking down at me, he gives me such a blank, nonchalant expression. His eyes are still void of life. I almost want the boy from the car back, because at least there wasn't pure evil behind those crystal blues.

He leans in and pinches my chin again, but I back away this time, jerking out of his grasp. "Don't you remember what I said in the car? You belong to me now."

I swallow down the lump in my throat, making it hard to breathe. How did I end up in this mess? And more importantly, how am I going to get myself out?

"You brought this on yourself. You had to come to my game. Had to blabber to my coach. You probably could have had me transferred out of your class and ended this right away, but I think you love it, Miss West. I think you wanted this, so this is the game we're going to play now. You wanted me—and now you've got me."

I'm speechless as he tosses my phone on the couch. I jump for it, opening it with a quick swipe to see what he did. There are no obvious changes. Home screen looks normal. My texts open directly to Thomas's last message— he was the last person I texted. It all looks perfectly normal.

"How long do you think this can go on?" I ask.

He's doing something on his own phone so he ignores my question for a moment. Then he looks up and flashes the image of my bare breasts, and I have to look away. "Until I know you get it, Everly. Until you understand the hell I've lived in for the last eight years. Until you truly know what you did to me."

I press my lips together and refuse to meet his gaze. The intensity of his stare bores into me, and I know for a fact with that photo and the one of us kissing that he's got me. I can't fight him now. At this point, it's more than my career as a teacher on the line. If those pictures get out, me making out with the teenager from my biggest case, my career as a journalist is over too. My entire life is on the line. He's right —he does own me.

"Fine. What do you want me to do?" I glare at him with hatred in my eyes. This is no longer a student/teacher relationship between us. He's treating me like the enemy so I guess that's what I am.

A smile creeps across his face, and it's the kind of smile from someone who has just won. "Nothing right now. But remember, you will not do anything without my permission. You don't go anywhere, talk to anyone, or even so much as touch that pretty little cunt of yours without my permission. Because I'll know. Understand?"

Every part of me wants to fight back. I want to scream, fight, argue, but I don't. Maybe it's because of the photo and the blackmail he's holding against me or maybe it is because of the guilt I still feel for what happened to him as a child. Do I deserve to live in this hell for it? No, but there's something in Cullen that still pulls at my heart, even if he is now the villain in my story.

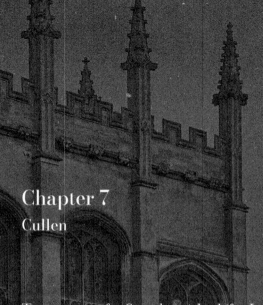

Chapter 7
Cullen

THANK FUCK for Saturday night shifts. I managed to make almost $300 in the six hours I worked tonight. And people were tipping well. Which put me in a good mood—good enough to swing by Miss West's before catching the bus over to Gina's where I could afford to get good and high.

I was not planning that stop at Everly's, but once I found myself there, I couldn't help but have a little fun with her. The idea for the kiss photo was brewing in my mind all night, but I didn't think about it too much until I was there and the opportunity arose. Then it was suddenly too easy.

Ripping her clothes off and snapping pictures of her perfect little tits on the couch—that was less of an idea and more of a...craving. I get this warm, fuzzy feeling every time I think about hurting her, and damn, that feeling gets me horny as fuck. Those pitiful cries for me to stop go straight to my dick. I'm not even going to bother feeling bad for that. I'm not some fucking rapist or predator, but I can't quite explain the way making Everly West suffer gets me off. Plus, she deserves it. It's a win-win.

Now I'm stoned off my ass at Gina's with the new

server, Allie, and she has her lips sheathed around my cock in the guest bedroom. She's on her knees, moaning loudly as she bobs up and down. My hand wraps around her pony-tail, and it's nice. I mean, having your dick sucked is always nice, but I was hoping for more than nice.

When she aims those big brown eyes up at me, and lets me thrust my hips forward and fuck her mouth until she gags, I don't feel any closer to coming. I'm just going through the motions. Using this girl isn't doing anything for me. My dick likes it, but my head is not in the game.

Then my mind wanders to a certain little brunette and how she felt in my arms, her tits pressed against my chest as I slid my tongue between her lips. Her voice still echoes in my head. Everly may be older than me, and I'm not really into the older woman thing, but her kiss didn't feel any different.

No, with my eyes closed and my tongue in her mouth, she didn't feel any older at all. And her age certainly didn't stop my brain from wondering what she might taste like if I had my tongue buried in a different set of lips.

My cock reacts to that thought, and I pump a little faster. Squeezing my eyes shut, I imagine it's Everly's mouth on my cock. We're in the lecture hall and she's wearing that dress she wore on the first day of school with the green sweater. I force her dress up to see the wet pussy underneath, no panties, of course.

Then I imagine spinning her around and fucking her hard from behind over her desk while she begs me to be quiet so no one hears. It only makes me thrust harder, so she has no choice but to scream.

At first I guessed Everly was a basic vanilla bitch, but now I'm seeing things different. She's such a perfectionist and control freak that I bet she'd love to be truly dominated in the bedroom. Little Miss Virtuous would probably love to be forced to her knees while I call her my dirty little slut with my cock down her throat.

Finally, my balls tighten, and I pull Allie's mouth off in a rush, so I can shoot my load all over her face. She keeps her mouth open as it lands on her tongue and cheeks.

After a moment, I turn toward the nightstand to grab her a tissue and help clean her up. She has a lazy smile on her face as she tucks the stray hairs behind her ears. Then she stands up to place a warm kiss on my lips, but I don't really return the kiss, not much at least. Allie's nice and all, but I'm not exactly feeling it with her. I mean, I just got off on a fantasy with my worst enemy while she blew me. Can't exactly say there are sparks here.

"Thanks, babe," I mutter as I slowly make my way toward the door. Just as I reach the living room, my phone buzzes in my pocket. It's past midnight at this point, but the alert is coming from Everly's security system. I gave myself access to all of her cameras when I had her phone. The notification tells me there is motion at her front door.

Clicking the app, I watch as a grainy night vision video shows a man stumbling toward the front door, leaning against a pillar on her front porch. Squinting at the screen, I recognize him as the guy I spotted kissing her on the cheek Friday morning before class started.

A red-hot burst of something unfamiliar courses through my veins. She's having a guy over? Now? After everything I just told her.

Did she tell someone what I did? Is she calling in reinforcements to protect her? If so, this woman has balls. I made it very fucking clear that running that mouth of hers would only get me more upset, and I am more than willing to shoot these pictures to the dean. I just thought I'd get more time to have fun with her first.

"Evie...let me in, sugar tits," the man in the video calls in a slurred tone.

A moment later, her front door opens, and I hear her answer him. "What the fuck is wrong with you?" she asks, grabbing him before he topples over into her flower garden.

She drags him into the house, and my blood starts to boil. Closing the app, I pull up my texts and jab out an angry message.

Me: You have thirty seconds to send him home.

It takes a moment before she types out a reply.

Everly: What the fuck? You're spying on me?

Me: If I don't see him walking out that front door, I'm coming over.

Everly: Relax! He's my best friend. He's drunk, and he's gay.

Me: So call him an Uber.

Everly: I can't, Cullen.

With my jaw clenched, I stare down at my phone. No, this bitch needs to know who's in charge. I can't let this shit fly. This isn't a joke to me. I feel only slightly relieved to learn he's gay, but regardless, he's in the way. I don't want anyone between me and her—they're just complications.

I mean, sure, I didn't really plan for things to get this intense, this fast, but seeing Everly again just fired something up in me. And I don't even know what my plan is, only that I want control over her in every single sense of the word. I don't want her to have even a sliver of freedom or happiness in her life without me controlling it. I need to know she did not win a perfect life while I suffered. I want her to pay.

Me: Send me a picture of him sleeping on the fucking couch then.

A moment later, a picture is already uploading to my texts. And sure as shit, the guy is passed out, still dressed, shoes and everything. One of his long legs is hanging off the side of the couch. It looks as if she draped a white throw blanket over him, and there is a bottle of water and aspirin on the table next to him.

Me: Now a selfie of you in your bed.

Another picture opens on the screen. It's dark in the room, but I can make out her pale skin and dimpled cheeks in the moonlight. Her head is on the pillow and I spot the pink polka dot lapel of her pajamas. She makes it a point to look enraged in her photo—tight-lipped and stern brow. I can make out the deep bags under her eyes, and I can't help but wonder if she cried after I left.

I can't fucking help myself as I hit the *Video Call* button.

She answers after one ring.

Taking my phone back into the guest room, I find it empty and close myself in. Everyone else at the party is lounging around the TV in the dark, watching some movie on Netflix, so they won't even miss me. Fuck, they probably forgot I was even here.

"Show me your pajamas," I say once her face pops up on the dark screen.

Still looking stubbornly irate, she pulls the phone away from her body, putting the entire pink polka-dot top into view. They are not by any stretch of the imagination sexy pajamas. They are sensible, button-up, soft pajamas that a middle-aged woman would wear if she no longer cared about exciting any man.

But for some fucking reason, my dick starts to rouse to

life as I see Everly in them. I remember the shape of her soft tits and how they barely filled my hand but felt good in my grasp regardless. Her nipples were already hard when I pinched one on her couch, the tight pink bud too inviting to ignore. I desperately want to touch them again.

"Unbutton your shirt," I whisper. I mean, you can't blame me for trying. I am still high off my ass.

"No. No more, Cullen. Tonight was hard enough. You got your pictures, but you can't blackmail me into doing sexual shit for you. That's where I draw the line. You might as well get me fired now if that's what—"

"Okay, okay...Jesus. Settle the fuck down."

"You hardly seem like the kind of guy who needs to blackmail his teacher into sexual shit anyway," she says, and I smile.

"As a matter of fact, I just came all over my coworker's face, so you're actually right about that." I don't know why I just told her that. Again...maybe because I'm high, but blackmail or not, it's a weird thing to tell a grown woman you have a semi-professional relationship with.

"Lovely," she mutters, not sounding very interested in that. "No girlfriend then?"

She's lying on her side in the dark, the phone propped on the pillow next to her. I mimic her position, flopping on the guest bed and holding my phone in a similar way.

"Fuck no."

"Why not?"

"Because every girl I date only wants to stick around for a few fucks before she loses interest and ghosts me. Wait—" It suddenly fucking occurs to me that I'm running my mouth, and I don't quite remember how that happened. "Since when do you get to ask the questions?"

"I'm a journalist, Cullen. It's my job. You're literally in my class."

"Yeah, well, no more questions from you. I'll be asking them from now on."

"Fine," she mutters. "Can I go to sleep now, sir?" She's mocking me, but I don't care.

"No. What's your friend's name?"

"Thomas. Why? You're not going to torment him too, are you?"

"Should I?"

"No. He's harmless. He was my editor, and he had nothing to do with your case. What's your coworker's name?"

"Allie," I reply. "Why do you let Thomas crash on your couch unannounced?" I ask, fighting off a yawn.

"Why does Allie let you come on her face? Did you force her to?" She isn't just killing my buzz—she's slaughtering it.

"My question first." Something about her question has me feeling defensive. I didn't force Allie to do shit. Not even close. She offered. It bothers me that she seems to think this is how I treat all women. She's missing the point—I treat her like this for a reason.

"I let him crash here because he's my friend, and he probably struck out at the bar, so he doesn't want to go home alone. It's something that happens in your thirties. You have to face your loneliness without seeing an end in sight, and it sucks."

I'm not going to fucking tell her I feel that shit, too, at only eighteen. Instead, I stick to crude instead of deep. "Have you fucked him?"

"My question first," she replies. We seem to be volleying on the invasive questions, and it's tit-for-tat.

"No, I didn't force her. Allie's been drooling for my dick since she started a couple weeks ago."

"Did you return the favor?" she asks. I purse my lips and let out an impatient-sounding sigh, because she owes me an answer first. She picks up on it right away.

With a huff, she says, "I told you he's gay."

"So? Maybe he was curious. Or just in the mood to try some pussy. Answer the question."

"No. We haven't had sex. So, what if we had?"

I don't know the answer to that question. Would I be jealous? Maybe a little, but I can't tell her that. Her eyes start to drift closed, and I can't tear mine away until I begin to drift too.

Sleepily, she adds, "You didn't answer my question."

"I don't give a shit about you banging your gay friend."

"I asked if you returned the favor for your coworker." Her eyes glare back at me through the phone screen, and I feel drawn to them. Everly has big round eyes that give me a flood of warmth when she really directs them at me.

"Miss West. Are you asking if I went down on a girl?"

"Well, you got off. Did she?"

"Not by me," I reply.

"That doesn't seem fair," she answers with a yawn. "For a guy who seems really hung up on things being fair and equal, that surprises me."

I'm cornered. Maybe I'm too stoned or tired to be mad, but I just stare at Everly as I replay her words in my head. Life isn't fucking fair. Nothing ever is, so why the fuck do I want revenge on this woman so badly? Why am I so stuck on her feeling what I felt?

She cuts off my thoughts. "I have to run errands tomorrow. Do I have to get permission from you if I need to buy food?"

"Yes. I have practice tomorrow. I want you to take me there. Do your errands while I'm practicing and then come pick me up at the end."

She lets out a sigh. "Fine." She doesn't even bother fighting it, as if Everly has just decided to play along. I don't know how I feel about that, but a small smile creeps across my face without permission. I had absolutely no plan to own her like this, but I'm glad I did. Not just for the convenience of having a ride and not having to take the bus, but this control I have over her is fucking hot. Shit like this shouldn't turn me on, but it does. That's probably why I'm thinking about her so much, wanting to fuck her in rough and dirty positions. It's not that I'm attracted to *her*, but the sense of power is coursing straight to my dick.

"All right, go to sleep," I say in a commanding tone.

She's already drifting off, but it's like she was waiting for me to tell her to let go. She nods before shutting her eyes.

"Don't hang up. Just set the phone down."

"Just in case my gay friend decides he wants to *try pussy*?" she asks in a mocking tone, without opening her eyes.

"Yeah," I say, "because of that."

She rests the phone on the pillow, so I'm looking at a dark ceiling on the screen. I can still hear her breathing, and before I know it, I drift off too.

Chapter 8
Everly

WHEN I WAKE up in the morning, my phone is still lying on the pillow next to me. Jumping up, I grab it to make sure Cullen isn't still on the screen, but it's dead. A feeling of dread and guilt courses through me as I realize it probably died sometime during the night and he could be trying to reach me.

Wait a minute. That's insane.

All of this is insane. He's my student, practically a kid, and I'm letting him treat me like garbage. My head is pounding, and I can tell it's not from the wine and more than likely from the crying and the overall trauma that took place in my own home. God, what the hell was that all about? I knew Cullen was intense. But we went from pill bottles and pearl necklaces to near-rape in like two seconds flat. I can't get the look on his face out of my head. The lack of life behind his eyes. He was just...lost to the fever of his rage like a sickness, and I couldn't reach him. I begged him to stop, and it didn't do me an ounce of good.

Maybe I had too much faith in him. Maybe I wanted to believe Cullen was the apple that fell very far from the poisoned tree, but I was wrong. The way he treated me last night—hell, the way he's *still* treating me today—I see him for what he really is. He's abusive, manipulative, and as far as I can tell up until now, an actual sociopath.

Or is he just a shattered man grown from a broken child?

No. *Stop it, Everly. Stop making excuses for him and letting him walk all over you.* I can't keep this up. Yes, that moment before bed was almost endearing. Yes, we had a brief connection, and this vitriol between us feels almost... intimate. But it has to end. It's exhausting. If he wants to leak those photos, then oh well. He can leak them. I'll lose my job at the university, but who cares? I don't love teaching that much anyway. I can always get a job somewhere else. Maybe I'll start fresh in a new city.

God, what the hell am I thinking?

It's too early for this existential crisis. First, coffee.

For good measure, I plug my phone in and head out into the living room when I get a whiff of brewing beans coming from the kitchen. Thomas is standing near the coffee pot in last night's clothes.

"I wasn't the only one drinking last night," he mutters, glancing at the empty wine bottle on the table. "You look rough."

I'm sure I do. I didn't even bother sparing a glance in the mirror, but I can imagine the bags under my eyes are intense and the look on my face probably says *very fucking hungover*. Thomas doesn't need to know I'm more hungover from the trauma than from the Merlot. So, I give him an innocent shrug and omit the part about my student stopping by and drinking half of it.

He fills his cup and then mine, half with cream before

passing it to me. "So, tell me all about your first week on the job."

Letting out a groan, I sit at the island and slump against the granite.

"That bad, huh?"

Just the idea of having to talk about my job while omitting any mention of Cullen depletes my energy and will to speak at all. I decide at that moment there's nothing wrong with telling Thomas about Cullen being in my class. I'm so used to telling him literally everything, but I can't possibly include the part about Cullen harassing me, stalking me, forcefully taking naked pictures of me, and basically ruling every aspect of my life.

"What's on your mind?" Thomas says, pulling me from my daydream. My friend is so intuitive. No one reads me better than him, but I don't think I'm being very subtle about this being the worst week of my life.

I let out a deep sigh. "Do you remember the Ayers' kid from *that* case?"

He flinches, his eyebrows pinching together as if he wasn't expecting me to bring that up. Which makes sense. It is sort of out of nowhere.

"Um...yeah. I remember him having a kid."

"Well, that kid isn't a kid anymore. He's in college."

"Okay..." he says, clearly waiting to see where this is going.

"And he's in my class."

His jaw practically hits the countertop. "You're kidding."

"I wish I was."

"Do you think he remembers you?"

Rolling my eyes, I try very hard to feel bad for lying to my best friend, but I'm afraid if I teeter too close to the truth, I'll cross the line and spill everything. So I lie right through my teeth. "No. I don't think he does. He was only ten at the time."

"I know but...that was big news back then. Your name was in the paper as much as the Ayers family was."

"Well, ten-year-olds don't read the newspaper, Thomas. And if he does remember me, then maybe he's moved on."

"You're lucky if he did. That case ripped that family to shreds, and it all started with your article."

Letting out a scoff, I glare at him. "Wow, thanks for reminding me, as if I don't already feel terrible enough about it."

I didn't exactly need the reminder. Cullen has been very clear about this since Wednesday.

"Speaking of," he adds, "I heard the lawyers are putting together a strong case for his appeal. I wouldn't be surprised if he gets out a lot sooner than the full thirty."

"That's insane. With all of those charges..."

"I've seen crazier."

We're quiet for a moment, both sipping on our coffees while he scrolls through his phone. Then for some reason I think about the files I opened last night. All the missing person cases are still unsolved. "Did you know how many people ended up displaced after his hotel chain closed?"

"Uhh...yeah. I mean, I figured it was going to be a clus-terfuck after that."

"Do you remember me trying to get the chief to approve my idea for the exposé on the women who never made it home?"

He grimaces. "Sadly, yes."

"What?" I snap, glaring up at him. "You don't think that was important? Hundreds of people were left homeless and displaced. We left it up to private non-profits to help them while the FBI did nothing."

"I'm not saying it wasn't a good cause, Ev. I'm saying... it's not our job. You wrote your article. You did your part. The rest is not on your shoulders."

Then why do I feel like it is?

After coffee, Thomas gives me a firm hug and heads out to the Uber waiting for him in my driveway. Waving to him from the porch, I suddenly realize I left my phone in the bedroom.

When I get to it, there are two text messages from Cullen.

CULLEN: My PRACTICE IS AT TEN. DON'T BE LATE.
Cullen: Aww...you feel terrible?

THE SECOND ONE DOESN'T MAKE SENSE. AND MY MIND is still lost in a fog, so I write it off as some Cullen hate-flirting and go back to the kitchen to pour myself another cup. It's still early so I don't need to rush into the shower just yet. It gives me a few quiet moments in my kitchen, but my mind is still ruminating on my conversation with Thomas.

Why was I the only one who seemed to care about the people left behind? I mean...I wasn't the *only* one. The people with the non-profits jumped right in to do everything they could, but where was the oversight? Whose job was it to make sure everyone made it home? Why was I the only one in the journalism industry to feel terrible about it?

Terrible.

I glance down at Cullen's text again.

. . .

AWW...YOU FEEL TERRIBLE?

I said that, didn't I? To Thomas, I said I already felt terrible about it.

My blood runs cold. How did Cullen hear that? Instinctively, I glance around the room, feeling like someone is watching me. Like I'm not alone, and it makes me sick to my stomach. Logging into my doorbell camera is one thing, but not being able to have a conversation in my own home, without him listening in, is *way too fucking far*.

Punching the green button on the phone, it starts dialing his number, and I hold it up to my face with my hand shaking. I'm done, and this ends right now.

Why does that thought make me feel almost...disappointed? That's a conversation for my therapist. For now, I'm buzzing with rage, waiting to hear his voice on the other end. As soon as it answers, I lose it.

"What the *fuck*, Cullen?" I scream. "Where are you?"

He laughs, his deep chuckle vibrating through my ear, and his nonchalance makes me even more irritated.

"It's not funny!"

"Relax. I dropped into your smart speaker. Only for a moment. You weren't answering my calls, and I knew your phone was dead. I wanted to make sure you were up. I heard you talking to your little bestie before I got off."

"*Not* okay!"

"I know, I know. Geez. But neither is making out with your student and flashing him your titties, but you did that, so I guess we're even."

"I'm unplugging that thing," I snap.

"Fine," he mutters. "Hey, it's almost nine. Don't be late. I need to be there in an hour, and it takes you at least fifteen minutes to get here." He's so casual about it, and the outrage I felt a moment ago fizzles out like a popped balloon.

I should argue. I should tell him no, and part of me almost does. But the truth is...I don't want to tell him no. It's actually nice to be...needed.

There's another one for my therapist. I need to book an extra-long session next week.

Will endure toxic, manipulative relationships in order to feel needed.

I'm like the poster child for self-worth issues—something I didn't even know I had. Should be fun getting to the bottom of that. I'm over here worrying about Cullen Ayers when I know I mean literally nothing to him. He doesn't care about me—not in a good way.

And yet, here I am, throwing on some more workout clothes I have absolutely zero intention to work out in before grabbing a bottle of water and running out the door so I'm not late. Cullen is sitting on the low brick wall outside his dorm when I pull up, and I do a quick glance around to make sure no one recognizes me as he climbs in.

"Morning, sunshine," he says, and I don't bother replying. I'm still mad about the speaker thing, and I want him to know it.

He keeps his duffel bag at his feet, and I can't help but notice how good he smells or how thick his arms look in that tight T-shirt. I never went after guys like Cullen when I was his age. I was so focused on finding a forever man, I tended to date the straight-laced type. That plan obviously backfired because the straight-laced boring types are never as polite or kind as they seem on the outside. I had my heart broken more times than I could count by men who only wanted me to sit down, be quiet, and blow them from time to time while they belittled me, spoke over me, and cheated on me. It was the oldest trick in the book, and I kept falling for it because they never failed at appearing like perfect gentlemen on the outside.

At least Cullen has the decency to look like a red flag.

"What's wrong with you?" he asks as I pull out of the campus parking lot.

Instead of answering, I glare at him. He knows exactly what's wrong with me.

"You're not still mad about the speaker thing, are you?"

"Yes, I am. And the kiss thing. And the naked photos thing. And the forcing me to drive you around thing."

"Like you had better plans today."

"Maybe I did. But even if I didn't, shouldn't it be my choice?"

"We went over this. You owe me, Miss West."

"Actually, I don't owe you shit, Cullen. Do you have to blackmail everyone in your life to be around you?" I snarl as we turn onto the main road.

"You're being a real cunt today," he says, and it's laughable how genuine it is. He has the nerve to act surprised by it too.

"Can you blame me? After everything you've put me through."

"And I'll keep putting you through it as long as I want. Are you miserable yet?"

"Yes," I reply, exasperated. "I am. Can we be done now?"

"Do I have to remind you how much you fucked up my life?"

"Oh my God! Get over it!" I yell.

"No, I don't think I will. I'll drag this shit out just to piss you off more. Maybe after practice, you'll drive me around and do my errands. And then I'll make you cook dinner for me like a servant. Then you can do my fucking laundry."

"A couple scandalous pictures will not buy you that much," I reply, huffing with a sarcastic laugh. "I'm not your fucking mother," I say without thinking. It just slips out. There's a beat of tension before he snaps.

"Pull over," he barks, his voice so deep it sends a chill down my spine.

"You'll be late—"

"Pull over!" There's a side street off the main road mostly hidden by trees, but when I glance around, I realize that if he wants to get out, here is not the best place to do it. There's nowhere to walk.

"Cullen—" I say as I turn toward him, but he cuts me off. His large hand snatches me by the back of my neck as he yanks me toward him. His lips press against mine in a bruising kiss. I'm caught off guard, letting out a yelp as he forces his tongue into my mouth. The kiss is full of fire and fury, ten times as angry as it is sensual. In fact, this isn't even in the same gene pool as a tender, loving kiss. It's really more like a punch to the face or a stab to the back.

Pulling back, he takes my bottom lip between his teeth and brings me just enough pain to hike up my fear level from alarmed to terrified. Up until this point, I haven't really kissed back—learned my lesson last night, but I haven't had much of a choice either. He knocked the sense right out of me with his mouth. But I also know there's a part of me holding back because I'm afraid this is just Cullen being manipulative again. I want to believe this is real, even if it is angry and hate-filled. I want to hate-kiss him as much as he clearly wants to hate-kiss me, but I'm keeping my wants and desires guarded until I understand what is going on a little more.

Letting go of my lip, he presses his mouth against mine and snarls, so I can feel his words as well as hear them.

"No, you are not my fucking mother, Everly. Don't you ever compare yourself to my mother again. You will never be like her. She wasn't a bitch like you."

I let out a gasp and instantly try to pull away, but he grabs me hard by the back of the neck, squeezing so tightly that pain shoots all the way down my spine. "You're hurting me," I say with a whimper. Still, he doesn't let up. Instead, he grabs my hand off the steering wheel and slams it against his crotch, and I lose the ability to breathe when I feel the rock-hard bulge in his shorts.

"Hurting you gets me hard, Everly. You see how fucked up I am?"

He's holding my open hand hard against his cock, and I don't close my fingers around it. *That* would be inappropriate, a voice in the back of my head reminds me. As if all of this isn't already super fucking inappropriate.

Our mouths are still touching as he breathes heavily against my face. Silence fills the car, and I stare into his eyes, noticing he's raging with anger, but there's something else there too. He's not quite dead behind the eyes like he was last night because today, they are also shrouded with lust. It softens his eyes, and I know what's coming before he even says it.

"Pull it out."

"Cullen," I whisper, pleading.

"You said those photos won't buy me enough, so let's get some more leverage. You can either swallow my dick or I can shove it down your throat. Your choice."

That should turn my blood to ice. It *should* make me

quiver in fear and scream until someone hears me. I'm behind the wheel; I could drive away right now, but I don't.

Because his cock pulses against my palm. And I hate myself for how much I want to touch it right now. Our fight changed the entire mood in the car from sarcastic to passionate. I'm charged and full of buzzing energy with nowhere to direct it.

Right now, with the smell of his cologne filling my car and those crystal blue eyes staring a hole right through me, I want to do so much more than touch him.

I hope my therapist is ready for this.

"The clock is ticking, Miss West," he mutters. Jerking me forward, he kisses my jaw before baring his teeth and biting all the way down to my neck. Heat floods my bloodstream, and I feel the moisture leak onto my panties.

How am I seriously considering this? I know there are a million reasons I should *not* do this—one of them being he's forcing me solely for the purpose of blackmail—but these reasons just fade into the background of my mind, out of focus and distant. I am too headstrong to let a man push me around like this, so why do I suddenly seem to like it? All I know right now is the fever I feel burning between us and the rock-hard length beneath my hand.

"I can't," I whisper, unconvincingly. It's about as much as the rational thought in my head can manage.

The hand on the back of my neck shoves me down hard until I'm bent over the center console and his groin is only inches from my face. "Fine. We'll do it the hard way then. I think I might enjoy it more this way anyway," he says, trying to shimmy down his shorts.

"Okay, okay!" I cry out because as much as I secretly want to have his cock in my mouth, I don't want it like that.

It would change everything for me if he truly forced me to do it.

Cullen is a man, I remind myself, as I slowly peel down the elastic band of his shorts with trembling hands. And when his cock pops out, it's all the reminder I need. Cullen is definitely a man. It's the perfect length, thick and veiny with a slight curve, and I can't seem to tear my eyes away.

There is absolutely no good, rational reason for what I do next other than the fact that my life has become unrecognizable in the past five days. I don't know what he's doing to me, but I'm not the same person I was. Five days ago, I would have been horrified by this primal, sick thing between us, but in that short time, I've almost gotten used to it. Whatever it is, it drives me to grab his hard length in my hand and stroke it without hesitation.

He reacts immediately with a deep groan that sends another hit of arousal to my panties. Before I lower my head to his cock, I glance back up at him. He doesn't look so angry. He just looks aroused and hypnotized by pleasure as something like awe reaches his eyes.

The grip on the back of my neck loosens to a firm embrace as I drop my head and wrap my lips around his cock. A shocked-sounding groan echoes through the car as my tongue draws circles around the head, getting it as wet as I can before dropping my mouth down to ease him into the back of my throat.

This is a full-service blow job. I'm not warming him up with kissing his head and teasing his length with my tongue. He's still technically forcing me to do this—as far as he knows at least—so I'm doing the bare minimum. I need to get him off fast so it can be over.

"Jesus, fuck," he moans.

Squeezing him at the base with my hand, I stroke his

cock with my mouth, not even bothering to go slow. I tighten my lips around the head every time my head bounces up, and I suck his dick like my life depends on it. Like it's a fucking race.

I don't need to look up to know he's recording this. In the corner of my eye, I see the phone, but he seems too focused on the pleasure to worry about the angle. This is what he wanted it for, though—something to keep me a slave to him. And why did I go along with it so easily? I should have fought him more.

Instead, I'm soaking my panties as I swallow his cock and the pressure on my neck is practically gone. Now his hand is in my hair, and his thumb moves back and forth as if he's caressing me.

"I'm gonna fucking come," he pants, and excitement pools low in my belly. I've never been so turned on in my life. "You better take it all, Miss West."

I squeeze my eyes shut as he presses me down a few times, jerking his hips up. I start to panic a little when I feel the head swell because I've never in my life either spit or swallowed. All of my other blow jobs end with the guy unloading somewhere on me or him. The idea of swallowing makes me freeze up. But it's too late as he lets out a sound as if he's being strangled, and something warm and salty fills the back of my mouth. At first, I gag, and I'm afraid I'm going to make a giant mess on his lap, but then I close my lips around his cock and force down a swallow.

It's not...terrible. The taste isn't as bad as I expected, and the way he rubs my head, brushing my hair out of my face as I lap up the cum around his cock makes me feel good.

More notes for my therapist.

Opening my eyes, I stare down at his wet dick then up

to his face. His eyes are still glossed over, staring up at the ceiling as he's coming down from the high of his orgasm. A wave of shame washes over me.

What the fuck did I just do?

Grabbing a tissue out of the glove compartment, I quickly wipe my mouth, cleaning up the drool and cum that leaked down my chin. I can't look him in the eye, but he's not exactly looking at me either. Keeping his gaze averted, awkward tension fills the inside of my car as he pulls his shorts back up and fidgets in his seat.

I would hand over the keys to my car just to know what he is thinking right now. Because he doesn't look half as angry as he did before the almost nonconsensual blow job. He looks a little uncomfortable, if I'm being honest with myself.

There are so many things I want to say as I pull the car back onto the road like, 'Guess you've got your leverage now,' or some empty threat about him releasing that video. I could easily carry on our argument from before and demand he put an end to all this, but is that what I want?

I don't know anymore, and that's a scary thought. How could I not know? It should be as simple as, *no, I do not want to be treated like this by a teenager with anger issues.*

But it's not that easy.

We don't speak a word as I drive him to his practice, dropping him off in the parking lot and keeping my face away from the field in hopes Coach Prescott won't see me. He silently gets out of the car, and as I watch him walk to the field, I notice he's carrying himself differently. He seems tense, with his brow furrowed and his lips in a tight, thin line as he glances back at me.

I'm desperate to be as far away from him as I can at the moment, so I peel out of the parking lot and drive as fast as I can to the grocery store. I just need space to clear my head. Cullen is in my brain like a tumor, warping reality.

Once I get to the parking lot of the store, I let my face fall into my hands against the steering wheel, letting out a muffled scream. I don't even care if anyone can hear me.

Can I go to jail for this?

No. This isn't high school. At best, I'll lose my job. That thought certainly doesn't make me feel any better about myself. I mean, what kind of thirty-two-year-old woman does this?

After about fifteen minutes of this parking-lot meltdown, I get out of the car and head into the store. From there, I run by the post office to drop off a box of returns and once that's done, I start checking my phone obsessively, waiting for Cullen to text me back for a ride home. These moments of normalcy in between moments of pure chaos are strange, but a welcome break from the trauma that is Cullen Ayers.

It's been two hours since I dropped him off and I've literally done everything I need to do today, so I head back to the field where I dropped him off. Sitting there in the parking lot, I watch the guys practice, running around and tackling each other, half of them shirtless, and I pick out Cullen immediately. He runs with grace, spinning and dodging the tackles as he dashes down the field with the ball under his arm.

It's a public park with a large parking lot, so I figure there's nothing wrong with just taking a walk while I'm here. I am in workout clothes, after all. Locking my door and taking the key, I get out of my car and join the rest of the walkers and joggers on the paved path around the green field. It's nearly impossible to keep my eyes off Cullen while I stroll. He steals attention like a beacon.

I get the strangest sensation in my chest as I watch him shouting to his teammates. I'm so angry with him, so frustrated with the way he treats me and being so unable to understand him, but I don't hate him, not really. I wanted to. If anything, I might have hated Cullen more before he showed up in my class. I hated what he represented, much in the same way I'm sure he hates me for what I represent. What would I do if I was in his shoes? Would I want to see him hurt?

My mind travels back to a moment in the car when I told Cullen he was hurting me and he used it as an opportunity to show me just how much he likes hurting me. Is this even about revenge anymore? Or is he just plain sadistic?

My gaze finds him again, and that unfamiliar sensation returns in my chest. It's strong, like a pulsing cocktail of anger, lust, and something else...intimacy? Attachment, maybe. Whatever it is, it makes me feel the distance between us like a literal pain. It wants to drag me closer to him, and if it had a pair of legs of its own, it would walk me right over to him. It says he is, in some way, mine.

And that is insane. It must be like some sort of psychological victimizer attachment. Is that even a real thing?

"Funny seeing you again," a familiar voice says on my second lap. I quickly glance over to see Eric Prescott standing nearby. I shake off the guilt in my expression, like he could somehow tell by my eyes that I blew Cullen in the car on the way here, and I force a fake smile on my face.

"I didn't know you guys practiced out here," I lie.

"Yeah, it's a better field for drills."

I swallow down the bile rising in my throat as I catch the way his eyes drift down my shirt, focusing a moment too long on my cleavage in this tank. Glancing at the players on the field, I notice Cullen staring, his expression shrouded in anger.

"All right, gotta get these steps in," I say with a forced laugh as I point at my smart watch.

"Take care." Even as I leave, I feel his eyes on my ass and I suddenly regret even getting out of the car.

Twenty minutes later, practice is over and everyone has left. Cullen sneaks over to my car and doesn't miss a beat as he climbs in. "What the fuck was that?"

"What was what?"

"Prescott. I want you to stay away from him." He tosses his duffle bag in the trunk this time, shutting it like this is nothing out of the ordinary.

"He's harmless," I reply, knowing it won't be enough to satisfy his sudden sense of possessiveness.

He jumps in the passenger side, and I'm anxious to get out of there as fast as possible. The coach is already gone, and I truly think he's harmless, but something about him has me feeling uneasy. On the bright side, at least the tension from the car ride here has dissipated. Even as I start driving toward campus to drop Cullen off at the dorms, I feel the question brewing. This is where I'm taking him, right?

"What's for dinner?" he asks, and I glance over at him.

I let out a frustrated sigh, although somewhere, deep down, I'm relieved. Even as I make the right toward my house instead of a left toward his dorm, I can barely see past the red flags. Cullen is taking advantage of me, abusing me, and I'm pretty sure I'm supposed to be miserable about it. Too bad I'm not.

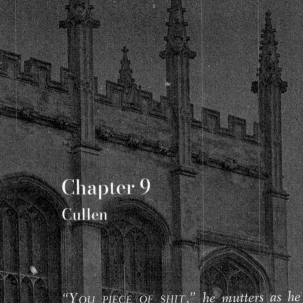

Chapter 9
Cullen

"YOU PIECE OF SHIT," he mutters as he slams the fridge closed. "You ate all the pizza."

I keep my mouth shut. That three-day-old pizza was the only thing he's fed me all week.

"Hey, punk. You better go to the store to get me something to eat. I'm hungry."

I'm twelve. How am I supposed to go to the store? But still, I don't argue. He doesn't like it when I talk back. He also doesn't like it when I ignore him, or breathe, or take up space in his house. Or eat, apparently.

His palm lands hard against the back of my head, but I saw that coming. Still hurts like hell, though. I wince over my math notebook and swallow down the lump building in my throat. I hate him so much, and when he gets like this, I focus hard on that hate. It's like a nuclear bomb goes off inside my head, one of those big mushroom clouds bursting through my brain. That's the hatred I feel for him, and I can't wait for the day when I'm bigger than him, so I can smack him in the back of the head like he does to me.

These thoughts make it hard to focus on my math homework.

"Your piece of shit dad couldn't leave you any money, so now you're my burden, I guess. It's fucking bullshit, that's what it is. I didn't want a goddamn kid." He leans down close to my ear, and the smell of beer singes my nose.

"My stupid whore of a sister never knew when enough was enough."

The bomb inside me goes off, and I burst out of my chair. I don't care that he's still twice my size. I swing at his face anyway. The beer makes him move slowly so, unlike every other time I try to fight him, this time I actually make contact with his face. My fist makes a cracking noise as it collides with his cheekbone. Both of us freeze, staring wide-eyed at each other.

I wish I could take it back.

"You're so fucking dead," he mutters as he snatches me by the hair and slaps me hard against my face. The whole time he pummels me with his fist, I just keep thinking about the day when I can get my revenge. Revenge on him. Revenge on all of them.

WIPING THE STEAM OFF THE MIRROR, I TRY TO CLEAR away the memory from the front of my mind. Something about being in Everly's home is bringing on the flashbacks of the seven nightmare years I spent in my uncle's house. Although this is nothing like that. Maybe because that was the last house I lived in.

From the time I was ten to seventeen, I had to share a home with that asshole. The only saving grace was the major growth spurt I had at fifteen, putting me at nearly six feet tall, and poof—just like that, he miraculously started leaving me alone. Shocker.

Then the idiot got arrested, and I managed to get emancipated at seventeen, so I never had to depend on anyone ever again.

Whatever is sizzling in the kitchen when I get out of Everly's shower smells like heaven. A home-cooked meal is so rare for me, I'll literally do almost anything for one, including blackmailing my professor, apparently.

A blow job and dinner both in one day. I must be doing something right.

I'll admit, the BJ was...unexpected. I had no intention of our morning commute going in that direction, but I'd be lying if I said I haven't been thinking of ways to get her mouth on me. Then, she got sassy with me in the car, and it brought out the aggressive side of me, which brought out the turned on as fuck side of me, and the next thing I knew, my dick was hard and she was touching it. It all happened so fast, and it threw me off my game. As sex almost always does.

All through practice, I couldn't land a catch or make a pass without the sudden reminder of her face in my lap, the wet heat of her mouth around my cock, slurping and bobbing on me like I had a knife to her throat, which for the record, I did not. If she wanted to put up more of a fight, she could have.

Fuck, I want her to do it again.

I want her to sit on my face while she does it next time, letting me suffocate on her pussy while she slobs on my pole, doing that delightful little thing she did when she tightened her lips on the head, practically milking my dick.

And...I'm hard again.

Standing in her bedroom in just my towel and looking

around at her jewelry and random pictures of her perfect middle-class family, I have to remind myself that Everly is the enemy. I *hate* her. She ruined my life, and she is literally the face I see every night when I close my eyes, remembering how I once had it so good compared to the constant shitshow my life has become.

Suddenly, hating her is becoming something different. Like I'm annoyed with her. Frustrated with how she lives her life, like she takes all of it for granted, never truly appreciating how good she has it. I hate that she's rolling over and taking my punishment when what I really want is for her to fight back.

I want to hurt her without *really* hurting her. I want her *to want me* to hurt her. Because there is no denying that my dick got hard solely from the way she cried out, and kissing her was not some sort of sensual foreplay. It was a punishment.

What the hell does that even mean?

"Dinner's ready," she calls from the kitchen. The bedroom door is open, and there is a direct line of sight from her to me, so I drop my towel. Might as well have a little fun with her, I guess.

With my bare ass in her view, I turn my head to see her looking at me with a deer-in-headlights look on her face.

"Ever heard of a door?" she asks, shaking off the hypnotized look in her eyes.

"Your turn to take a picture, Miss West."

"No, thank you." She groans.

I let out a laugh as she turns away. After getting dressed, I find her in the kitchen, stirring something on the stove while flipping through her phone. She's in a pair of green workout pants and a loose top that has a cut-out along the back, exposing her porcelain skin. I want to walk up to her and run my fingers down her spine. I want to bury my face in her hair and press my body against her, pinning her to the oven. For some reason, I want to claim every piece of Everly, as if having her as mine is some sort of punishment for what she's done to me.

I mean, a good hate-fuck isn't exactly off course.

Everly is a woman with a sense of maturity in her body and mannerisms I don't find with the girls at the restaurant or at school. She's not so self-conscious, constantly hiding her body and flaws, or flaunting it like she thinks she's made of gold. I think for the most part, Everly doesn't care what other people think. I can't explain what has me so attracted to her.

My eyes land on the nape of her neck where the soft hairs have fallen from the ponytail, inviting me to touch them. My fingers itch to reach toward her, but I hold back.

Noticing me standing there, she glances my way. "Grab a plate."

Doing as she says, I pick up a white porcelain plate off the counter and walk up to her like a waiting child. This little playing-house routine is weird, but I like it.

As she scoops up a chicken breast smothered in some creamy, delicious-smelling sauce and a heaping spoonful of rice, I watch her face. She looks miserable, and I wonder if she really is or if she's just playing the part since I'm still technically *making* her do this for me.

I want inside her head. I want to see everything she's thinking at every moment, and I've never felt that way with anyone before. Does she really want me gone? If I walked out that door right now, ending everything, would she be disappointed or relieved? I'm sure even if she was disappointed, she wouldn't let it show. She would never give me the satisfaction of knowing I got under her skin.

We eat in silence. Well, I should say she eats in silence. I inhale every bite of it, not even registering it's gone until I stare down at my empty plate. She glances at it, too, and avoids my eyes as she refills it without a word.

"Thanks," I mutter when she sets it down. I should be more embarrassed by how fucking hungry I am, but she's being too nonchalant about it. Still, I hate feeling like a charity case. I was born with a silver spoon in my mouth that was abruptly torn away without warning, and what the fuck did I do wrong to deserve that? Nothing. But here I am, feeling like a fucking piece of shit in her dining room, forcing her to feed me like I'm a damn child.

Today she asked if I had to manipulate everyone to be around me, and I hate that it still bothers me. I don't have to manipulate the girls who eagerly drop to their knees for me. I don't have to manipulate the guys on the team or Gina or my other friends at work. Everly was just being a bitch, but the question still pisses me off, which just winds me up even more.

After dinner, she cleans up while I wander around her house, nosily picking at every single thing I can. Her laptop is open on her desk, and I'm tempted to start scrolling through it, but the second I get close to it, she snaps at me.

"Leave it alone."

"You got a porn stash you don't want me to see?"

"Yes, that's exactly it," she replies sarcastically.

"Let's watch it."

She's stepping forward to stop me when I wrap an arm around her waist and pull her close. I was looking for a reason to touch her—that's not even worth lying about. "When are we going to talk about that little incident in the car today?"

"We're not. I was planning on forgetting it ever happened."

"Oh, it happened," I reply, leaning my face close to brush my nose along her jawline.

She lets out a shaky breath as I feel her tremble. "You're sending mixed signals, Cullen. You hate me, remember?"

"Oh, I remember. Ever heard of a hate-fuck?"

Her eyes flash toward mine, our gazes locking in a heavy stare, so many things left unspoken between us and so much we don't even need to say. Intrigue and lust are thickly wrapped around us, and it makes me forget what I was supposed to be doing in the first place. I'm trying to make her pay for what she did, not make her feel good.

Something feels wrong, and it makes me freeze. She's not fighting me, not stopping me as I lean my lips down and rest them against her neck. Last night, she gave me hell, just trying to escape my touch. Now she trembles, leaning in toward me, and I realize this train has fallen off the tracks.

I'm not here to make Everly West feel good or fuck her or give her what she wants. I'm here to make her miserable, but in less than a week, I've found myself at her house in some sort of domestic foreplay, and it pisses me off.

Fuck this.

"I'm going home," I say in a low tone, and she stiffens, looking up at me.

It's like she just had the same dawning realization I just did. She looks like she wants to protest, but that's not right. She should be relieved I'm leaving. Gathering her composure, she pulls away.

"Am I driving you?"

"No, I could use some air. Don't leave the house and no visitors."

"Yes, sir." She gives me a defiant glare, her shoulders

back and her lips pressed into a fine line. That's more like it, I think.

"See you in class," I mumble as I head toward the door. Grabbing my bag, I head out and hear her quietly reply before I'm gone.

"See you in class."

Chapter 10
Everly

It's fifteen minutes into class when he finally marches in, causing a disruption I try to ignore as he takes his seat on the top row. The class is still mostly unsettled by Cullen after our little dispute during our first week of class, where he literally called me a cunt. I do my best to settle their insecurities by not reacting to him during class.

Our eyes only meet for a split second, but I have a hard time looking away from him in those tight jeans and a T-shirt that hugs his body so snug I can see the soft ridges of his muscles. I lose my train of thought for a moment and I see the way it makes his mouth turn up only slightly at the corners. He likes getting inside my head.

It's been almost three weeks since he came over. He says it's because of his work schedule with practice and school work, but I can also tell that Cullen needed a little space. Our first week was intense, and it ended strangely. He mentioned hate-sex that night, and while it had me on edge, it also made me almost...excited. The dynamic between us changed too quickly for his liking. I wasn't fighting him so much, and we were almost getting along. I don't think that was ever his intention, so he took a few weeks off.

He still video calls me every night 'to make sure I'm home and alone.' We spend the entire time shooting questions back and forth. I tell him about my terrible boyfriends, my family in upstate New York, and my decision to move from the newspaper to teaching. He's talked about his uncle, how he's never had a steady girlfriend, and his plans to finish college so he can start his own business, although he doesn't know what kind.

I feel like I know Cullen now after so many years of thinking I knew him and hating him for the version I had in my head. I can't speak for him, but I'm starting to get the feeling he feels the same. He's not *as* cruel as before. But I don't want to get comfortable just yet. He's just waiting for the right moment to strike again.

"Knock, knock," a voice calls from the doorway after I finish my lecture. I'm in the middle of assigning the next reading assignment to the class. I pause as I look over and see Coach Prescott standing in the doorway. He has a bright smile on his face as he nods his head toward the hallway.

"Got a second?" he asks.

My mouth falls open. I'm literally standing in front of two hundred students in the middle of a class. No, I do *not* have a second, but he doesn't seem to care about that. It takes everything in me not to look at Cullen.

"Just a second," I reply as I reluctantly follow him to the hallway.

Cullen has demanded I attend his games and practices all week, and while I don't hate that so much—there could be worse punishments than watching sweaty college boys tackle each other on a field—it has garnered a little bit of attention from his coach, who never fails to corner me into conversation every time.

"I hope to see you at tonight's game," he says, trapping me between the wall and his body, as one hand rests on the wall next to my head.

"Of course. I'll be there."

"Maybe we can finally grab that drink after the game."

Eric has literally spoken about his wife. She's come to the games. I have *met* her.

"I don't think that would be very appropriate."

"I can't help it," he replies, leaning in. "I can't stop thinking about you. Just have a drink with me. No harm."

"I should get back to class."

"Think about it," he says. I make the mistake of lifting my gaze to meet his eyes, and he takes the opportunity to lean in and press his lips to mine. It's all wrong, and I instinctively push him away. I slip away toward the door, but when I glance back at him, he's smirking at me. He thinks I'm playing hard to get or something, but he's seriously delusional.

By some miracle, I manage to make it through the rest of class, feeling Cullen's eyes on me throughout the hour, trying my hardest not to glance up at him. I know he must be irate about Eric's little visit and judging by the way he doesn't move when the rest of the students start packing up to leave, he's about to make his feelings known to me.

After giving the students their assignments, I dismiss the class. Naturally, a handful of them linger to ask me questions or to start their excuses early. The assignment isn't even due for another month and they're already giving me stories about broken laptops and long work hours. Once I send the last kid away, my eyes lock with Cullen's, who is still sitting in his seat, reclining with his legs wide and staring down at his phone.

"What the fuck was that all about?"

I force myself to relax. I haven't done anything wrong here.

"It's nothing."

"Why are you lying to me?" He doesn't move from his seat, and I start to feel a sense of fear in my gut. Please don't cause a scene or make a big deal out of this, I pray silently to myself. But this is Cullen we're talking about here. If he was able to handle things rationally, we wouldn't be here.

"I'm not lying. He asked if I was coming to tonight's game, and I said yes. That's it."

"You're leading him on. I see you flirt with him. You're too fucking nice and now he thinks you want to fuck him."

"I am not leading him on! The only reason I go to the matches is because you tell me to! It's not my fault if he takes that personally."

He's silent for a moment, glaring down at me like an angry god on his mountain. That white mop of hair is washed out in the lecture hall's fluorescent lighting and it gives his eyes a deep, menacing shadow.

"Maybe you should just fuck him then," he says darkly, and my body stiffens.

"What? No! He's married, and I'm not even attracted to him. I'll let him down easily."

Finally, he stands. "No, if he finds out you're coming to the games for me, it jeopardizes my place on the team, so you'll just have to go through with it."

"And what if I don't?"

"You know exactly what will happen, Everly."

He's testing me. Or pushing my buttons, I don't know, but the fact that he's considering this is making me sick.

Does he really care so little about me that he would let me do that? After everything, the *you belong to me* talk and the late-night video chat conversations. He's telling me to fuck someone I don't want to for his fucking scholarship? Someone he can't stand.

I'm not buying it. I refuse to believe it for a second. Last time Cullen and I were alone at my house, I could sense the desire in the way he touched me. I bet it's freaking him out how much he wants me to himself, being so much older than him. Someone he's supposed to despise. But I'm not going to fall for this little dare of his, so while the words to argue are perched on my lips, ready to fire back, I stop myself. And I watch his expression as I whisper, "Fine."

He flinches. It's subtle, but it's there.

"This is what you want, Cullen. You want to blackmail me into doing whatever benefits you, so I'll do it. I'll sleep with your coach, just so he doesn't find out about you and me and whatever the fuck this is. So *you* don't lose your precious spot on the rugby team."

It's silent while I finish packing up my bag. Feeling exasperated, I let out a heavy sigh that shakes me down to my bones. When I turn around, he's standing right in front of me. So close I can smell the soap on his skin. The citrusy spice scent of whatever it is he uses, body spray or cologne, I don't even know, but it's intoxicating.

He takes another step closer, and I feel myself getting lightheaded. He is wearing a fierce, stone-faced expression, those intense blue eyes aimed right at me. This is the closest Cullen has gotten to me since that night at my house, and I feel the same shock of arousal low in my belly just from his nearness and the anticipation of what he'll do next.

I can't want him the way I do. It's a dangerous line we're walking on, one I've already crossed, and I really can't afford to toe it again, but I'm feeling reckless. Like I want to break every single rule just to see what will happen. Just to feel something, even if it's despair, loss, or fear. I need a hit of life, and Cullen is that hit.

The air between us is electric, charged with something I can't put a name on. I want to call his bluff on Eric, but I can't, not yet.

"When should I do it? After the game? And how many times should I fuck him? Will a blow job suffice?"

He pounces, slapping his hand hard over my mouth and shoving me backward. My ass hits my desk as he crowds me, a look of pure vitriol in his eyes.

"I changed my mind," he snarls. "I think I'd rather have your mouth around my cock, and I could never stick it there again if you let him touch you." Fire skitters down my spine as he presses against me, his hips pressing firmly into my belly. My hands grip the desk behind me, and I'm torn between wanting to submit to him like a sacrificial lamb or tear into his confident bullshit facade because I see through it all.

He always likes it better when I fight back, so I go with the latter. This is just a hint of Cullen's jealous side, and I want to see it all. I'm tearing down the walls around him. Grabbing onto his arm, I yank it away from my face.

"No. I want to fuck him. That's what you wanted, so that's what I'm going to do."

He shoves me harder against the desk, the rock-hard length in his pants pressed to my belly. As he brings his face closer, his eyes stay laser-focused on mine. "You touch him, and you're dead, Miss West."

"Then why did you say it?" I ask in a breathy exhale. "Or rather, why did you take it back?"

"I told you. Because I don't share."

"Because you don't hate me as much as you want, admit it," I spit back. My heart is racing in my chest, and I'm starting to feel dizzy.

"I can still hate you and want to fuck your brains out. Want me to show you?"

"You're lying," I reply, and it sounds like a dare. I'm playing with fire, and I know it.

He spins me quickly, bending me over the desk as he slams his hips hard against my backside. I let out a gasp that turns into a low moan when I feel his erection through his pants slide down the crease of my ass.

"What's wrong, Everly? You've never heard of hate-sex? A revenge fuck. Angsty, depraved, and dirty as sin."

My mouth goes dry, and I can't respond.

"Is that what you want? Because that's sure as fuck what I want, and that's why that asshole will *not* touch you, understand?"

When his hands grip a handful of my hair, I shudder. Arousal warms my belly as he yanks my head backward. There was some reason why I shouldn't do this. I distinctly remember there being a reason I'm not supposed to do this.

But God...I want it.

Without warning, he sucks hard on my neck, his mouth cruel and rough, making me gasp, heat skating its way across every square inch of my body.

"I'm going to fuck you, Everly."

My eyes close tightly as he growls those words that send me flying into some other consciousness. Then I feel his hand crawling up the back of my thigh. He presses it between my legs, inching them apart and lifting my skirt as he does. My body both welcomes and rejects it as a flutter of nervous excitement is left in the wake of his touch.

"Cullen," I whisper in a weak plea. It's a poor attempt to sound convincing.

"Do you want to say no? Do you want to fight me off, but let me take it anyway? Even if you fight me, Everly, I know you really want it."

"We can't," I say in a gasp. I should stop this. I know somewhere in the back of my mind I'm the older, more mature person in this scenario, and it's up to me to draw a hard line here, but my brain has no real control over my body. I'm literally the one who pushed him to this point.

"I'm going to fuck you with all of the hate I feel for you."

"Not here," I reply in a breathy groan, realizing I didn't say no. I didn't say no at all.

What I just said was basically yes—just not right now.

"No, not here." One hand is still pulling painfully on my hair while the other teases the inside of my thighs. His mouth is next to my ear and he breathes me in like a predator would delight in the scent of its prey.

My breath escapes me as the thought of not having him right now makes my chest feel heavy with disappointment. Even though I just said, 'not here,' the truth is that I want him right now. I can't believe a moment ago I was teaching class and now, he's all over me, soaking my panties and making me want him to fuck me hard on my desk.

"You sound almost disappointed, Everly. Do you want me here?"

Fuck, are there cameras in here? Can we really do this? What would happen if someone walked in? My eyes glance toward the door. It is *not* locked and someone could waltz in at this very moment. Right now, I don't care. In fact, I think the danger of it makes it even hotter.

The back of my skirt is lifted up to my ass as Cullen

pushes his hips against mine, dry humping me from behind, and making me see stars with the way my arousal slams into me like a truck.

God, I want him to unzip his pants and just fuck me right here. I don't even care that I could be caught, lose my job, and be in the headlines all over again, but for much worse reasons. I don't care. The feel of his perfect cock entering me with force would be worth it. My body is on fire, flames licking at my belly as he grinds his impressive length against my ass.

"Fuck me," I whisper, shamelessly. So fucking shamelessly. I should be the very definition of ashamed right now, but I'm not. I just don't care.

The hand in my hair releases, and his fingers wrap around my throat instead. He jerks me backward until his mouth is at my ear. "Oh, I want to. I want to fuck you so bad right over this desk. I want you to have trouble walking tomorrow. I want you to fight me, hate me, scream my name as I make you come against your will. And I will make you come, Everly. I will fucking ruin you for every man who ever dares to come into your life after I'm done with you. After me, you will be doomed to boring, unfulfilling sex until you die, and you'll beg me to do it. You want me to ruin you, don't you?"

"Yes," I gasp.

His teasing fingers finally dip into my panties, touching me along my soaking wet lips, and my body jolts in response. The sensation of his touch only makes me hungrier for him. Like alarms ringing in every nerve ending of my body, his fingers finally making contact with the one spot I want them to bring me life.

"Cullen, please," I beg, but he doesn't give me what I crave. Instead, he teases me. Slipping his fingers through the folds, he slides a finger in roughly, making me cry out. Then, he pulls it out and spreads the moisture all over, pulling his hand out and touching his wet fingers to my lips.

"Taste yourself," he whispers, and I do. It's erotic and filthy and sends my heart racing, a strange new feeling sprouting in my stomach, like being turned on by something that also makes me feel wrong and dirty. It's so much better.

After he pulls his fingers out of my mouth, he puts them in his own, sucking them dry like he's licking ice cream off them. I find myself shoving my hips back against him, *needing* more.

"I can't wait to ruin you, Miss West. But today, I have a class to get to."

The sudden absence of his body against mine is almost painful as he tears himself away. I'm standing with my skirt above my waist, feeling absolutely wrecked. And looking it too. I quickly pull down my skirt to cover myself. There is a flush in my cheeks as he grabs his bag from his seat and walks to the door.

"Keep your phone on you," he says calmly. I notice the obvious bulge in his pants as he retreats. My gaze is glued there as his own eyes glance down, acknowledging what I did to him. "Afraid people will see me walking out of here with this?"

I don't answer, turning away, feeling so wrong about how badly I want to suck the arousal right out of his cock. When I glance back at him, it's like he can read my mind, a devious smile lifting one side of his mouth.

"Skip the game tonight. Go straight home. Wait for me there."

"Yes, sir," I reply sarcastically.

He spins around and crowds me again. "Save that for later."

I shudder at his words.

"Bye, Cullen."

He laughs, heading for the door, leaving me feeling very fucking unsettled. Whatever this is between us is just wrong.

I can't deny that I do love the way he holds power over me, the way he makes me feel, but what does any of this mean to him? Am I just a toy to him? Something to fuck with, like a brat tortures a tiny ant. It makes my chest ache to think about it like that, because I can't deny that Cullen means more to me than he's supposed to.

I am looking forward to this *hate-sex* he's talking about, but is it really hate-sex for me? I don't hate him, not anymore—if I ever truly did.

Chapter 11
Cullen

I PLAYED LIKE SHIT TONIGHT. My head was somewhere else, and it cost us the game.

It's fucking Everly. She's in my head. Every time I think I have the upper hand, and I have her right where I want her, she throws everything off. When I catch the scent of her perfume or touch the soft curves around her hips, I forget what I was supposed to be doing.

It's annoying as hell.

The whole *fuck-my-coach* demand was a total test. I wanted to hear her beg me not to make her do it. I would have been happy to see some tears and watch her sweat with anxiety, but noooo. She had to go and *agree to it*. Too fucking easily, too.

I know she was bluffing. She knew I was bluffing, but it wasn't supposed to work that way. And the fact that I'm not one hundred percent sure she was bluffing ended up filling *me* with anxiety. Not the intended outcome there.

Because you don't hate me as much as you want, admit it.

That's what she said, and it echoed through my head the entire game. She's wrong. I still do hate her, but I've gotten addicted to hating her, toying with her, making her life all about *me*. Nothing has really changed, only that I'm enjoying all of this more than I thought I would.

And I'm about to enjoy it even more because the plans I told Everly about after class today will finally get this craving out of my system.

The bus stops at the corner down the street from her house. My hair is still wet from my shower after the game. Coach had the team on clean-up duty in the locker room and on the field as punishment for our shitty performance on the pitch. That was *after* we ran an hour's worth of drills with the assistant coach. Prescott was in a shit mood tonight, and I know it was because his hot date never showed. So just before we took off on our post-game jog, he bolted.

What a piece of shit that guy is. And Everly thinks I'm the bad guy.

A couple blocks away from her house, I get a notification on my phone. It's her doorbell camera, and I freeze on the sidewalk as I open the app.

As soon as the livestream loads, my breathing stops. Standing right in front of her door is Coach Prescott. His voice carries through the speaker, and the first thing I notice is it's slurred. Glancing at the time, I see it's a little after ten —way too late for a casual drop-in. He leans on the door frame, smiling at her with a look that has me feeling very fucking irritated.

What the fuck is he doing there?

His body language and the small talk between them makes it pretty obvious he is flirting with her. He has an arrogant, I-can-do-whatever-I-want attitude, and I know that's hypocritical coming from me, but he's not messing with just anyone right now. He's messing with Everly, and she's *mine*.

Just as I'm about to pound the pavement and sprint to her door, I stop.

What happens when he finds me there? Will it ruin my scholarship? He could have me thrown off the team for fraternizing with a teacher. It would be a big scandal, one even I can't afford. And I've had my fair share of scandals with my family.

Releasing the photos I took of Everly—and the hot as fuck video from the car—would have the same effect, but she doesn't need to know that I have no plans to actually release those. Or maybe she already knows. Fuck, I don't even know at this point.

Walking slowly toward her house, I listen in on their conversation on the doorbell app.

So far it's just small talk. He's telling her about moving to the area, leaving out everything having to do with his wife, of course. Everly is nodding in agreement, but I recognize the tension in her voice.

He's making her uncomfortable, and it's making me want to put a hole through something. That's *my* job.

"You mind if I come in and use your restroom?" he asks, and my spine straightens.

Absolutely not, motherfucker.

"Tell him no," I whisper to no one who could hear me.

"Um...sure. Don't mind the mess," she replies in a clipped tone. They move out of my view on the camera, and goosebumps erupt along my arms, and a very bad feeling raises the hairs on my neck. This time, I pick up my pace and practically jog to her house.

When I get there, I see his truck parked in the drive. Checking to make sure no one is outside, I quietly sneak around to the window that looks out from her living room. Standing in the shadows outside the window, I peer inside to her brightly lit home. She has sheer curtains hanging over the window, so I can barely make out her form, but I can hear everything clearly.

Everly is standing in the entryway between the kitchen and dining room when Prescott emerges from the bathroom. They continue their conversation in the living room. Even through the hazy curtain, I can read her body language. Her arms are crossed and she's cornering herself to put distance between them.

"I should really get to bed. It was nice of you to check on me, though," she says. She moves toward the front door and he reaches out a hand to grab her by the arm.

When he pulls her against his body, she struggles to get away. Then, he kisses her and she lets out a shriek. "Stop!"

"Come on, baby. I won't tell anyone."

I'm frozen in place, but the blood pumps wildly in my ears as I fight the urge to break this window and climb through to fuck him up. If she can just turn him down, tell him to fuck off, he'll leave.

"I think you should leave," she says, this time louder than before. She manages to evade his grasp and stomps toward the door. They're out of my sight now, but I stay to listen to everything.

She can handle it, I tell myself. She just needs to get rid of him.

"I'm sorry for coming on a little strong," he says in a low tone. "But with the way you're showing up everywhere I turn...I know you want this, too."

"Eric, I'm sorry for sending you the wrong signal, but—"

There's a scuffle, the sound of something hitting the wall, and I freeze, waiting to hear if that was him hurting her or her hurting him.

"Why are you fighting me?" he yells, and when she cries again, her voice is muffled, like he has his hand over her mouth. "Don't be a tease now."

"Get off of me!" she screams, and his voice is low and grunting. My heart is hammering in my chest. "Eric, please!" This time she's not yelling, she's *begging*. And something in me snaps. I seem to black out for a moment because I'm suddenly tearing through the front door in a panic, rage and desperation warring in my head.

My jaw is clenched so tight, I'm afraid my teeth will shatter.

They are against the wall, his face pressed against hers, kissing her while she clearly struggles to move away, but he has her pinned against him so she can't move. Both of their heads snap in my direction, and I see red. Something wild and angry takes over as I charge toward them.

Grabbing him by the back of his neck, I rip him away from her in one fluid motion. He goes crashing to the floor, staring up at me in shock.

"She said to stop," I snarl at him.

"Ayers...what the fuck?" he stammers, getting to his feet, but just the vision of him trying to stand up to me has me wanting to break his spine in two. A raging violence courses out of me as I throw my fist down, landing hard against his nose as he crumbles back to the floor like the pathetic piece of shit he is.

My gaze travels to Everly, who is now huddled against the wall, watching me as I yank Prescott back up by his collar, only to land another vicious punch to his face. Blood splatters against the floor.

"Cullen, stop," she cries.

But I don't want to stop. I want to keep punching him until I'm satisfied or maybe until he's dead. Whichever comes first.

"What the fuck are you doing here?" he asks, glaring up at me.

"Don't you worry about that. All you need to worry about is getting home to your wife before I call her myself!"

Fear washes over his expression as he stares up at me. It's clearly registering to him that I have more on him than he has on me or Everly at this point. He scrambles to his feet, staring at her for a moment, and just seeing his eyes on her brings out the possessive side of me. I grab him by the arm and throw him against the wall. "Don't you fucking look at her," I snarl as I wrench his arm up his back and hear the deafening crack in his shoulder before he falls to the floor screaming.

"You little shit! You're fucking dead."

"Oh, I'm dead?" I ask. His arm is hanging limply from his shoulder as he struggles to argue with me. He is red-faced with anger, and I have to remember—this is my coach. He's a man I'm supposed to look up to. A man who should be smarter, stronger, and better than me, but he's not. Like every other man I've tried to idolize in my life, he's a fucking letdown.

Now I'm really pissed because he just threatened me, as if he has any place. He'd be better off if he just laid on the floor like the pathetic piece of shit he is. "See those, idiot?" I say, pointing to the cameras perched in the upper corners of Everly's living room. "Those are cameras, you dumb fuck. Recordings I have access to, so if you want to stay out of jail, I suggest you stay the fuck away from Miss West."

"Jesus," he mutters, and he looks genuinely remorseful. Not for what he did, but for what it will cost him. Then he looks up at her and then at me. "This is why you're coming to all the matches, then."

When I rear back my arm, ready to make his ugly face even uglier, she holds up a hand. "Cullen, stop." Then she looks at him. "It's not what you think. Keep Cullen out of it."

The color drains from my face as I glare up at her. Did she just fucking defend me?

"Whatever," Prescott mutters as he struggles to his feet. "Both of you can fuck off."

When he reaches the door, I give him one more push. I stand my ground in the doorway until he's out of sight, stumbling to his truck. His drive home should be fun, and explaining his condition to his wife should be even better. Either way, I don't give a shit.

Once he's gone, I lock the front door.

Spinning around, I look for Everly, but she's disappeared into the bedroom. Knocking on the closed door, I hear her sniffling on the other side. Pushing it open, I peek in to find her washing her face at the sink.

"Leave me alone, Cullen," she snaps.

I almost ask if she's okay...like I've forgotten she's the fucking enemy.

"Better yet, why don't you get the fuck out of my house?"

With a scoff, I glare at her. "I just saved your ass."

"Why? Why would you save me, Cullen? Don't you want to ruin my life?"

Jesus. Not like that.

There are red spots speckled across her cheeks and nose, and her eyes are bloodshot with tears.

"You think I should have let that piece of shit have his way with you? Nasty. I was doing you a favor."

"Tell me, Cullen," she says, drying her face. "What's the difference between him and you? What makes what he did so much worse than what you've done?"

I stand there silently, my lips shut in a tight line. What the...fuck?

"You want me, Everly. You..."

"I what? I deserve it? Is that what you wanted to say? Because if you wanted me to be miserable, then you've succeeded."

"You're miserable because of him, not me."

"Is that so?"

Why is she saying this? I didn't try what that mother-fucker just tried. I'm *not* that guy.

"It's over, Cullen. You've accomplished what you came here to accomplish. Can you please leave me alone now?" Fresh tears fall across her face.

"We're not done," I say quietly.

She takes in a heavy breath and lets it out in a deep sigh that rolls off her shoulders.

"Don't you see? You clearly don't need to worry about ruining my life," she sobs. "I'm doing that just fine on my own."

Tears stream down her red face, and I clench my fists. "What, you think you did that? You think you invited him in?"

"Didn't I?" she cries, wiping her face on a white hand towel.

Letting out a heavy exhale, I roll my eyes. "Fuck, Everly. That guy is a tool. You didn't invite him or deserve that shit. Sure, I want to make you pay for what you did to me, but you didn't deserve *that*."

"Well, men like that seem to love me, and I only have myself to blame. I'm an asshole magnet," she says, lifting her arms and dropping them against her sides. "So, haven't I had enough abuse for one night, Cullen? Can you just leave?"

It takes me a moment to realize that I'm one of the assholes she's referring to, and it sours something in me. It shouldn't come as a surprise, like at all, but it does.

Without a word, she turns off her light and crawls into her bed, turning her back toward me. Standing there for a moment, I watch her cry silently, feeling both helpless and angry.

Turning away, I'm ready to leave her here, but then I see the mess he left when he attacked her. Papers from her desk are all over the floor. Her laptop is lying closed beneath them, so I lean down and pick up everything, even the over-turned chair they must have knocked over.

A familiar name catches my eye in the papers, and I pick up a printed copy of the police report issued when they took my father. Beneath that are scribbled notes on yellow lined paper and tax documents and missing person reports. My blood chills as I rifle through the documents that contributed to my father's downfall.

Young girls in school pictures smile up at me under the words, "Missing child." There are so many of them, and conflicted emotions collide as I stare back at them. Too many feelings, and they make me uncomfortable, so I gently stack them back up on the desk.

I can't start catching the sympathy bug if I want to stick with my plan, and it's been a long enough day as it is. I'll sift through those thoughts later.

It takes me about an hour to get everything cleaned up, so when she wakes up in the morning, she won't have to deal with seeing what happened tonight. No one needs that reminder.

Silently, I slip out the front door and head toward the bus stop.

Chapter 12
Cullen

Wednesday nights are always slow as fuck. I'd take the first cut, but I need the money, and Allie knows it, so she leaves around nine. With only one table at the moment, I pull out my phone after delivering their food.

Typing out a quick message, I smile wickedly.

Me: I'm bored.

 Everly: I'm working.

 Me: Show me something good.

 Everly: Like what?

 Me: You.

 Everly: Was that...a compliment?

 Me: I'd call it persuasion.

 Everly: What are you persuading me to do?

 Me: Send me a picture of you at this very moment. I want to make sure you're at home grading lame-ass papers instead of fucking someone you shouldn't be.

THE PICTURE I GET BACK IS OF HER LEGS RECLINED ON her couch, propped up on the coffee table with her slippers and a glass of red wine. Her laptop is on her lap with a notebook and pen by her side. I shouldn't be smiling at that, but I can't help myself. Fuck, the effect Everly has on me is so strange. I've never really hated someone so much before and enjoyed just fucking with them to the point that it makes me feel...good.

ME: *I THINK YOU CAN DO BETTER THAN THAT.*

THE NEXT PICTURE IS THE TV AND AN EPISODE OF what looks like *The Vampire Diaries*. What is wrong with this woman?

ME: *IF YOU DON'T SEND A PICTURE OF THAT PRETTY PUSSY soon, I'm going to make things bad for you.*

I CAN'T SEEM TO BITE BACK THE SMILE THAT'S PULLED across my face. I don't know if she'll actually do it, but I know there's a good chance that if she does, I'll be catching a different bus tonight. But I don't want to do that. I like dragging things out with Everly. I like having her panting for me, wanting shit she knows she shouldn't want. I like to imagine she hates herself for how badly she wants my cock. Bending her over the desk, just to watch her squirm, was the most fun I've had in a long time.

We've cooled things off since the incident with Prescott.

I was so ready to go over there that night and fuck her brains out and finally get all of this tension between us—or just make it more intense, I'm not sure. I was ready to find out, though. And then that asshole ruined everything. I saw what he did to her, and not just literally but emotionally, mentally. How she blamed herself, how she blamed *me*. How she...compared us.

I'm still hellbent on revenge and making Everly understand the consequences of her actions, but right now that looks more like control and less like hate-sex. Although, the thought really hasn't left my mind in the past two weeks.

EVERLY: *PLEASE DON'T MAKE ME. IT'S SO WEIRD.*

DENYING HER REQUEST, I LAUGH, TYPING OUT A CRUEL response.

ME: *NO FRONTAL VIEW EITHER. I WANT A CLOSE-UP, LEGS open, lips, clit, and all.*
   Everly: *No way.*
   Me: *Or I can go show the guys in the kitchen this little video I have on my phone.*
   Everly: *You wouldn't.*
   Me: *You sure about that?*
   Everly: *I hate you.*
   Me: *I hate you too, baby.*

I THROW IN A KISSY FACE EMOJI FOR FUN.

After taking my table their check and the to-go boxes they requested, I feel my phone vibrate. My cheeks grow hot as I make conversation with the family, knowing what's waiting for me in my pocket.

Leaving them, I head toward the kitchen and pull out my phone. Swiping it open, my mouth goes dry, and I have to press myself to the wall, so no one sees the photo over my shoulder. It's just like I asked, a full view of her pussy. With her thong pulled to the side, the shot captures her perfect pink folds, but it also shows her face as she reclines on her couch. She's biting her bottom lip, staring at the camera, looking hot AF.

Jesus. I didn't know Everly could be so sexy. Maybe it's the grainy low lighting of the photo, but she looks like the hottest chick I've ever seen and not at all like my thirty-two-year-old journalism professor.

I need to be with her right now. I'm dying to know what she tastes like and how smooth she would be if I could run my tongue along the length of her sex.

Fuck, I want her. This waiting shit is hard, and it's not the only thing that's hard now. I didn't quite expect her to be like...this. I didn't expect any of it, least of all her actually sending me the picture and me liking it this much. Pocketing my phone, and rearranging a little bit, I return to the table to get their credit card and run their tab. I can't get the image of her out of my head. My mouth literally waters thinking about it. What am I doing? Getting horny for my teacher, for *her*.

This has got to be some mommy issues bullshit, right? Some repressed childhood trauma, getting horny for the woman who ruined my life. At this point, I don't even care. I just need to have her, to fuck her brains out, and I plan to. I plan to keep my word about ruining her. The only reason I want to make it mind-blowing for her is because I know once I do, she'll be fucked for the rest of her life, never able to find an ounce of pleasure without remembering what I did to her.

After the table is cleared and I have some time, I head for the breakroom in the back. It's rarely used, and it's mostly for us to take our meals and store our shit. Right now it's empty and private, so as soon as I shut the door behind me, I hit the *Video Call* button on Everly's number.

She answers, looking pensive and chewing on her lip.

"Normally when someone sends you a nude pic, you don't take so long to respond."

"Worried I didn't like it?" I ask.

She glances away. "I don't care if you like it."

"I can't believe you actually did it."

"Well, that's sort of the thing about blackmail."

"Did you really think I would show the horny chefs in the kitchen a video of you blowing me from the driver's seat?"

"You're such an asshole."

"Is that anyway to talk to your student?"

"Go back to work," she mutters, taking a sip of her wine. So that's how I got the pussy pic. She's tipsy. Whenever Everly has had a few glasses of alcohol, it's amazing how much she loosens up. Makes manipulating her so much harder because she'll literally do anything. Takes all the fun out of it.

"Show me again," I say in a low tone. She rolls her eyes before setting her wine glass down.

"Where are you?"

"In the breakroom. I'm alone. Just show me."

"Cullen..." she whines, and I love the way my name

sounds on her lips when she's trying to tell me no. It's like she's scolding me, and it makes me feel powerful.

"Show me now," I reply, my voice thick and dark, and I palm myself over my pants just thinking about her pussy in that picture.

"Promise me you're alone."

I quickly scan the room, but she still looks nervous, so I rush to the single bathroom, flipping on the light and locking the door.

"Show me now."

With a hesitant expression on her face, she peels open her robe, giving me a view of her bra and panties before lowering the phone and spreading her knees. Peeling her thong aside, she aims the camera right at her beautiful pink pussy.

My breath comes out heavy and loud. "Touch it."

"Cullen, no." She's putting up such a weak fight, it makes me laugh.

"Do it, Everly. I need to see you touch it."

With the slightest huff, she obeys. Her fingers run through her lips, and I groan. I notice how her mouth opens, her breath hitching, and her eyes darkening in lust.

"Finger yourself for me," I mutter.

My phone screen is the only thing in the world that exists as I watch her delicate middle finger run down from her clit to her entrance, where she slowly sinks it in to the knuckle. There's a soft blissful sigh as she moves, her hands familiar with her own body, finding her pleasure instantly. The dim light in the room catches on the moisture coating her finger, and I think I'm going to lose it.

I'm still torturing her, right?

When I hear her next breathy inhale followed by a tight groan, I can't keep from touching myself. With one hand, I tear open my pants and reach in, wrapping it around my cock. A soft grunt escapes my lips as I do. Heat travels straight to my groin as I watch her slowly fuck herself with her middle finger, her pussy swallowing the digit down and her hips lifting as she does. When she pulls it out, she brings the moisture to her clit, lubricating herself in tight circles.

"What are you doing to me?" I grumble, my voice echoing in the small bathroom as I stroke myself.

"What am I doing to you? What about me? This is insane," she replies, her voice soft and sweet. It occurs to me she's technically doing this because I'm still blackmailing her, threatening her, but look at her. She's enjoying it. She loves it, and I think she likes that she *has to* do it. She likes having the choice taken away because, without that choice, she's innocent. She's doing it because I'm telling her to and I'm letting her have that pleasure.

"Are you touching yourself?" she pants.

"Fuck yeah," I grunt, pointing the camera to my dick and back up to my face.

"Let me watch," she says.

Flipping the camera screen, I let her see in the mirror across from me as my fist pumps my dick faster, knowing I need to get back to work as soon as possible.

She lets out a sweet moan as her fingers pick up speed, alternating between fingering herself and rubbing her clit. Her head hangs back on the couch, her legs hanging wide and her back arched in pleasure.

"Everly," I whisper her name, the sound of it like satin on my lips.

Her heavily-hooded gaze stares back at me as she watches me stroke myself.

"I'm going to come soon," she says in a high-pitched cry,

and I bite my lip, loving the way her hand picks up speed and her chest stops moving.

"Come for me, baby," I manage to groan out just as my balls tighten, the head of my cock swelling as my own orgasm rushes to the surface in a hurried chase. I don't have time to draw this out as much as I wish I could. I have to get back to work, but they can wait another minute for me as I come all over my hand.

Everly makes a noise like she's gasping for air. Her fingers press hard on her clit and I stare at the phone, feeling breathless myself. She doesn't hide as she loses herself to the throes of pleasure, contorting on the couch and stretching her head back to ride the wave. It's fucking beautiful—a visual I will never forget. This woman is... unexpected. She's so fucking intense, insatiable, and unpredictable. I want to push her, press her for more, test her limits, see her reactions. The desire to own her grows stronger every day.

This was supposed to be me blackmailing her, but my lust for her has clouded everything. Now all I can think about is using Everly until I've wrung her dry, stealing my own pleasure from her body. Once I've done that, I'll have her out of my system—I know it.

"Fuck," I mutter.

"Oh my God," she says at the same time, and together, we seem to wake up from this strange, hazy dream. She moves the camera away from her body and to her face as she glares wide-eyed at me. "What are you doing to me, Cullen?"

I move to the sink, propping the phone, so I can clean myself up. A small dribble of cum landed on my pants. Fucking great.

"I could ask you the same thing."

"I'm serious," she replies in a low, serious tone. "This isn't a joke to me. What we're doing...this could have some dire repercussions for me. Are you just playing with me—"

"You want to talk about dire repercussions, Everly?"

"Tell me why you're doing this."

"Doing what?" I snap back.

"Making me act this way."

The sincerity in her eyes is shrouded in fear. I realize she may be enjoying this chemistry between us, but given the choice, she wouldn't indulge in what we're doing.

"Because I know when this started you said it was to make me feel what your last eight years were like, and I'm willing to bet your teenage years were nothing like this."

She's not wrong there.

"Yeah, I guess it started as torture, but now I'm just using you."

There's a glimmer of disappointment in her expression. That's not what she wanted to hear.

"What's wrong? Don't like that answer?"

"I don't like that you've never actually opened up about the last eight years. I know you hate your uncle, but I want to know why. If you want to make me see what that case cost you, then I want you to show me."

Well, fuck. I didn't expect that.

"You're such a fucking journalist," I mutter.

"Yeah, I am."

"A dirty fucking journalist." That puts a small smile on her face, so I quickly punch the *End Call* button and shove my phone in my pocket.

I quickly wash my hands, so I can get back to work. I'm so tempted to go to her house tonight. Fuck, the temptation is all-consuming, and I hate how much I have to fight it, but I will. Not because I don't want to mess with her or fuck her, because I do. I want both of those things badly. But I'm not going over there because whatever is happening with Everly is overwhelming me. It's doing things I didn't expect, making me feel things I didn't see coming, like *wanting* to go to her house, just to go there. Just to be around her. And that won't work.

She wants me to show her how bad the last eight years were, so that's exactly what I'm going to do.

Chapter 13
Everly

THERE ARE random moments during my day where I literally freeze and cringe, thinking about what I did with Cullen last night. While making coffee this morning, pouring shampoo on my head in the shower, parking my car on campus. People greet me in the office of the English building, and I have to force a smile, all the while thinking, *if they only knew.*

I didn't have a choice, though. I was being blackmailed, so I really shouldn't feel so ashamed, when he literally made me do it.

Didn't he?

I mean...as far as anyone else is concerned, he did. No one needs to know that video call was the hottest moment of my life. How I haven't come that hard in a long time or how I want to change my panties every time I think about it.

When I get to my office, I spend the morning grading papers, planning my next class, and thinking about Cullen. He's in my mind, consuming every thought. His face is there in my memory between every sentence I read and every word I write. I hear his voice, smell the soap on his skin, taste him on my lips.

It's gotten out of hand already.

I find myself checking my phone every few moments, wondering what he's doing. Wondering if he'll be coming over later. Wondering if he's thinking about me.

Oh my God. Stop.

This is ridiculous.

To distract myself from thinking about him again, I open the USB drive, the one from his father's case. I keep going back to it every time I get a moment. I don't know why. Something about being with Cullen has me thinking about those missing person cases and I can't shake the feeling there is unfinished business there.

I get the impression that the deep, unshakable shame I feel when I'm with Cullen is about more than just the dirty things we do. It's like he's a walking reminder that I started something but didn't finish it.

So, I fish out the files again, picking up on the research where I left off. A couple weeks ago, I created a spreadsheet, tracking where the Ayers' employees ended up, something I bet no one else has done since the case was last opened. There's not much to go on. It's mostly dead ends.

For some reason, I keep ending up on the nanny in the photos with the Ayers family from about fifteen years ago. After digging through some old (and probably falsified) employee records, I can't find a single one on her. There are just some pictures of her with the family, but only until Cullen was about five, when she suddenly disappeared. So, she was out of the picture long before I wrote the article, which explains why she wasn't included in any of my other research.

I waste away the next hour or so scrolling through

photos of missing person cases, looking for anyone who could match her photo. It's depressing, seeing so many runaway teens, and I don't even know why I'm so focused on this one girl. For all I know, she could be nobody, deported somewhere or quit working for the Ayers. She could be completely inconsequential.

Then I notice how affectionate she is with Cullen in the photos.

And it dawns on me—this is someone who loved him. It's obvious in the photos and the way she held him. This is what he needs, even if he was a small child when she saw him last. She's the closest thing he can get to a mother now, so if I can find her...maybe it will make things right. Give him back what I took away. That's a ridiculous notion—I know that—but it doesn't change how badly I want to try.

The rest of my day crawls by. I have an afternoon class before I finally get a text from Cullen. I'm packing up my things when I read his message, an unwelcome burst of excitement as I see his name on the screen.

CULLEN: *I HAVE PRACTICE TONIGHT.*
　　Cullen: I want you to be there.
　　Cullen: I have plans for you after.

I CAN'T HELP THE GROAN THAT RUMBLES THROUGH MY body. Sex should be a major nonnegotiable here. I absolutely *cannot* have sex with Cullen. Sure, we almost did it that one time, but I wasn't thinking clearly. I'm thinking very rationally right now, but still...my body wants what it wants. I am consumed with this desire and dying to know what Cullen would be like with me. That rage-filled hate-sex he was talking about sounded like something only an idiot would pass up.

ME: SHOULD I BE SCARED?
Cullen: I would be.

SHIT. I DON'T KNOW IF HE'S BEING COY OR SERIOUS. Cullen is so hot and cold. He's harsh and cruel, but then he rescues me from Eric and video chats me—it's all so confusing.

There's a knot of anxiety in my stomach. After packing up my stuff, I finish a few things in my office before heading toward the rugby pitch across campus. A subtle feeling tremors under my skin as I reach the stands. There are a set of bleachers on either side of the field. The guys are already on the field, and I hear the assistant shouting orders as I cross the parking lot.

The day after the attack, Coach Prescott retired for the rest of the season. The rumor around campus was that he had personal problems at home, but he was spotted a few days later in a cast with purple bruises across his face, and the rumors only got juicier. I stayed out of it. I have my own problems without getting involved in his.

I spot Cullen as he starts to run toward the end of the field. Truth be told, I know nothing about rugby, but with all those guys in short shorts, colliding against each other as they work up a sweat in the mud, I don't think knowing the rules is really essential.

Climbing the bleachers, I take a seat on the third row up, just high enough to see the players while being inconspicuous. There are other people watching too, mostly girls, probably girlfriends. And for the most part, I look like a devoted team fan. But I pull out my notebook and phone to get a little work done while I'm here too, mostly more research on the open cases.

Glancing up, I notice Cullen. He's impossible not to watch. Like a magnet, my gaze refuses to settle on anyone else. He has the ball, running down the field, and it's like he anticipates everyone else's moves, jetting left and right before his opponents do. When he gets himself cornered, he passes the ball and sprints down the field.

I bite back my smile, feeling this strange, protective feeling wash over me. After all the hell this boy has put me through, I let my mind wander to the things he's told me about his childhood. The years of hell he endured after I saw him last. How could anyone hurt him? It makes my blood boil and tears sting my eyes just thinking about it.

After the assistant coach blows the whistle, Cullen glances up toward me and our eyes lock for a moment. There is so much intimacy in hatred that I realize as he stares back at me that I've never been as close with anyone else as I am with Cullen. My heart pounds in my chest, bleeding warmth throughout my body from the eye contact alone.

Fuck, what is happening to me?

Please, heart. Don't fall for this one. Please.

Still, I can't look away. The black roots of his hair are growing out in stark contrast to his bleached white locks. With those dark brows and crystal blue eyes, Cullen Ayers is a fucking masterpiece. How are girls not swarming him like bees in search of honey? He's gorgeous, shining like a diamond on that field. The piercings and tattoos crawling up his neck don't hurt either.

"Get your head in the scrimmage, Ayers," the coach

yells, and Cullen nods at him before turning back to the team.

As hard as I try to keep my focus on my research, I can't seem to tear my eyes away from the practice for the next hour and a half. I even find myself getting sucked into the rules and strategy, watching Cullen as he makes the forward passes, and a little part of me panics every time he gets crushed in the tackles. As soon as he jumps up, he glances at me. He wants to know I'm watching, and I am. The eye contact between us grows in intensity, making me even hotter as I sit out here in the cool fall air, bundled in my coat.

Just before seven, the practice ends, and I head to my car before him, so we're not seen leaving together. As I climb in, I spot him coming toward me, and my pulse quickens. This is the first time we've been alone since that video call yesterday.

As his eyes lock with mine, I have to remind myself he hates me. Cullen is not interested in me, not like that. The sexual attraction between us is fueled by revenge, and that's it.

Don't you dare get attached. Don't do it.

He throws his bag into my trunk and drops into the seat next to me, but he doesn't hesitate a moment before grabbing my face and pulling me to him for a bruising, violent kiss.

Time stops, and I let out a yelp just as he fuses his lips to mine. And he tastes *good*. Kissing Cullen is like visiting a private place all on your own, where there are no rules or witnesses. I don't necessarily kiss him back, but when his tongue presses its way into my mouth, I let it. He nips at my lips as he consumes me, and I try to stop time. I don't want to open my eyes and face his disdain for me anymore. I just want to exist in this kiss.

Finally, he breaks the contact, and I suddenly register how much passion is coursing through this car like a fog we're both breathing. I have to stop it or we'll be tearing off each other's clothes in no time. And that can't happen.

"You reek," I mumble against his lips.

"Just fucking drive. You can soap me up at your place."

Was this what he meant when he said he had plans for me? God, I hope so.

A thrill runs through my veins as I pull away, trying to clear the fog from my head, so I can put the car into drive and head toward the main road.

Chapter 14
Cullen

THANK God it's a short drive from the campus to her place because I don't know if I can wait any longer. It was never supposed to be like this, but I'm not complaining. I've been thinking about her all day, how she'll sound as she begs me for mercy, and I get hard every time.

As we pull up to her house, I pull her face to mine for another bruising kiss. She lets out a whimper as I wrap my hand tightly around her throat, squeezing as I shove my tongue into her mouth, desperate to own her body more than she owns it herself.

I can't explain why kissing Everly has me so addicted to her taste. There's a little resistance with her hands pressing gently against my body, but I know her body wants what her mind doesn't, and fuck, that turns me on.

When we finally pull apart, we both hurriedly exit the car and rush inside. She walks ahead of me into the house, and the sight of her ass in that little black pencil skirt has me on edge, so I grab her by the hair, jerking her backward. She lets out a cry as I crash my lips to her neck, nibbling, kissing, and biting. Her purse and keys drop to the floor and she clutches the edge of the kitchen counter for support.

Pressing myself against her backside, I want her to feel what she does to me. She responds with a shove backward, grinding herself on my dick.

"Shower, now," I grunt, smacking her hard on the ass.

There's a gleam of hesitation in her eyes as she turns toward me. I know what she's thinking. She's searching my expression for a sign that I'm going to fuck her or hurt her, or both, and as much as I want to—*and I want to*—I'm not. Not yet. I love the holding out, the making her want it. The fight for anything that gives us relief. And what I have in store is perfect.

Her cheeks are flushed, her eyes hooded with lust, like it's the only thought on her mind—need, want, lust. When we reach the master bathroom, she turns to flip on the shower before spinning back toward me to pull up my shirt.

It's the first time she's really taken control, letting herself express how much she wants me, and I like it. Everly wants me, and even though it's not like she's the first woman to want me, the attention warms a part of me that's always felt cold and dead before.

Our reflection in the mirror catches my attention, and I turn to see us. She's still in her work clothes, the top of her head only coming to my chin, while I'm shirtless with my tattoos and white hair. We are mismatched. She's nothing like the usual girls I hook up with, who flaunt a lot more skin than Everly, and have faces covered in makeup. But this woman is delicate, natural and gorgeous in a completely different way. We look like we belong with two totally different people, and for some reason, I try to memorize this image of us together. The whole picture is all wrong, and there's something fucking beautiful in that.

While I'm staring at the mirror, she glides her hands along my abs and up to my pecs, skimming her fingers softly over my nipples, toying with the barbell through each one. And even though my skin is still covered in a thin sheen of sweat, she leans forward and kisses my chest.

A groan builds softly from the base of my chest, growing louder as her mouth finds my nipple and her teeth bite the piercing there.

Fuck, I'm not going to make it.

Her tongue travels across my tattooed chest and up to my collarbone like she's tasting me, enjoying the flavor in her mouth, and I capture her lips again, kissing her harshly. She's getting herself so hot, which is only going to make things so much worse for her.

Her fingers peel down my shorts, and my cock bounces out, slapping her on the belly. Just when I expect her to touch it, she doesn't. Instead, her hands glide down my ass and over my thighs as she pulls my shorts and boxers to the floor. I toe off my sneakers and reach down to tear off my socks until I'm standing naked in front of her.

She's toying with me, touching me everywhere but where I want, so I grab her by the back of her neck, noticing the wicked way she smiles as I do, because she knows. She knows I'm pissed with the way she's denying me.

"You better fucking touch it, Everly, or I'm going to shove it down your throat."

"Is that supposed to be a threat?" she replies in a breathy cry.

Without denying me any longer, she wraps her soft hand around my cock, squeezing it tightly at the base, and I clench my jaw, shoving my hips forward so I can find some friction.

"Get naked now."

With that devious smirk on her face, she pulls her shirt over her head and quickly unclasps her bra. Getting the full view of Everly's tits, my mouth waters. She's just so damn perfect—long limbs and soft curves that make me want to grab a handful of every inch of her body.

And that's what I do. The process of tearing off her panties and skirt is not graceful in the least because I'm too ravenous for her, desperate to touch her everywhere. I'm ready to have this part of her—the most intimate, private part of Everly West, the woman responsible for my undoing. She belongs to me; she's mine to fuck, touch, break, and play with. A wicked sense of power rushes over me as I grab her body and pull it against mine. I could do anything with and to her, and it's a sensation I'm getting high on.

"Get in," I groan, smacking her ass.

She flinches, her breath hitching before she steps into the tub, and I follow, pulling the curtain closed behind me. Surrounded by steam, I run my hands along her naked body, all the way down to the bare skin between her legs. Sliding my hand roughly along her sex, I plunge a finger in. She lets out a gasp, and I clutch her tighter. She's so warm, wet, and tight, and I need her. But I can't let myself get lost in this perfect sensation. I have to keep the upper hand with Everly.

Spinning her around so her back is against me, I hold her tightly across the chest with one arm as I plunge my fingers in again. Writhing against me, she cries out as I stroke her relentlessly. I want her as close to coming as I can get her. Clutching onto my arm, she hangs from my hold as I zero in on her clit, rubbing it so hard I know she's teetering somewhere between pain and pleasure.

"Cullen," she gasps in a plea. She's begging me for more.

My dick is pressed against her back, and I squeeze her closer. God, I want to fuck her so badly, but I can't. I have to keep my head.

Drawing her closer and closer to her orgasm, I rub faster, harder, until she's clenching her body, right on the precipice, then I stop, pulling my hand away. She lets out a garbled cry as I shove my fingers, wet with her arousal, into her mouth. She sucks obediently while her backside rubs against my cock, but she's not going to get what she wants. Not at all.

"Remember last night, you asked me to show you what the last eight years of my life have been like? This is how it was. Imagine having everything you wanted just out of your reach. Imagine seeing someone else live the life that was meant for you. Imagine being denied pleasure again and again and again."

Putting my fingers back where they were, I do the whole thing all over again, bringing her to the very edge of pleasure and then stopping just before she boils over.

"This is how I plan to punish you, Everly."

And I do, again and again, working her up and letting it die down. She starts to struggle against me, crying out in pain and frustration until I know it hurts like hell.

"Cullen, please!" she shrieks, and it's the beautiful sound of her begging that gets me even harder.

"You don't get what you want, Everly. You just get to see it long enough to want it, but you'll never be satisfied. Just like I was, having my whole life ripped away," I mutter into her ear. She pants, her fingers digging into the tile wall of her shower. Pumping some body wash into my hands, I stroke my cock with it, getting it nice and covered.

"Now press your legs together as tight as you can."

She freezes for a moment, probably because she knows

I'm about to be cruel, and there's nothing she can do about it. When I feel her legs clench, I squeeze my cock between her tightly clamped thighs, using her body as my fuck toy without giving her any pleasure. She can only feel my cock enough to want it, to have it so close but not close enough. Not how she wants it.

With my hands on her thighs, I press them together even tighter, fucking her soft flesh, and it doesn't take me long. I know her moans aren't from pleasure but from misery, and that gets me off. I pull away from her in time to come all over her back, leaving her desperate for a release she's not going to get. I wonder how bad it hurts, to be so close to coming without getting to. I hope the ache is visceral.

Once I come down, and I look at her, with her shoulders tense and her expression closed tightly, not revealing how much she hates me at the moment, I almost give in. I *almost* feel bad. All day she probably thought she was going to get what she wanted tonight. Instead, I took what I wanted and left her with nothing. Or worse, I made her want it more. Then I denied her.

But I can't feel bad for her. She's the enemy. All I have to do is remember her face in the courtroom that day, her smug grin plastered all over every news article about my family, having the best day of her life while I had my worst. That's enough to take away my sympathy for her. It's enough to remind me I have every right to make her miserable, and that I should be enjoying it. I just wish I did.

She's noticeably angry with me. We wash up together before getting out, and I take my time with her, soaping up every inch of her body, not out of lust but curiosity. Then she does the same thing for me, but she's not enjoying it like she did before.

Just before we get out, I take her chin in my hands and tilt her face up to see mine. "I am going to use you as much as I want, and when I've had my fill, then it will be over. Okay?"

She swallows, and I swear it looks like she might cry. She wanted more. It's obvious. Maybe she thought this would become a real relationship, maybe she thought I cared about her, and I've just crushed her hopes. I remember that feeling very fucking vividly, wishing as a kid that we wouldn't lose our house, wishing my mother would wake up, wishing I could live literally anywhere else in the world than the nightmare home that was my uncle's. I know very fucking well the crushing disappointment she's feeling right now, which means I've done what I came here to do.

Which means I should leave. I know that. But when we get out of the shower, I'm exhausted. I slip on a pair of sweatpants and my body doesn't want to move, so I fall into the warm embrace of her oversized couch.

"I was going to order Chinese. Are you hungry?" she asks.

"I'm hungry as fuck. Can I get some Kung Pao chicken?"

She nods and picks up her phone, without really looking at me. Oddly enough, after everything I've put her through, this looks like the most miserable I've seen her.

After the food arrives, we end up on the couch. There's a football game on, and I watch with a carton of chow mein on my lap while she works on her computer. It's comfortable, and I don't just mean her house, which is a lot fucking nicer than my dorm room. But it's also relaxing just being with her, in the silence, not being alone. If I wasn't here, I'd be watching the game on my phone alone in my bed. Instead, I'm curled up on a plush couch with hot food and the smell of some candle thing she's burning in the foyer that makes her house smell like apples and cinnamon. There are picture frames on her shelves with her and her parents, looking happy as can be. It's homey as fuck.

I find myself wondering what my life would have been like if my father had never been caught. Our home was nothing like this. It was huge, with so many rooms I didn't have to see anyone if I didn't want to. There was always someone to clean for me, cook for me, drive me wherever I wanted to go. Forget Chinese takeout and apple and cinnamon candles.

My mother would still be alive. Her bright smile and warm voice are clear in my memory, but the more I search for memories *with* her, the more I come up empty. My mom was truly an angel, perfection personified, but I didn't get enough time with her as an actual mother. Instead, I remember nannies who held me close at night, read me stories, tied my shoes, told me jokes and made me laugh. There were a few different ones through the years, and they grew colder and more like employees as I aged, but there was one in my distant memory who was the kindest, warmest, and most nurturing.

Even thinking that makes me feel like shit, like I'm desecrating the memory of my own mother by thinking of women who were better.

And what about all of those people my father stole from their homes to manipulate them into working for him? How can I sit here and complain about the mansion ripped from me when they were living in God only knows what kind of conditions?

My stomach turns and I lose my appetite. As I toss the box of noodles on the coffee table, I try to focus on the game, pushing away the sick feeling of self-loathing that creeps up from time to time. How is it my fault that I was dealt such a shitty hand? Why do I have to feel like shit for the things someone else did? My dad, Everly, fuck, even my own mother didn't need to overdose on those pills and leave me alone, but she did.

"What is it?" Her quiet voice pulls me from my thoughts. Glancing toward Everly, who is sitting on the chair next to the tall lamp, curled up under a blanket, I feel a sudden burst of emotions. I can't figure out if I want to hold her, hurt her, or make her get on her knees and blow me, but I *want* something. I want something so badly I could choke on this want.

"Nothing," I mutter instead. She wouldn't understand.

She closes her laptop and lets out a sigh. "Cullen, talk to me."

"You're my therapist now?"

"No."

"Then what are you?"

She rolls her eyes, shrugging her shoulders. "You tell me."

"Do you want me to leave?" I bite back, feeling defensive, but also self-deprecating, like I want her to say something mean to me just so I can feel something from her. I'm hating myself right now so she might as well join in.

"Honestly?" she replies, and I narrow my eyes.

"I dare you to be honest."

She leans forward, glaring at me without a hint of hesitation. "No, I don't want you to leave."

"You should," I say. Self-loathing and desire stir in my gut like poison.

"You don't think I know that? I'm so fucking mad at you *all the time*, Cullen. For everything. But...for some reason, and against my better judgment, I don't want you to leave. I like having you here, and I guess I shouldn't admit that because you are not in the mindset to give me what I want, but you wanted me to be honest, so there you go."

I swallow the brick in my throat. She's right. I shouldn't give her what she wants, but I like it here too, so I don't want to leave. Instead of pulling her to this couch with me so I can hold her like I want, I turn back to the game and leave our conversation at that.

If anything, this whole thing with Everly has made me realize I am tired of being alone. It's not *her* I want, but the idea of having someone who will listen and be with me in this comfortable silence is growing on me. I've been alone long enough, and Everly is the first one to make me want to change that.

Chapter 15
Everly

I WANT TO KILL HIM. That much is obvious. My body is still throbbing from the shower, wanting release more than I've ever wanted it before. Wanting him inside me, really inside me. But I think I knew by the second time he toyed with me he wasn't going to give me what I wanted.

The football game ends at nine-thirty, and I start to feel restless. I'm not sure if Cullen is going to want a ride home or if he'll stay. And I don't want to ask, afraid he'll say it's time to go. I really shouldn't want him here as much as I do. Even if he sleeps on the couch, even if he gets off again and I don't, I'm still happier with him here. It's better than nothing, and nothing is what I had before.

He doesn't move as the TV transitions into some late-night show. I let out a yawn, moving to clean up, and as I pass by the couch, he grabs me by the leg, wrapping his arm around my thigh and tugging me closer.

"I'm sleeping here," he says, and I swallow.

"Fine," I reply, doing my best to look like I don't care. I pick up his half-eaten Chinese food carton and try to move away, but he still holds me in place.

"I know it's fine."

"I'll bring you a blanket," I mumble, biting my lower lip.

"Why? You sleeping on the couch?" With that, he yanks me onto his lap.

"It's not for me," I answer. Glancing back at him, his eyebrows shoot up and his mouth drops open.

"You want to be sassy now? Okay then." In a swift movement, he stands up, taking me with him, his arm wrapped around my waist as he hoists me up and heads for the bedroom. I manage to empty my arms onto the coffee table without spilling too much. A laugh bubbles out of me as he tosses me on the bed.

I put up a fight, crawling away, but he grabs me by the ankle, jerking me toward him. Letting out a scream laced with laughter, I push away from him, but he's so much stronger than I am. Plus, I don't really hate the idea of being at Cullen's mercy, not anymore.

This thing between us has morphed from actual torment to superficial torment, like we're playing the parts, fulfilling roles. He is my punisher, and I am welcoming my discipline.

"Come here, you little brat," he commands, and I hear the playfulness in his tone. If I didn't, I wouldn't push him the way I do. Underneath it all, I did really fear Cullen, and maybe I still do. And while we are far from being friends and even farther from being lovers, we can still play with each other. Not everything needs to be so serious all the time.

He climbs onto the bed, covering my body with his. He wrestles my wrists from my chest and pins them above my head.

Looking into his eyes with a dare on my face, I say, "Don't start something you can't finish."

He hears the challenge in my voice and smiles wickedly. "I don't think you deserve to finish," he growls, abruptly kissing my neck. His lips and teeth are both soft and rough, kissing and nibbling, making me squirm with the too-good and too-painful contradiction, which is really just Cullen in a nutshell, isn't it? I want all of him and none of him at the same time.

His feelings for me are clearly more of the love-to-hate variety, and as much as I tell myself to be careful, to not get too invested, too excited about the idea of him in my life, I can't help it. I'm already used to it. I'm already addicted to the drug, desperate for more, the highs and the lows. Desperate for all of him.

"But I've been so good," I murmur sweetly as I wrap my legs around him.

"I did say I would ruin you for all other men, didn't I?"

"Yes, you did," I reply.

When he pulls away to look down at me, there's still a warm expression on his face, not so much the wicked smile, but something closer to affection, and it makes my heart pump faster, a warmth spreading through my body at the sight of it.

But as soon as it's there, it's gone. He steels his features, almost as if he just realized he wasn't playing the part. With it, my smile fades too.

The fire has gone out. The fire that was rocketing us closer and closer to sex, animalistic and wild. Without it, we are just two people who want to fuck each other, and that is all, and suddenly that doesn't feel like enough.

He feels it too.

"Not tonight," he mumbles as he climbs off me. I don't bother arguing, because I understand. Cullen let his guard down. We both did, and it ruined the moment. Sex with our guards down is too dangerous. The last thing either of us need are real emotions getting involved. Sticking to the warm blaze of hate is easier. Hate we can hide behind. Hate can conceal the truth.

He spends the night anyway, and I let him crawl into my bed next to me. We both scroll through our phones absentmindedly in the pitch-black room until I set mine aside and roll away from him, falling asleep quickly.

Somewhere during the night, I wake to something kicking me hard in the legs. My bed is shaking and it's accompanied by grunts and moans. I'm not used to having someone in my bed, let alone someone in the midst of a nightmare, so I hesitate too long, too afraid to move.

"Cullen, wake up!" I call out as I flick on the bedside lamp.

When I get my first look at him, I feel sick. He is pale, covered in a glistening layer of sweat, and there is a look of terror etched on his sleeping face.

"No, no…" he moans, and his body jerks again.

Tears spring to my eyes as I reach for him. I place a warm palm against his face and cover his trembling body with mine. My lips are close to his mouth as I coax him awake.

"Cullen, it's okay. It's just a dream. Wake up."

He jolts and his eyes open, wide and terrified. Even when he looks at me, it's like he's looking through me.

"It's me," I say, and then his eyes focus on my face and he takes a long, heavy breath.

"What the fuck do you want?" he snaps at me.

"You were having a nightmare."

He looks visibly offended, climbing out of bed in a rush as if to get away from me.

"No, I wasn't."

"Cullen...yes, you were. You were shaking and saying no—"

"Shut the fuck up, Everly!"

As he slams the door to the bathroom, locking himself inside, I fight the urge to cry. Climbing out of bed, I pad silently to the bathroom and knock on the door. He doesn't answer, so I gently pry the door open.

I'm greeted by Cullen's back, the muscles taut with stress as he leans over the counter, gripping it tightly in his hands and hanging his head. Tears pool in my eyes, watching him try to catch his breath, so full of the violence and rage that was planted there by someone else long ago. Cullen was cursed from the start, thrown into the fire by those who were supposed to protect him.

Approaching him carefully, the moisture in my eyes spills over as I press my hand softly to his spine. He flinches and I clench my eyes shut, waiting for him to lash out. But he doesn't, so I replace my hand with my tear-soaked face, pressing a soft kiss to his back and wrapping my arms around his waist.

"I'm sorry, Cullen," I whisper.

Any moment now he will push me away, yelling at me or hurting me to get his revenge. I'm ready for it, which is why I'm surprised when one of his hands covers mine.

We stand there for a long time, finding comfort in the silence, before I finally pull him back to bed. There's not another word spoken between us before we both fall back to sleep. This time, instead of turning away from each other, we are face to face, our legs tangled and our hands entwined.

Chapter 16
Cullen

"This assignment is bullshit."

"Will you keep your voice down?" she says with wide eyes as I storm into her office, dropping the assignment she handed out today on her desk. "It's Friday night, Cullen. Don't you have a social life?"

"I was going to go to Gina's to get high and maybe get laid, but you give better blow jobs than Allie."

"Jesus Christ," she mutters, looking flustered as she jumps from her seat and shuts the office door, making sure no one overheard me.

"Relax, the building is empty. What are you still doing here anyway?"

"Working," she says. I reach over and grab the notepad next to her laptop. She freaks out, trying to grab it out of my hand before I can read it. Of course that only makes me want to read it more. I have to stand up to keep the notebook out of her reach. Her handwriting is sloppy, but I make out some random names, dates, and then I see my last name scribbled on the page more than once.

"What the fuck is this?"

Then I remember the stuff I found on her desk at home a few weeks ago. Everly is still doing research on my family, or at least something to do with my dad's company and the people he employed.

She lets out an exasperated sigh. "I was doing some digging on the case and I found out some of the women that worked for your father were never really followed up on...so I'm following up on them."

She has a sheepish look on her face. I sit down and drop the notepad on her desk. "And?"

"And...a lot of the girls made it home or are still alive today."

"Why do I feel like there is a but coming?" I ask. Everly is worrying her bottom lip as she stares up at me like she's testing my reaction.

"But...not all of them made it home. At least not that I can tell. Some are international, so there's really no way for me to tell for sure. But these American women, they just...disappeared."

"You think they were murdered or something?"

"Well, what would *you* think?"

"You really do love a case, don't you?"

"You're not mad?" She sits down opposite me and looks genuinely worried as I read over the stuff she wrote.

I ignore her question as I pick up the other papers on the desk. The same faces peer back at me that I saw the other night, the same faces that have been haunting me ever since. What if Everly's research could actually mean something good for these people? Could she really help find some of these women? My eyes travel up to see her face. She's staring at me, her eyebrows lifted in anticipation. She must really be getting under my skin because something about this has me feeling something like excitement or...interest.

"Need some help?"

She bites her bottom lip, trying to hide the hopeful expression on her face.

"Yes."

"Order us a pizza. Let's take these back to the house. I'm hungry."

"Okay..." she replies hesitantly, taking the pad of paper from my hand.

THREE HOURS LATER, EVERLY AND I ARE SITTING ON her couch, which is covered by papers with random scribbles and notes all over them. A half-eaten box of pizza is under the stack of missing person files we've already been through.

"Do you have the file on H. Tierney? I just found a police report for her filed three years ago," I ask. Everly spins around and grabs the stack off the floor, flipping through quickly until she finally pulls out a stapled file. She reads it for a moment before chewing her lip and tossing it back in the pile.

"I already had that on file."

My brow furrows. "What are you talking about? Why is it still in the missing pile if you know where she is?"

Her shoulders slump from the other side of the couch. She's giving me that *grown-up* look, like I'm an idiot and she knows so much more than me. It irritates me so I knock my outstretched leg against hers. "What are you talking about?"

"She has a warrant out for her arrest in Minnesota, Cullen."

My brows pinch inward even more. "So what?"

"So...they're mostly for drug charges. A DUI, I think. If we report her location to the bureau, they'll find her."

I suddenly deflate. Everly tosses the packet back on the stack and goes back to what she was doing. But this is still bothering me. Questions swirl around in my mind. How long has Everly cared about right and wrong gray areas so much? How is this any different than what happened to me? My blood starts to boil as I stew over it.

I knock her leg again. "What is your problem?" she asks, looking up at me.

"Why is she worth sparing?"

"What do you mean? I'm just trying to do what you said."

"You used to be all high and mighty about your job and putting the truth first to catch the bad guys, remember?"

"Yes, I remember."

"So...what happened to all of that?"

"Right and wrong aren't so black and white, Cullen. No one is getting hurt if we just let this lady live in peace in Nevada or Arizona, where she's living now," she says it so casually, like it's nothing.

"Aren't you the same person who started all this to make sure everyone was accounted for?"

"Aren't you the one who's forcing me to face the consequences of my actions?" Her voice is louder than mine, her face a little red, and it hits me. Everly isn't going back on her word. She's not being a hypocrite or a liar. She's...listening to me.

It grows silent between us as she continues typing. I can't take my eyes off her. It makes me wonder what I'm still doing here. She's clearly not really suffering from her punishment anymore and I'm not even really torturing her. So, what are we doing? What are we?

I set my computer down on the table and stretch out along the chaise end of her couch, reclining until my head rests along the pillows. She keeps up her work and I feel content just watching her.

"You look tired," she says softly, glancing at me.

"I'm getting an A on this assignment, right?"

"You have to write the article first." She teases me with a gentle smile. The computer screen illuminates her face, framed by her dark hair that reaches her shoulders and the blunt bangs at her brow. I want to reach out and touch her delicate nose, run my fingers along her jaw and kiss the place where her shoulder meets her neck.

"We got a lot done tonight, Cullen. How are you so good at this?" she asks, not even noticing the way I'm admiring her.

"I'm just good at this, I guess."

"You can sleep now," she says, looking my way.

"Lie down with me, and I will."

She does a double take, as if she didn't think I was being serious, until she actually saw the look on my face. I'm not threatening to hurt her or tease her. I just want her to cuddle with me. It takes her a moment to react. Then, she places her laptop next to mine and pulls her blanket along with her as she stretches out on the couch, resting her head in my lap. I know we could go to the bedroom, but I don't want to disrupt this moment.

My hand rests in her soft hair, and once I know she's comfortable, I reach back and turn off the lamp. I stroke her head as we drift off, and I can't stop thinking about what Everly just said.

Right and wrong aren't so black and white.

I'm not quite sure if she was referring to the missing person cases...or me.

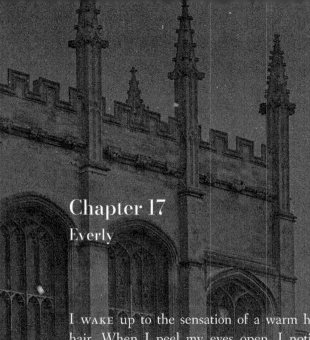

Chapter 17
Everly

I WAKE up to the sensation of a warm hand stroking my hair. When I peel my eyes open, I notice it's still dark outside, but there seems to be a shred of light creeping up the dark sky through my living room window.

It's so peaceful and quiet, and I almost don't want to move, but I can feel from the touch of his hand that Cullen is awake. I turn my head to see his face, and he's staring down at me sleepily. There is no hatred or anger in his eyes. And I realize that he's being gentle with me, touching me with affection and not violence, not trying to hurt me or scare me, and it makes my heart swell. All of those warnings I gave myself about not getting attached to this boy, this *man*, are pointless now.

I'm lost. Swept away in his current, and I know somewhere down the line, the tide will spit me out somewhere, and it's probably going to hurt like hell. But it's too late to go back now. I stare back up at him in the tender early morning hours before light has even entered the space between us. Then I nestle my cheek against his lap and feel the stiff length in his sweatpants, hard against my face.

He strokes my hair again.

He's not forcing me, and I know I don't have to, but I want to. So I lift my head and slowly pull down the elastic waistband of his pants and reach for his cock. I am not hurried or frantic as I slowly wrap my hand around him, watching his face for signs of pleasure when I squeeze. His eyes threaten to close as I stroke him once, then twice.

With my gaze on his, I shift closer, so I can run my tongue along his shaft. He moans and presses his fingers subtly against my head.

He wants more, and I want to give it to him.

I don't even care that I'm not going to get off. I'll do it just to watch the way he comes and to hear the sounds he makes as I unravel him piece by piece.

Swirling my tongue around the head of his cock, I watch him, and he groans, shifting his hips. This time, I take him into my mouth, letting him slide across my tongue, going deep into my throat.

"Everly," he whispers, and a bolt of lightning strikes me at the base of my belly, just from hearing him say my name in a lust-filled moan. Coming onto all fours, I pick up my speed, leaving the quiet, solitude of the morning behind us as I suck his shaft deep and fast into my mouth, the wet sounds and groans replacing the silence we just woke up to. On every upstroke, I squeeze his head, sucking hard with a groan of my own. I'm ravenous for him.

"Fuck, I'm going to come," he pants, and he starts to tense. I'm pleased with myself, happy and satisfied like I don't need anything else, but the warm jets of cum never hit the back of my throat.

Instead, I'm jerked violently off his lap. He yanks me up until I'm in his arms and my face close to his. One hand grasps me by the back of my neck as he slams our mouths together. When he growls into our kiss, I know everything in this moment is different. I don't know what happened or if it was a multitude of things, and I'm quite sure it will only exist in this delicate witching hour, but Cullen isn't treating me like he normally does.

Suddenly, I'm being thrown flat on my back against the couch, and my breath leaves me on impact. His fingers are quick as he digs into the waistband of my pajama pants, tearing them down in a frantic motion.

I don't expect him to do what he does next, so I'm reaching for him when he drops to his knees and buries his face between my legs. The warmth of his wet mouth is intense, so intense, I let out a strangled cry as his tongue punches hard into me. It's almost too much, but it's him, and he's touching me, and I let myself melt into that thought.

"Cullen," I gasp, arching my back and burying my hands in his hair.

He moans, pressing his mouth harder against me, his tongue going deeper. Hooking his arms under my thighs, he practically fuses his lips to my body.

When he finds my clit, I lose my mind. His tongue ring strokes over the sensitive spot over and over, and I'm carrying so much pent-up arousal, I think I might combust already.

"Don't stop," I cry out. "Please don't stop." I'm so afraid he will. I can practically feel it already, the sudden absence of him, teasing and tormenting me, and I don't know what I'll do if he does. I'll lose it for real.

But he doesn't stop. He settles in with no end in sight, and I abandon myself to the pleasure. I don't care that he's my student or that he supposedly hates me. I don't care about any of it because right now, none of that matters. It's just us, him and me and this fire between us, burning like an inferno.

"I need you, Cullen," I groan as I feel my orgasm creep closer, and it's perfect, but it's not what I want. With him still between my legs, I tear off my shirt and reach for him. "Please."

As he pulls his face away, I let out a sigh, thinking he's giving me what I need, but he doesn't. Instead, two fingers thrust hard into me, and he groans, his voice deep and guttural. Pumping them hard, he puts his mouth back on my clit, and I melt like wax into the cushions of my couch.

"What are you doing to me?" I say with barely enough air in my lungs to breathe. Everything is so potent, I want to cry. I want to sob and scream, and tear open my heart and give it to him. I almost can't handle it anymore. "I'm coming," I pant.

Instead of pulling away, like he would have yesterday, he sucks harder, thrusts deeper, and everything that happens to my body takes me to a different plane of existence. It's like all the passionate emotions I'm feeling are fused with every nerve ending in my body, so my climax shoots out from my heart and almost kills me.

My orgasm quakes and quakes and quakes, and I can't stop it, and he doesn't let up. I think after a few moments it won't ever stop, and I let out a cry—a real one, tears streaming down the sides of my face. I reach for him again.

"Cullen, please!"

He's on top of me in a heartbeat, devouring my mouth the way he was just devouring my sex, making me taste myself. Making me *like it*.

I feel his thick erection heavy on my belly as he kisses me. My eyes are squeezed shut, tears still streaming when I wrap my legs around him, inviting him in.

"You still want to fight me?" he mutters darkly against my mouth. "You still want to pretend you're not mine?" When I try to shift my hips to meet his cock, he takes a hold of my face under my chin to keep me still. "Fucking open your eyes, Everly."

There is moisture on my lashes, but I stare at him, our eyes locked in a blazing hot gaze as he presses his cock to my entrance. "Still think you're not mine?" He shoves a few inches in roughly, and I'm met with a burning pain. Then, he pulls out just a little and shoves back in, this time seating himself entirely inside. Cullen isn't my first, but it's my first time *like this*. This rough, fast, hard sex is new to me, and he was probably right when he said he was ruining me.

Let him.

Once he's fully inside me, we let out a heavy groan, a collective celebration for this moment we've both been waiting for. He settles himself in deep until our bodies are joined as one. My legs wrap around his hips, trying to keep him in this spot.

"Tell me you hate me now," he grits out as he pulls back and slams in again. His hands clutch me hard, one behind my neck and the other around my waist.

"I hate you," I whisper, as another batch of tears flow out of my eyes. I'm not sad or scared or hurt, but the intensity of the moment forces them out, and I can't stop them now.

Cullen shoves his hips against me again and again, fucking me hard. My eyes won't leave his face, desperate to capture this look of pain and pleasure he's showing. And I want to take my words back. I know he wanted to hear me say I hate him just to play the part, but I don't hate him. I feel something as ardent as hate, but that's not it at all.

So as he thrusts, chasing his orgasm, feeling what I did a

few moments ago when he tongue-fucked me into oblivion, I do what I wanted to do before. I reach up and take his face in my hands, drawing his lips down and kissing him tenderly, loving this sweet boy who isn't so filled with rage and spite. This version of Cullen may be mine, but I'm hoping they are all mine in some way. After only a few weeks with him, day in and day out, I want to believe that I have some claim on him, a part of Cullen Ayers to keep forever, a part I helped mold, and even if it's in hatred, I want to know that his emotions are tethered to me.

With his lips pressed against mine, he shutters and jolts and comes hard inside me. And I don't care about consequences or how stupid it was to let him fuck me without protection. I'm on the pill, and every other stupid thing I've done with Cullen has worse risks than this one. Because right now, I need him inside me. I need his risks and his trust.

He buries his face in my neck, letting his heart catch up. I feel it pounding hard against mine. When he finally pulls away, he catches the tears on my face with his thumb and lifts it to his tongue while gazing into my eyes. There are words hanging on his lips, and I wait for them, but he keeps them to himself. Instead, he stays with me in this silent moment for a little longer.

The sun has risen and filled the room with dim light when he finally climbs off me, leaving my body cold in his absence. He leaves me on the couch and disappears into the bedroom.

When I hear the shower start, I peel myself off the couch and follow him. He's staring in the mirror. I want to reach for him, hold him, stroke away his pain, but he doesn't let me. Turning away, he climbs into the shower and leaves all the words unspoken.

Standing there a moment, I replay everything in my head, the things he said to me during sex. I know I'm making a huge mistake trusting him and throwing myself into my enemy's arms, but I can't help myself. I am too far gone.

I follow him into the shower and wrap my arms around his tall frame from behind. "I am, you know," I whisper.

"What?" he asks.

"Yours."

His chest slowly expands and deflates in a long, heavy breath. Then he pulls me around until I'm wrapped in his arms under the hot spray. With his lips on my head, he replies, "I know."

Chapter 18
Everly

"Okay, what's his name?" I nearly jump out of my skin as Thomas approaches me from behind during my walk across the quad on the way to my Friday morning class.

"You scared the shit out of me," I say, stopping and turning toward him. "They really do just let anyone on campus, don't they?"

He laughs, looking as handsome as ever in that tight-fitting polo with slacks that stop right at his ankles and expensive-looking shoes on his feet. "They really do. Now, tell me," he says, pulling me to the side so we can talk, letting students move around us. "Who is this mystery man that's been keeping my best friend from me for the last nine weeks?"

"You're being dramatic. I've just been busy with work."

"I'm calling bullshit, Everly. Don't forget I know you better than anyone."

I let out an easy laugh, rolling my eyes at him. Just then I spot a certain white-haired, tattooed student approaching us from behind Thomas.

Oh fuck, no. Please don't...

Too late. Cullen strolls right over to where I'm standing and throws an arm around my shoulder. Thomas reacts with wide eyes as he glares at the *college student* getting a little too cozy with his *teacher*. It's a miracle I still have my job at this point. I try to shrug off his arm, but he doesn't budge.

"Well, hello," Thomas says, and I can tell that he doesn't recognize Cullen right away. Who would? "Speak of the devil."

"Who, me?" Cullen replies with a wicked smile. *Devil, indeed.*

"Thomas Litchfield," my friend says, extending his hand. God bless my cool-headed best friend for not showing how shocked he must be to see Cullen and me together. With him on my shoulder, I must look like I'm in the middle of a midlife crisis, robbing cradles and dating teenagers. It's embarrassing, and I know for a fact that Thomas will give me hell about it later.

Then, it gets even worse as the man at my side reaches his hand out and replies, "Cullen Ayers."

Blood rushes to my ears and time stops. Thomas seems to freeze too. With his hand halfway to Cullen's, he pauses, and his gaze shoots up to Cullen's face. Recognition registers and his eyes get as wide as saucers.

It's only for a minute. He quickly regains his composure and shakes Cullen's hand, acting as cordial as ever.

"So, what were you guys talking about before I showed up?" Cullen asks.

Thomas clears his throat. "I was just telling Everly that I haven't seen her in forever. My suspicion involved a new boyfriend, and I guess I was right."

"Cullen is not my—"

"Yes, I am." He squeezes me closer, pulling my face up

toward him and planting a quick kiss on it. I swat him away and glance around to make sure no one else has seen us. If my other students see me standing here with Cullen, intimately, I can kiss this job goodbye.

Thomas looks more amused than concerned. He always did love juicy drama.

"Well, I'm having a dinner party tonight," Thomas adds with a bright white smile. "Everly has to come. I haven't seen her in weeks. Cullen, you are welcome to—"

"No!" I snap. This entire conversation is pure torture.

"Sounds fun." When I glare at the boy with his arm still hanging around my shoulders, I want to punch him or pull out that ring in his eyebrow. It still wouldn't be as painful for him as this is for me. Just when I thought his constant torture had come to an end...

"Great! Well, it's at my place at seven. I look forward to seeing you both there."

I give Thomas more of a grimace than a smile, which makes him laugh even more as he leaves us and heads toward the campus parking lot. As soon as he's out of earshot, I turn and slap Cullen hard on the arm.

"What is wrong with you?"

He cackles maniacally in return. "What? You don't want me to meet your friends?"

"Not even a little bit, Cullen. There is no way we are going to that party."

"Oh yes, we are."

"Why would you want to go to a boring dinner party?" I ask as we walk together toward the English building. "It'll just be some of Thomas's lame friends and at least one guy he'll be trying to hook up with. Someone way too young for him and out of his league."

"Sounds fun." He chuckles, and I glare at him as he

holds the door open for me. I have to stop at my office first to get the copies I printed for today's class but also to get Cullen alone for just a minute before said class.

The last week has been different and, in some ways, more terrifying than the ones leading up to it, only because this time, things are good—very, very good. He stays over every night and we are having sex as often as we possibly can in the short time between me picking him up from work or practice to when we leave for campus together in the morning. The cruelty has stopped for the most part, but I still enjoy a touch of Cullen's harsh edges when I can get them.

He follows me to my office and no one seems to notice as I close him in my office with me, latching my body to his the moment we're alone. We only have a few moments, maybe five spare minutes before I have to run to class. But it's enough to at least let him kiss the life out of me, and touch me as much as he possibly can.

I'm pressed against my desk as he settles himself between my legs. There's a hand at my throat, just squeezing gently below my ears as his mouth ravishes mine.

"I wish you had enough time to suck me off."

I glance down at my watch. *Fuck.* Class is supposed to start in less than five minutes. The room is probably full already. If Thomas hadn't held us up, we definitely would have had time.

"I wish, but I have to run."

"I hope I don't get in trouble for being late, but I have to do something about this." He grinds the steel shaft in his pants against my hips, and I stifle a groan.

I can get through this next hour. It won't be easy, but I can do it.

"Clean up after yourself," I say, planting one last kiss on

his lips. Then, I painstakingly remove my body from his, taking my swollen, red lips with me to class, leaving him in my office.

As I reach the lecture hall, rushing in two minutes late, I have a hard time focusing, knowing Cullen is currently stroking himself in my office, hopefully thinking of me.

Looking up at my class, as we approach the end of the semester, I get a wave of nostalgia as I remember how it felt to walk through these doors that first week. How scared I was of him, how mad, then how...obsessed. I don't know what I feel about Cullen anymore—it's too confusing to put words to, but right now, at this very moment, I'm enjoying it. Probably far more than I should.

Just as I start today's slideshow, he makes a clamoring entrance, letting the door slam shut, and I make it a point to look disappointed in him. He winks at me and bites his bottom lip, tonguing the piercing there. It makes my knees go a little weak, and for a second, I forget what I was going to say.

God, Everly...what are you doing?

I'm not stupid. I know this can't possibly last long. Cullen will get bored, especially now that I don't fight back, and he'll move on. There's really nothing stopping him from sleeping with other girls as it is, and as intensely dejected that makes me feel, I have to accept it.

Cullen is mine for a moment, not a lifetime. So I might as well make the best of it.

Chapter 19
Cullen

How DID I end up here?

We're sitting on Everly's friend's patio, string lights glowing overhead, and a bowl of paella on the table in front of me. I mostly agreed to come to make Everly squirm because I know how uncomfortable this is for her, but now I'm regretting it because I'm bored as fuck.

All these people do is talk, and her friend, Thomas, spends the entire night staring skeptically at me. He won't bring anything about my father or the case up, not here. He has company and that would be embarrassing. Instead, he watches me with a quizzical lift to his lips.

He spends the other half of the night flirting with a twenty-year-old barista named Nico.

Nico is oblivious. It's almost sad to watch.

Next to me, Everly won't stop fidgeting. She's either rolling up the edges of her napkin nervously, or biting her bottom lip, or shifting in her seat, like she's waiting for the inevitable bomb to drop right here on this dinner table.

Just for clarification, the bomb is me.

She's expecting me to make a scene or pick a fight.

There was a part of me that liked to watch her suffer so much, but I don't know where the fuck that part of me went because now I just want to run my hands down her arm to soothe her.

So that's what I do.

While some douchebag named Chad is going on and on about his lame-ass trip to South America, I run my fingers down the back of her arm until I find her fingers. When I link her hand with mine, she stiffens. Her eyes dance to her friend and then to me, but I remain casual, like it's nothing. Picking at the Italian bread on my plate, I zone out on the weird guy's story and think about Everly. I have no fucking clue how this shit happened or where my feelings for her came from, but unlike every other girl that I fuck, I actually want this one to be there when I wake up.

"What is your major, Cullen?" Thomas asks, and it pulls me out of my silent daze.

Glancing up from the table, I meet the eyes of everyone who seems to be waiting for my answer. "Well...it was Communications, but I'm thinking of changing it to Journalism."

Everly's head snaps in my direction. "No, you're not."

I raise my eyebrows at her. "Do you have a problem with that?"

"I don't believe you."

"Why not?" I argue with a smile.

Her mouth is hanging open, and she realizes she can't really answer that out loud. What she's thinking is that I can't be a journalist because her job is the whole reason I have hated her for eight years. The one thing that brought a downpour of hate and revenge on her when I came back into her life. She's thinking it, but she can't say it.

Her eyes narrow at me as if she's trying to gauge if I'm being serious.

"What can I say?" I ask, lifting her hand to my lips, planting a kiss on the tender skin of her knuckles. "You're a good teacher."

Thomas clears his throat across the table, and Everly's cheeks grow the reddest I think I've ever seen them. Someone else at the table quickly picks up the conversation and they all start talking again while I'm caught in a silent moment with the woman next to me.

EVERLY LETS ME DRIVE HER CAR HOME SINCE SHE HAD at least four glasses of wine. I can see the loose smile on her face and the subtle heaviness in her eyes that she's tipsy.

"Did you have fun?" she asks.

I shrug. "It was fun making you so uncomfortable. Watching your friend try to flirt with that guy was kind of fun."

She laughs. "He probably will score, you know."

"Oh, I definitely think he'll score. By the time we left, Thomas was literally feeding him crème brûlée from his cup, and that's not a euphemism."

Everly cracks up, giggling in her seat. Her cheeks are red from drinking, so when we pull up to a stoplight, I reach over and run my hand up her thigh, squeezing as she looks at me. The bright lights from the car behind us reflect in the rearview mirror, lighting up her face in a cool glow.

"I still can't believe you went to a dinner party with me." She looks embarrassed.

"Why?"

"Don't you have anything better to do on a Friday night?" she asks.

"Like what?"

"I don't know. There must be other girls. Plenty of them throwing their pussies at you, I'm sure."

A laugh breaks through my lips as I glare at her. "I don't want their pussies. I want yours." As the light turns green, I release her thigh and make the turn into her neighborhood.

"Even when I give it to you willingly?" she asks, and that question makes me pause.

She's getting at something, and I know it's because of the wine that she's being so flippant with her words. She thinks I only wanted her when there was a struggle, and I guess that was true, at first. "Yeah, of course. What are you getting at?"

"I thought we were just...messing around. I'm not getting my hopes up for anything more."

"You said you were mine. *I* said you were mine. Are you changing your mind now?"

"I'm just saying, if you fucked someone else...I wouldn't be mad." She can't even look at me as she says that, and I really fucking hope she's lying.

"Yes, you would."

"I mean, yes, I would be upset, but I just...I don't know. I want to know where we are...*what* we are."

My brow furrows and I start to get irrationally angry with what she's saying. "Well, if you fucked someone else, I would be very fucking mad. Is that clear enough?"

"Why? I'm not your girlfriend, Cullen." Her words slice like a knife, and I slam on the brakes, glaring at her.

"The *fuck* you're not." My fingers squeeze around the steering wheel as she shifts in her seat to face me.

"What are we then? First, you hate me, and now you don't? Now, I'm your girlfriend? It doesn't make sense, Cullen."

I don't reply as I continue silently down the street to her house. It doesn't make sense, but the more she pushes the conversation, the more irritable I get. Talking about this shit isn't really my thing.

I glance again in the rearview mirror, noticing the car behind us again as we reach another light.

"Why do you keep looking back there?" she asks. There's a hint of irritation in her tone. I didn't mean for this conversation to get so heated tonight, but I feel the same fucking restlessness she does.

"Nothing. This car has been behind us for a while and I don't like it."

"You're being paranoid. Clearly something is bothering you."

"I'm fine," I snap, and she looks ahead.

She's silent for the rest of the ride, and I steal a look at her before we reach her house. The car behind us passes without slowing down and I realize I am on edge, and I don't know why.

It's what she said—that this is fucking weird and I'm not even a fucking relationship guy, but I feel so goddamn attached to her. I don't want to explain it or label it; I just want her to be there for me to fuck, touch, and talk to. There's a visceral craving in my bones to make Everly *feel*. And it used to be about pain, but now there's so much more there.

When I walk into the house a few minutes after her, she's already on the bed. She's still in her thin, black dress, and she's pulling off her strappy heels. I stop at the door and watch her.

"Do you hate me?" I ask. I'm genuinely curious. She used to be so fucking vocal, told me everything she thought about me, fought back, but now...she's just complacent.

She won't look at me. "No."

"You have a problem being my girlfriend? The other day you said you were mine."

This time she looks up at me. "No." For a moment, she looks confident, but then her concern starts to show. "But, Cullen, you won't want—"

"Shut the fuck up."

I know what she's about to say. I won't want her for long. And damn, I don't know. Maybe I will get tired of this after a few months. Maybe it is phase. But right now, it sure as hell doesn't feel like one. Whatever this is, I feel it in my bones, and I guess this is why people make stupid fucking decisions when it comes to love. It's a tricky bitch.

"If I'm your girlfriend, are you going to be nice to me?" There is so much courage in her eyes as she asks that.

"Probably not. Do you want me to?"

Her eyes close as she lets out a heavy breath.

"It's not about me being fucking nice to you, Everly—it's about you being *mine*. And about you and me being *us*. It may not be like other relationships, and people would probably think it's fucking crazy, but you know that whatever it is, it works for us."

She opens her eyes and nods. As her lips part, my dick twitches. Every tiny movement this woman makes drives me nuts. I need her more than I want her.

Still standing across the room, I cross my arms and lean against the door frame. "Now, get on your knees and crawl to me."

She moves to lift the hem of her dress, and I hold up a hand. "Keep it on. I want to stain it with my cum."

I watch her swallow, intense eyes still focused on me as she lowers herself to her knees. My cock reacts instantly to the sight of her on all fours, looking at me like I'm a god as she crawls slowly toward me. Licking my lips, I hold back, even though I want to move. My cock is crying behind my pants, begging to be taken out and touched.

As soon as Everly reaches me, I bend down and hold her under the chin, tipping her face up toward me.

"You are so beautiful on your knees."

Pulling her up so she's kneeling in front of me, I pry her lips open and her chin drops, revealing her perfect pink tongue. She's staring up at me, and it reminds me of that day in her car, the first day I hurt her and how good that felt.

"Am I a monster, Everly?"

She doesn't respond, and when she tries, I press my thumb into her mouth until I feel the back of her tongue. Tears brim in her eyes as she fights the urge to gag. The sight of her with my thumb down her throat is so degrading and hot as fuck. I love how much she loves it.

Leaning down until our faces are close, I smile wickedly.

"Can you love a monster?"

She moves to reply, her eyes widening as I spit into her mouth again, just like last time. But this time, I pull her mouth to mine, replacing my thumb with my tongue, kissing her deeply. She cries into my mouth and I love the taste of her, especially when she kisses me back. And that's enough of an answer for me.

She can love me for what I am.

I dig my fingers into her hair, ravaging her mouth until we are fused. Then I drop to my knees in front of her and pull away from our kiss, pressing her back to all fours so her face is inches from my waiting cock. She knows what to do, quickly unbuttoning my pants like she's starving for me. A moment later, she has me in her mouth, taking me deep without any foreplay. No kissing or licking or teasing.

Pleasure sweeps like lightning up my spine, making me sway in my spot, and I pump my hips forward, meeting her thrusts. I'm going to come way too fucking fast if she keeps this up, and I'm not ready for that yet. I want to keep her like this.

"Slow down," I bark, grabbing her hair again and pulling her mouth away. Keeping hold of her head, I slide my shaft across her tongue again, and she closes her mouth around me, sucking slow and hard. My heart hammers in my chest as I watch her. Fuck, she's good at this. I swear I could watch her suck me off for the rest of my life. I love it that much.

Leaning over as she works me with her mouth, I grab the hem of her dress and tug it up to expose her ass. A groan rumbles through my chest.

"Miss West...are you not wearing panties?"

She smiles around my cock, giving her ass a little wiggle.

God, I need it.

I run my fingers down the crack of her ass while she gags on my cock, and I run circles around her tight asshole. She moans sweetly in response.

"I'm taking this tonight," I say in a husky whisper.

She tenses.

"Has anyone ever had your ass, Everly?"

There's a moment of hesitation before she shakes her head, and my heart hammers faster, liquid fire running through my veins where there should be blood.

"It's mine, baby. Get my cock nice and wet and turn around."

"Cullen," she whispers with a hint of fear in her tone. A string of saliva hangs from her lips.

"Are you afraid it's going to hurt?"

With a small nod, she stares up at me with innocence in her eyes and I want to fuck it out of her.

I pull her mouth up to mine again and kiss her, this time with more tenderness than before. I can practically taste her fear. Her fingers clutch onto my shirt, and I trail my mouth down her jawline to her neck. My touch finds its way down to the warm folds between her legs, and I discover the moisture there, dipping a finger in and making her cry out in pleasure.

"Do you have any lube?" I ask against the soft flesh of her neck.

She swallows against my lips. "Yeah."

"Where is it?"

"Nightstand."

"Wait here," I mumble. She licks her lips, her gaze saturated with lust as I leave her on the floor to get up and find her lube. In the bottom drawer of her nightstand, there is a tiny bottle of lube next to a pack of condoms and a black vibrator. Wickedly, I grab the vibrator, sliding it into my pocket so she can't see it. Then I kneel behind her, where her bare ass is still perched in the air waiting for me.

I lean down and plant a kiss on her lower back, and she flinches. Then, I run my tongue from her pussy to her ass, and the gasp that escapes her lips is beautiful. I will probably never get tired of shocking her. My thumb runs circles over her puckered hole, and she stays silent.

I dribble a little lube on her crack, working it in. My cock can barely wait another second, but as much as I love hurting her, I don't want to *actually* hurt her. I like forcing her to do a lot of stuff, but this one will actually take some trust. So I make my cock wait while I ease my finger in. She's so tense, it's a vise grip.

"Relax, Everly."

"I'm not used to relaxing around you."

With my opposite hand, I grab a handful of her hair and pull her upright so my mouth is next to her ear. "Do you think I really want to hurt you?"

"Yes."

"You're wrong. I want you to be my dirty little slut. I want to fuck your brains out and make you come so hard you see stars. Can I do that?"

She lets out a sweet little breath and nods. "Yes."

As she returns to all fours, I lube up my cock and continue working her hole, slipping a second finger in when she finally relaxes. She hums, pressing her hips back like she's just realizing how good it feels.

I give her small pumps with my fingers, and the muscles in her body seem to melt with each thrust. Then, I work in a third finger and she barely notices.

Pulling out my fingers, I put a little more lube on her ass and line up the head of my shaft. She tenses again, shutting me out. I grab her hips and press forward, but she's too clenched. So I land a hard smack on her ass, and she yelps, dropping her head toward the floor.

"I said relax, Everly."

When I try to press inside again, this time, she lets go, and I slip past the ring of muscle. She lets out another gasp, and I can barely fucking breathe. It's so goddamn tight, and when I push inward, her ass devours my cock.

"Oh my God," she cries out. It's not exactly a moan of pleasure, but she's not telling me to stop either. In fact, her hips nudge backward, urging me in further.

It takes everything in me to keep from blowing my load already. "Your ass loves my cock, Everly."

"More," she breathes in a raspy plea.

Holding her soft hips in my hands, I slam myself in as

far as I can go and she practically screams, but this time it's pleasure-laced and hungry for more.

"Oh, fuck," she says, resting her forehead on the floor.

"Dammit, Everly. This is so fucking beautiful."

"More, Cullen, please." She sounds so desperate, like her life currently depends on me fucking her ass.

I take it slow at first, easing out and back in, losing my fucking mind every time her tight entrance swallows me in, strangling my cock. I touch her spine, running my fingers along her back, feeling the goosebumps erupt under my touch. Her body is on fire. I can see the heavy breaths she's taking by the weighted movement of her rib cage with each inhale. There's a soft sheen of sweat along her skin.

It's the most beautiful shit I've ever seen.

That's when I reach into my pocket. Twisting the vibrator at the bottom, it comes to life, buzzing loudly as I press the tip to her clit. The sound that comes out of her mouth is fucking magical. She gasps for air, pumping her hips back and calling my name between breaths.

This is the closest I've ever felt to her—or to anyone.

"Cullen. More. Oh fuck. I'm—gonna come."

Our moans and cries of pleasure bleed into every inch of this room. This feeling, the sounds, the vision of her on her knees taking my body in her. It's all too much.

"I'm comin' too, baby," I grunt out.

Her fingernails dig into the wood floor as she screams, her body pulsing through her orgasm. I hold her hips in my hands while she spasms in pleasure. It lasts forever, so just as I feel my climax coming, I pull out and paint her black dress white.

Once my cock is spent, I yank her body up again, holding her by the throat and running my tongue up the side of her neck. Then I find her lips and kiss her. She melts into my arms, letting me hold her, touch her, stroke her.

My chest feels like it's about to crack in two. Why is everything with this girl so fucking intense?

She's still resting with her back to my chest as we try to catch our breaths. After a few minutes, I pick her up and carry her to bed. Then, I cover her body with mine, rolling her until she's resting her head in the crook of my arm.

We fall asleep that way.

Chapter 20
Cullen

ME: *Pick me up without panties on.*
        Everly: And what if I don't want to?

"Who is she?" Gina asks, leaning over the bar and breaking me from my concentration. I'm trying to formulate the perfect reply to Everly's bratty message.

I hide my phone as I turn around to glare at the nosey hostess. "None of your business."

She holds up her hands in surrender. "You never come hang out anymore and you're always on your phone, so I figure there must be someone. A girl at school?"

"You could say that," I mumble.

My phone pings again, and I grind my teeth. I missed my opportunity to reprimand Everly for her last message.

Sneaking a glance, I bite my tongue to keep from snapping at Gina.

EVERLY: *I WILL IF YOU BRING ME A SLICE OF TIRAMISU.*

Me: *Tiramisu for pussy?*

Everly: *I never promised sex. I said I'd pick you up without panties.*

Me: *Which will result in me getting pussy.*

Everly: *So, do we have a deal?*

Me: *We don't negotiate. You do what I say, remember.*

Everly: *I'll go back to my original response. What if I don't want to?*

Me: *Then, you'll be punished.*

Everly: *Promise?*

I FIND MYSELF SMILING AT MY PHONE, BUT I CATCH IT and shove the feeling away. The past couple months have been strange. Everly and I have fallen into a rhythm. I spend most nights at her house, and she does everything I tell her to like laundry and driving me around. On the nights I have practice, she works on the bleachers, and on the nights I work, she stays home and checks in until I get off.

She wanted to put a title on it, and even though I know what this is, I hate the idea of giving it a label. She's mine. I'm hers. And I'm comfortable with that. The shit from our past feels so distant now, and when I have to remind myself who she is, it takes actual mental work to remember that I'm supposed to hate her.

So, I just stopped trying.

Last night, she admitted she thinks I'll get sick of her, and the thought has wormed its way into my brain. All day I've been thinking about it. Am I stupid to let her get attached? Am I getting attached? I've never even been in a real relationship, let alone felt the heartbreak of losing one.

It has me feeling anxious. Should I cut things off early to avoid the pain? Should I be spending my weekends with people my own age, drowning in pussy?

Fuck, that would be stupid. I've gotten laid more in the past two weeks than I have in the last four years. Everly is a fucking animal. She has zero, and I'm talking zero fucking shame in the bedroom. I love how fearless she is and totally unafraid to get exactly what she needs out of every single time we do it. The back and forth banter between us—me trying to deny her and her fighting me for it—is an actual turn-on.

"You should come over tonight," Gina says in a sing-song, high-pitched voice. I notice the way she's pushing her tits together, and I absently wonder if this is because she thinks I have a girl now, like suddenly I'm more attractive to her.

"Nah, I can't."

"Plans with your girlfriend?" she asks with a smile stretched across her face.

"I don't have a girlfriend," I reply.

"Well, you have something."

Biting the inside of my cheek, I make my way around to my tables, picking up checks and delivering drinks and trying not to think about Gina's words, the strange way I feel about Everly, and the nagging reminder that the way things are now won't last forever.

Why did Everly tell me I could fuck other people? Was that her subtle way of telling me she wants to fuck other people? Did I force her into this shit with me and now she's trying to give me all the hints that she wants out? God, my head is going in circles, and it's making me feel really fucking insecure—and it's all Everly's fault.

During a short break, I open my phone and see a text from Everly.

EVERLY: WHAT TIME DO YOU GET OFF? I FORGOT MY *laptop charger in my office, and I need to run back in.*

IT'S SO FUCKING CASUAL LIKE A GODDAMN relationship and I grow irritable for no reason at all. Ignoring her message, I act on impulse and head toward the front to cash out my last table.

"Hey, Gina," I call toward her. "I'll come over tonight."

"Oh yeah? Bringing your new girl?"

"Fuck no. Is Allie coming?" I ask, and something in Gina's demeanor changes like she reads the sincerity on my face.

"I don't know. Maybe."

Good, I think. It's a test. That's all. Maybe being around my friends will clear away this Everly fog I'm suddenly feeling today. It might be the palate cleanser I need, a quick reset button. It's not cheating. Everly doesn't want to be my girlfriend, so I don't need to feel bad about this.

Still, I feel a pinch of guilt as I type out my message.

ME: NEVER MIND PICKING ME UP. I'M GOING TO A PARTY *after work.*

I DON'T BOTHER TELLING HER ANYTHING ELSE, LIKE whether or not I'll be coming over after the party, because I frankly don't know. I want to. It feels like home already, and

I hate the idea of going back to my dorm room, but Everly's house is not my home, so some distance is good. We both need the reminder.

EVERLY: OKAY.

THAT'S IT, AND I STARE AT HER RESPONSE FOR A moment too fucking long. Why does it bother me so much? Why the fuck do I care? The silence between us feels like drawn-out torture so while I clean my station, I try to formulate my response, but I don't even know what I'm trying to say. All I know is I don't like her getting in my head, turning the tables on me like she fucking owns me, when it should be the other way around. Everly needs a reminder of who she belongs to.

ME: DON'T GO ANYWHERE. I'LL SLEEP AT THE DORM tonight. I have a game at ten in the morning. Be there.

EVERLY: OKAY.

THERE'S THAT FUCKING ANSWER AGAIN. WHAT THE fuck! Why does it feel like I'm the one being punished right now? I can feel her disappointment through these fucking text messages and it's grating on my nerves.

I consider canceling on Gina and just going back to Everly's so I don't have to deal with this shitty attitude I'm in now, but I don't. I finish up closing my station and paying out my tips to the bartender and busboys, then I grab a ride with Gina to her place.

On the way over, I get a notification on my phone, and while Gina's droning on and on about something, I glance down and see Everly leaving through the front door camera.

What the fuck? I told her not to go anywhere.

ME: WHERE THE FUCK ARE YOU GOING?

HER REPLY COMES BACK MORE THAN FOUR MINUTES later, but it feels like fifteen.

EVERLY: *I TOLD YOU I LEFT MY CHARGER AT THE OFFICE, so I'm going to get it.*

ME: IT'S LATE AS FUCK, EVERLY. STAY HOME. YOU CAN *get it in the morning.*

"I'M GOING TO STOP AT THE LIQUOR STORE. STAY IN THE car," Gina mumbles as she pulls up to the parking lot of a big warehouse-size liquor store. I barely acknowledge her, just glad for a moment of privacy, so I can talk to Everly alone.

As soon as Gina is out of the car, I hit *Call* on my phone.

"Will you just calm down?" Everly says as soon as she answers.

"I told you not to go anywhere."

"Just knock it off, Cullen. I'm not a fucking child, and I need my laptop charger so I'm going."

"Why won't you just listen to me?"

"Why do you care?" she yells. Her voice carries through the phone, and I can tell she's driving and the call is connected to her Bluetooth speaker.

"Because you seem to be forgetting I am in control here. You want me to just leak those photos, don't you?"

I didn't know silence could hurt so much, but the lack of response out of her when I threaten her with the photos, the ones I haven't brought up in over two months, feels like a knife through my chest.

"I thought we were past this, Cullen. Where the fuck is this coming from?"

"You said yourself you're not my girlfriend, Everly, so I guess I'm back to being just your annoying student."

"I seriously don't understand you, Cullen, but we can't keep doing this. I can't—"

"That's what I thought."

She lets out a sigh that sounds sad as fuck, and I hate myself for a moment. I'm ruining this.

"Why does it have to be like this? Do you really want to blackmail me?"

I stare out the window at the bright lights of the liquor store, and I can't see any way out of this. Everly wants me to admit feelings I can't fucking admit. She wants me to let go of shit I can't let go of. Any stupid dream I had of being able to be in a normal fucking relationship was cursed eight years ago...and she's part of that reason.

"Yeah, I guess I do."

"Fucking leak them, Cullen. I don't give a shit anymore." The resignation in her voice almost makes me want to punch a hole through this window.

"I will. Then we're done. That's what you want, isn't it?" I'm feeling frantic, desperate and seething with anger. I've lost control of her. I guess in a way, I've lost her completely.

"No, Cullen," she snaps. "That's not what I want, and you know it. I don't want to be done with you. I just want to be done with this version where you think you need to control me all the time, punish me for how miserable you are. I'm done with that. So go to your friends, leak the fucking photos, I don't care. Hell, I'll send them to the dean myself if you want. I don't belong to you anymore...not like that."

The phone goes dead, and I want to punch something. A rage burns through me, but I have to bite it back, so when Gina gets in the car, and sees my obvious change in mood, she looks worried.

I just need to go to this party, get high, and let Allie give me another blow job in the guest room. I have to do that, because it's who I am. Because a guy like me just doesn't belong with a woman like Everly. It was never going to work.

"Everything okay?" she asks.

"Yeah, let's just go."

There's a moment of hesitation before she pulls away from the curb. She can clearly see I'm not in the mood to party. My phone says Everly just got to campus a few minutes ago, but I don't know why I even care. So I shove my phone in my pocket and stay quiet for the rest of the drive to her house.

When we get to Gina's, there's a crowd of people in her living room and a skunky cloud hanging over the room. Her boyfriend offers me a beer and a hit of the joint, both of which I take enthusiastically. The sooner I get buzzed and high the better because, right now, my brain is on an Everly loop and it needs to shut the fuck up.

I make eye contact with Allie across the room, who is currently sitting alone, so I peel myself from the wall I'm leaning against and walk over. I decide that I should get more than a blow job tonight. I should fuck her and let it be the final nail in the coffin.

"Hey, stranger," she says in her sugary-sweet voice as I drop into the seat next to her.

"Hey," I reply gruffly.

"Rough night?"

I nod, staring ahead. I can't look at the girl next to me. She's pretty, beautiful even, but there isn't a fire burning between us. There would never be a moment with Allie like I had with Everly last night.

But there she goes again, stealing every thought in my head when I want to focus on something—*someone*—else.

"What's on your mind?" Allie asks as she leans into my lap, rubbing my leg.

I can't answer her question, so I let her touch me instead, and I wait for the weed to kick in.

But it never does. Instead, I have to suffer through Everly's words echoing on repeat in my mind.

I DON'T BELONG TO YOU ANYMORE, NOT LIKE THAT.

Chapter 21
Everly

THE PARKING LOT is dark and empty when I pull up to the building. I park near the front door, which is technically a spot for the dean, but it's almost midnight, so I doubt she'll be needing it right now.

After I put the car in park, my shaking hands grasp the steering wheel, and I let the tears fall as I rest my head against the back of my hands.

Why is everything with Cullen so intense? Why is he suddenly sabotaging something that I thought was so good just last night? What we did last night was easily the hottest and most intense thing I have ever done in bed, and it wasn't all about where I let him put it. It was about this moment that brought us so close, a give and take that I realized was so fucking perfect, I thought for a moment I found my perfect match.

Everything Cullen wants is exactly what I want to give. I need his dominating sense of control, and he needs my trust. Last night was pure harmony, and up until a couple hours ago, I had faith we could actually see this through.

I was wrong.

I still have so much I want to say to him, and the words are burning inside me, but I have to let it go. I have to let *him* go.

He's just a teenager, Everly. Why would you possibly think this could work out?

Nearly an hour later, after I've exhausted my tears and put myself through enough emotional turmoil, I get out of the car. I'm so focused on the fight with Cullen that I don't take a good look around the area as I run up to the door. I have an exterior door key for this purpose, but as I reach the top of the stairs, I let out an ear-piercing scream as I nearly slam into someone coming out. It's a man, and he's tall with pale skin and copper red hair. I don't recognize him, but I'm still so new here, so I don't know everyone at the office yet.

"Excuse me," he says, putting his hands on my arms to stop me from falling down the stairs.

I'm staring wide-eyed, a chill running down my spine, which I assume must be from running into a stranger in the middle of the night at an empty building.

"Excuse me," I mumble.

He brushes past me and takes off toward the empty parking lot, red warning signs going off in my head as he leaves. Maybe it was just another professor working late, I think in my head.

Something about going into this building right now seems like a bad idea, and every one of my instincts is telling me not to. So, I'm just standing on the stairs for a moment, deliberating what I should do next.

I'm being paranoid. There are security cameras inside. I'll be fine. I just need to run in and grab my charger. It will take two seconds. Glancing back at the stranger, he's already halfway across the parking lot, so I quickly unlock the door and run in.

Once I get to my office, my phone buzzes. Looking down, I see it's a message from some random app and not a text from Cullen, and my heart falls at the realization.

It's really over. Let it go.

But I can't stop thinking about him at that party. Is he going to sleep with someone else? A sting of jealousy sours in my stomach at the thought, and I literally have to sit down. How the fuck could I let myself get so attached to a student? A reckless, angry, hurting, broken student, who gets pleasure from my pain? Cullen is still so damaged from his upbringing, and he probably hasn't had professional help since, so now he's using me as an outlet to heal his pain. I can't let him do that anymore...no matter how nice it was at times. How much I loved watching him play rugby. Feeling his touch next to me on the couch and sharing Chinese food. The way he smelled straight out of the shower.

Another tear streaks down my face. I can't really let him go, can I? Not like this. Not this easily.

Deciding I will call him when I get back to my car, I walk across the room to my desk and grab my cord before bending over to pull it out of the wall. That's when I notice the drawers of my desk are open, papers thrown all over the floor. Was someone going through my office?

When I stand up, a figure in my periphery catches my attention. I let out a scream as my eyes land on the silhouette standing in the doorway.

With a black ski mask, he stands against the door frame, leaning casually with his arms crossed. It's dark, but with his tall figure and all black outfit, my mind immediately settles on the realization that it's Cullen.

"What the hell are you doing? You gave me a heart attack!"

There's a brief moment when the rapid pulse of my heart slows and the fear in my stomach dissipates because he's here. Not at a party and not mad at me for fighting with him. And everything feels right.

But silence spills out between us.

I can just about make out the shape of his eyes in the dim haze of the auxiliary lights. My heart hammers in my chest as I glare at him. Maybe I underestimated how angry he is. Maybe this whole time I've completely overestimated us, thinking there could be any genuine feelings here, and the whole time I've just been a toy to him. I've pushed him too far, and he's here to make me pay for that.

"What is your problem?" I mumble, trying to sound confident but failing.

As he charges toward me, I feel the first real wave of terror I've ever felt with Cullen. I scream out his name as his hands wrap around my throat, pinning me hard to the desk as my back slams against the surface. I don't bother to fight back, not at first, because somewhere deep down, I know he won't really hurt me. Not too much at least.

But as he squeezes harder, cutting off my airway, I panic. He's too angry, so lost in his rage, he could really kill me, and this will be how I go, at the hands of someone I've come to care about so much that I let him. I'm *letting* him do this.

Once my lungs begin to ache, my body fights back. I manage a kick to his groin and he falters, but not enough to free me from his grasp. My fingers claw at his shirt, then his neck, not registering why something isn't right about the bare white flesh against my nails. Where are his tattoos?

My mind only registers one thing—he's going to kill me.

It becomes obvious to me after my vision begins to blur. My eyes search his features for the familiarity of the man I know, but before I can find them, everything fades to black.

Chapter 22
Cullen

"Do you want to go to the bedroom?" she whispers against my ear.

My mind is in a haze, but not nearly as removed from reality as I would like. The living room is dim, and I can make out the sounds of people kissing on the opposite sofa. There's laughter coming from somewhere behind us, and Allie's hand is stroking the inside of leg.

My dick is not responding.

I should say yes. I should go to the bedroom with her, fuck her just to get it over with, and move on with my miserable, stupid life. I'll never be able to go back to Everly after that so at least it would put me out of my misery.

"Cullen," she whispers. She pulls my face toward hers and presses her soft, wet lips against mine, letting out a soft hum, even though I'm not moving a muscle to kiss her back. "I want you to fuck me."

There's a slur to her voice, and six months ago, those words would have been music to my cock, but today, they make me want to run away. I literally can't even bring myself to kiss her back.

"I can't, Allie." My own voice sounds far away, like someone else is speaking.

"You have a girlfriend, don't you?"

Fuck, do I?

"I don't know."

"No one has to know, Cullen." Her hand drifts between my legs again, but this time, I snatch her wrist before she can touch me.

"Ow!" she shrieks when I pinch her too hard. And as fucked up as it makes me, the sound of Allie's cries makes me miss Everly intensely. It brings back memories of the first time I really hungered for her, craving her pain and the control she would let me yield over her.

The shit that woman woke up inside me, the way she fought back just enough. The trust she put in me. The way we fit...

I jump up from the couch in a rush like I just fucking realized that I have somewhere to be—because I do.

"What the hell is wrong with you?" Allie cries from her seat.

"I have to go." I don't even bother saying goodbye or asking for a ride. I just bolt out the front door. Glancing down at my phone, I realize it's too late for the bus. Instead, I pull up the ride app and order a car to take me to Everly's. For good measure, I check her location just to make sure she's home.

My brow furrows when I notice her icon still settled on the campus on the city map. Why the fuck is she still at the campus? It's been over an hour since I spoke to her. Paranoia floods my nervous system.

I call her phone, with no answer, two times before the car arrives. She must have left her phone at her office. It's the most likely scenario, but it does nothing to settle my worry.

As we pull into the parking lot, I am flooded with relief when I spot the lone car parked by the English department. Her car is still here, which means she's still here.

"Thanks," I say as I jump out and check inside Everly's car for her. She's not there, so I lean against the driver's side, waiting for her to come out.

I only pace around for about two minutes, but with all these thoughts running through my head, I'm feeling impatient, and it feels like twenty minutes go by. I call her three more times, feeling more irrational and panicked with each passing second.

What the fuck is taking so long?

If she's planning on working all night in there, I'm going to kill her.

After jogging up the stairs, I check the door, but it's locked. I give it a quick bang, but there is no sign of life inside. Where the fuck is she?

Suddenly the door bursts open, and when I expect to see Everly on the other side, I stare in shock at the figure that rushes past me. He's in a black ski mask, and he's fast.

"What the fuck?" I blurt out from pure shock. It's the middle of the night, and some dude just came running out of the English department like he just robbed the place. Quickly, I catch the door before it closes, and I stand there speechless as he runs away.

Then, my blood turns to ice.

Everly.

My mind goes silent as I bolt into the building. The

only light is dim, like the building's on night mode, so I can hardly see where I'm going. There's an empty receptionist desk at the front, a mailroom behind it, and a hallway on each side.

"Everly!" I scream in a panic before bursting down the hallway on the right. Rushing into the room, I freeze in the doorway. She's lying on the floor, her dark hair covering her face. My blank mind only processes panic.

I'm reliving a moment from my childhood. I see Everly, and I see my mother, and I fucking pray. Don't make me go through this again.

Please be okay. Please be okay.

Snatching her body up in my arms, the first thing I notice is that her eyes are closed and I'm relieved that I don't find her lifeless stare glaring back at me. Desperation and panic mute every thought in my head as I shake her. Then I feel for a pulse, but my hands are shaking too much to make one out.

"Everly, please wake up!"

Clutching her body to my face, I listen for a heartbeat and feel subtle movement under my cheek. When I try again for a pulse, I find a soft beat under my fingers. She's alive.

"Come on, baby. Please wake up," I whisper, pressing my lips to hers.

Time seems to be moving both slow and fast at the same time. I need to call 9-1-1, but I'm too focused on just getting her to wake up. I need her eyes on me, but I'm starting to lose hope.

I pull out my phone and shake out the numbers, but just before I hit *Call*, she jolts, knocking it out of my hand. Her eyes are wide and full of terror, and even as I stare at her with immense relief, she glares back in horror.

"No!" she screams, pushing herself out of my arms.

"It's me, baby. It's me."

"Get away from me!" she cries, her voice catching on a sob.

"Ev, it's me, Cullen. You're okay now."

Her hands reach for her throat, and her face twists into anguish as she presses herself against the wall, holding the opposite hand out to stop me from coming closer.

"Please don't hurt me."

"I would never hurt you, Everly. It wasn't me."

"It was you! You just want to torture me, and I thought you were going to kill me. I can't do it anymore, Cullen. I can't let you hurt me anymore." Tears stream down her cheeks and the pure agony on her face pierces my heart. It shatters everything, every moment when I thought I could control her, own her, punish her. It's all so trivial and point-less now as I see the very real suffering on her face.

She must be hysterical, thinking it was me that hurt her, but right now, as she cries and flinches every time I even dare to come near her, I realize that to her, it *could have been me*. She thinks I'm capable of truly hurting her like this.

"What are you doing?" she cries as I pick up my phone.

"Calling 9-1-1."

She hiccups, watching me from her curled-up position on the floor. And I can't bear to look at her. I can't face the terror in her eyes, what she really thinks of me hidden in that fear.

"He didn't...hurt you, did he?"

Her eyes are searching my face, and I know this is hard for her to understand. That man had a mask on, and she probably did think it was me. Now she can't even trust me enough to answer the question. She still thinks I'm toying with her.

"Nine-one-one, what is your emergency?" the woman on the phone says.

"Yes, my..." I stop myself. I can't say girlfriend, not now, it feels wrong. "A woman was attacked. We're in the English department at Florence University."

"Is she conscious right now, sir?"

My eyes meet hers. "Yes, she's sitting right here next to me. She's pretty shaken up."

"I'm sending a patrol car and ambulance to your location now."

The dispatcher asks me a list of questions about Everly, her attacker, her wounds, and I feel so disoriented answering them, but I don't take my eyes off her for a second. She begins to soften, not ready to touch me yet, still holding on to some doubt in her head that I didn't just try to kill her, but I gather by the way I found her and the fact that her pants are still perfectly intact that he didn't do anything worse. It gives me some form of relief. Still, the thought of that man, the one I let slip right by, touching her, scaring her, nearly killing her, has my blood boiling.

I want to find him, and I want to kill him. A burning rage courses through my veins.

It was probably a drunk kid on campus, maybe just out to scare women for no reason. Maybe his plans were worse and she fought him off or he heard me coming before he could do more, but I still feel fucking sick thinking about it.

When the ambulance arrives, I hang up from the call with the operator, since I have to run to the front door to let them in. Everly reaches for me before I can get out the door.

"Wait, Cullen," she whispers.

Kneeling down in front of her, I stare into her eyes as she reaches for my face. "It wasn't you, was it?"

I wince, letting out a long sigh. "Of course not."

Another sob racks through her body as she wraps her arms around my neck. The way she squeezes me tight, clutching to me like her life depends on it, changes everything. With my arms around her waist, I hug her back.

Is it too late to fix the damage I've done? How the fuck was I supposed to know fucking with her would end with me feeling this way?

"Oh, Cullen," she says through a wet, strangled gasp.

"It's okay. I'm here," I whisper.

There's a pounding at the door, and I know it's the paramedics, so I take her with me as we walk toward the front to open it. There is a police officer and a couple of paramedics waiting for us, the glow of red and blue lights lighting up the night sky over the campus.

I see the way they look at me as I help Everly to the ambulance. And it doesn't matter that I was not the one who hurt her tonight. I hurt her before, and the guilt of that is enough.

The next hour goes by grudgingly slow. They ask us a million questions, stare at me skeptically, and give her a quick checkup, checking the swelling on her throat and the knot on her head.

During the entire ordeal, she won't let go of my hand, and I don't want to leave her, especially when the older cop comes over and asks for her to give him the entire report of the incident. I cringe through the whole thing, clenching my teeth so hard it makes my jaw ache.

"Are you sure you don't need a more comprehensive exam?" the male cop asks, and she cringes. Fuck, we both do because we know what he's asking. Did the man rape her? I watch her face as she answers him.

"No," she replies, shaking her head, and they're staring at me again. I know how this looks. I know with my piercings and tattoos and abnormally dyed-hair, I look like trouble. To them, they see a woman who's being manipulated, and to them, it probably was me.

"Sir, would you mind giving us a moment to talk to her alone?" the cop asks, and I feel my fists clench. She must feel it, too, because she squeezes my hand tighter.

"It wasn't him," she replies immediately. "I know what you're thinking. Trust me, I get it, but it wasn't." When her eyes meet mine, there's certainty in her expression, and it calms me. She knows it wasn't me. They could haul my ass away, make me sleep in a jail cell, but as long as *she* knows it wasn't me, that's all that matters.

The cop lets it go, and after she assures them she's fine and doesn't need to go to the hospital, they leave. By the time I take Everly to her car, I'm more exhausted than I think I've ever been in my life. I'm still so on edge with so many questions swirling in my mind, but it's all too much for me to process right now.

I drive us to her house in her car, and the entire time she doesn't let go of me, and while that's something I know I should love, right now, I hate it. I wish she would let go of me. I wish she still hated me the way she did before. The way she *should*.

Getting out of the car at her house, the cool air nips at my skin. I notice the way she clutches her arms tighter to her body, and I find myself staring at her. So many thoughts echo through my head.

She and I have balanced on this strange plane of familiarity. We belong in each other's lives, but not because of intimacy or love, but because of trauma. It binds us in a strange climate of distrust and vulnerability. I don't truly know Everly any better than I might know an actual girlfriend or friend, but I've rooted myself in her life without consent because, somehow, I got the impression I was entitled to do so.

She didn't deserve that. My rational brain knows that, but for some reason, my rational brain is struggling for control these days.

"Are you okay?" I ask as we step inside her dark house.

"Yeah." She's still so shaken, and I find myself feeling completely inadequate. Nothing I say or do is enough. This woman was nearly killed tonight, strangled on the desk of her office by a complete stranger, and I'm standing here talking to her like I haven't tried to make her life a living hell for the past several weeks.

"I should probably go," I mutter, keeping my place by the door, suddenly afraid to come inside.

"What?" The genuine shock on her face is endearing.

"You've been through enough. I'll let you get cleaned up and rested."

She lets out a heavy sigh, sounding very frustrated with me as she turns away. Spinning on her heels in the kitchen, she glares at me.

"Fine. Just go."

That's it?

"I'm not your boyfriend, remember? You told me that. And you're right. I'm not your boyfriend. I would be a terrible fucking boyfriend, Everly. All I know is how to be cruel and controlling. Those assholes broke me. If you need someone to come over and hold you while you cry, well, then you better call your friend, because I'm not that guy."

"Fine!" Her voice cracks as she yells, but she doesn't

move from her spot, like an angry statue staring at me from the kitchen.

"You really shouldn't be so angry," I argue back. "I'm offering to leave you alone. It's the nicest fucking thing I've ever done for you."

She scoffs, her eyes filling with tears, and it's like nails on a chalkboard. I've made her cry before, all those times because I was antagonizing her with a purpose, but now, she's not crying because of me. She's crying *for* me, and I hate it. I need to get out of here right now.

"Just go, Cullen. I think we've tortured each other enough."

"It's over. I'm done."

"Thank you." Her voice sounds so small.

My hand rests on the doorknob, and I don't understand why it's so hard to leave. I need to. I should, but something is holding me here. I've gotten so comfortable in this house, with her, my fucking professor, that I'm finding it hard to walk away.

If I care about her at all, I need to fucking leave.

With a quietly muttered "Goodbye," I open the door and disappear into the darkness. I could go home, but the vision of that asshole hurting her is burned into my memory and it feels wrong leaving her alone. So I slide against her front door, settling on the concrete of her patio, and I stay that way all night. Just close enough and far enough to keep her safe.

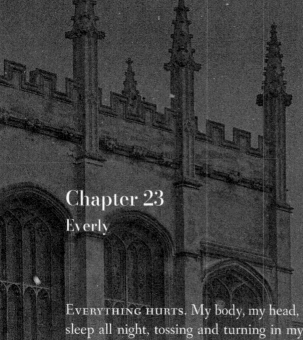

Chapter 23
Everly

EVERYTHING HURTS. My body, my head, my heart. I barely sleep all night, tossing and turning in my bed. I can't stop thinking about the attack and Cullen leaving. When sadness tries to occupy my thoughts, my brain tends to go into overdrive, like some sort of defense mechanism to keep me from thinking too much.

And with how miserable I'm feeling without Cullen here, my thoughts are out of control.

Someone tried to kill me tonight. That much is obvious. And I think Cullen is still under the impression it was just a campus predator, but I know better. If he wanted to rape me, he would have.

Is this because I've been spending so much time with Cullen, and someone isn't happy about that? Who else would even care?

I always knew there was a risk when I got involved with the Ayers case, but that was so long ago. I assumed it had all passed since then. So why now? Is George Ayers just now seeking his revenge?

Sleep finally wins the battle against my anxiety just

before sunrise, and I sleep restlessly. It feels like I have one foot in my dreams and one foot out, as if I'm keeping an eye out for him, waiting to feel him climb into my bed, to touch me, to kiss me, to take my body for himself.

God, I wish he would.

If only Cullen could get out of his own head, stop trying to use the present to fix the past. It's like he's punishing himself for letting himself feel anything other than anger and hate. He's vulnerable, afraid, and after the years of abandonment and abuse he endured, vulnerability triggers his fight-or-flight. Cullen will never fully let go. Which means he can never truly be mine.

In my fitful dreaming, I see his face in the courtroom again, but instead of the dark-haired emotionless boy, I see the white-haired man who radiates pain. I feel the daggers of his hatred as he stares at me across the aisle, and I ache for him. I beg him to hurt me, to make me pay, to make me whole.

When he finally eats up the distance between us, coming to me like a predator about to devour its prey, I give him my body. Arching my head back, I let him take the most vulnerable part of me, waiting for the kill, crying for him to hurt me, but when I feel his fingers on my skin, it's not pain that follows, but pleasure.

And it's all wrong. His touch is sweet and beautiful, and I fight against him, eager for the revenge-driven Cullen I know. As he looks down at me, tears pour from his eyes, and I instantly snap myself out of the dream.

My eyes fly open. Panic clutches my chest in a vise grip, making it hard to breathe.

Something is buzzing against my nightstand, but my mind takes so long to wake up that I ignore it until it stops.

Sunlight shines through the curtained windows, clouding the room in a warm haze.

I just keep replaying the dream in my head over and over until my phone starts buzzing again. Grabbing it off the table, I notice there are notifications covering the screen. Texts and missed calls, mostly from Thomas. Could he have found out about the attack already? I know someone from the campus should be contacting me today to talk about it, but I'm not quite ready to start all of that. First, I need coffee.

Then I see a notification that there is movement at my front door, and I freeze in terror. Opening the camera app connected to my doorbell, I gasp, covering my lips when I see a tall, lanky figure lying on my front porch. I touch the grainy, black-and-white image, running my finger over his light hair and closed eyes.

He slept out there all night.

Before I open Thomas's messages, I climb out of bed and head straight for the front door. Cracking it open slowly, I watch him as he starts to stir awake. He's using a cushion from my patio furniture for a pillow, but he must have been freezing out here all night.

"Do you want to come in?" I ask when he peels his eyes open. For a moment, I swear he's about to say yes, but he shuts down before the words come out.

He sits up with a groan, hugging his knees to his chest. "No. I called Thomas about an hour ago. He should be on his way."

That would explain the text messages and phone calls. "Let me give you a ride home then."

The word *home* lingers uncomfortably between us. This is his home, or at least it felt like it for a moment in time.

"No. I'll take the bus. I have a game today."

"Do you want me to come?"

"No." His eyes are focused downward, and it shatters my heart.

I just wish he would stop trying to be a hero now. Stop thinking about all the things he *should* be doing and do what he wants, and just as I'm about to tell him that, I spot Thomas's car pulling up to the house.

Cullen jumps up and puts his back to me, walking straight toward the street and right past Thomas as he gets out of his car. My friend stands there looking confused, glancing back and forth between Cullen and me. Tears pool in my eyes, but I only shrug and retreat back into my house.

I head for my coffee pot, firing up a cup with a couple buttons. The machine growls to life as the aroma of espresso fills the kitchen.

"What the hell is going on?" he asks, and the question breaks me. Tears spill out over my lashes and down my cheeks. He doesn't say another word as he swallows me up into his arms, rubbing my back and giving me a warm chest to cry into.

AN HOUR LATER, THOMAS AND I ARE ON MY COUCH AND I've filled him in on everything.

"Jesus, Everly. Are you okay? You were almost killed last night."

"I don't think so," I say, shaking my head. "If he wanted me dead, he would have killed me. I think it was a warning."

"A warning? From who?"

"Cullen and I have been looking into the case again, opening up old files, and I don't know if someone caught on, but..."

"You think Cullen's dad is responsible for this?"

I shrug in response.

"Does Cullen know this?"

I don't answer. Cullen and I don't need anything else between us. There's so much already, and if I tell him that I think his dad still has dangerous connections or that someone is still watching me after all these years, it would only create more of a fission between us.

"I think a little space would be good. Put the case away for a while. I'll stay with you."

He puts out a hand, and I take it, linking my fingers with his. "You don't have to do that, Thomas. I'm fine."

"Like hell you are. Everly, I've known you for a decade, and you are not fine. You do this thing when life gets rough, where you act like you're so tough and strong, so no one has to see how scared or sad you are. If you're not okay, that's okay." He brings his face close to mine, kissing my forehead, and I shatter into a million pieces.

I don't just cry, I sob. Resting my face against his shoulder, I let it all out. I cry for my loneliness, my failures, for Cullen, for the pain he went through as a child, for all of the love my stupid heart has built up for him, and I cry for my future because he did what he set out to do.

Cullen ruined me for all other men because I know there is no possible way I could ever love anyone more.

Chapter 24
Cullen

"THERE's some lady up front asking for you?" Gina finds me at the soda fountain by the bar, watching me with a hand on her hip. I don't answer her, staring at the cups as they fill with dark, syrupy carbonation.

"Cullen, did you hear me?"

"I heard you," I reply coldly.

I know it's *her*. I haven't shown up to her last three classes. It's been a week since the attack. I've watched her doorbell enough to know Thomas has been staying with her every night, and she doesn't leave her house after dark.

Gina lingers for a moment, like she wants to ask me about the mystery woman at the hostess station. I know in her mind she's thinking she's too old to be my girlfriend and too young to be my mother. Finally, Gina leaves and I ready myself to go back to the dining room, where I know her waiting brown eyes will find me.

Carrying the drink tray, I focus my attention on the table. Dropping off their drinks, I take their order with minimal enthusiasm, and the entire time I feel Everly's gaze on my back. After putting the order into the computer, I hear her approach me from behind.

"Cullen."

I hesitate, making her wait a moment before I turn toward her. It's not that I'm punishing her—it's that I'm not ready to look into those brown eyes again.

"Hey," I say finally, turning her way.

The impact of her gaze hits me like a ten-ton brick to the chest. She looks tired, dark circles under her eyes, her hair not quite as kept as it used to look, and the urge to gather her into my arms, to feel her tiny weight against my body, is intense.

When did this happen? When did the craving to hurt her get replaced by the craving to protect her? When someone else hurt her? Or when she thought that someone else was me?

"You've been missing too many classes, and if you don't turn in your final assignment, you're going to fail."

"I don't know what to say."

"Say you'll come to class on Monday. It's the last week of the semester. I just need you to turn in the assignment, Cullen. You can't lose your scholarship."

"So, you're here as my teacher."

She swallows, her eyes lingering on my lips. "What else would I be here as?"

The silence lingers between us. Out of the corner of my eye, I see someone at my table raise their hand, and I take the opportunity to break the tension. "I have to go," I say, leaving her standing there to see what the annoying lady at my table needs. As she gives me her complex cocktail order, I glance up to see Everly disappearing through the front door.

That's it then. She was here as my teacher, maybe even

as a friend, and that's the way I wanted it. I broke this shit off on purpose, so I should be glad. Everly was always fucking mine, but it wasn't supposed to be like that. Until I sort some shit out in my head, I need her to just stay the fuck away.

THEY CUT ME EARLY FROM WORK, AND GINA DOESN'T even bother inviting me to her party tonight. I've been in a shit mood all week. We lost our match last night, and I haven't been studying for my finals at all, so if I pass all my classes and keep my scholarship, it will be a goddamn miracle.

And if I'm not at work or on the pitch, all I do is think about Everly. Fuck relationships, and dating, and women. And love. Most of all, fuck love.

I hate going to my dorm since I've barely taken the time this semester to get to know my roommates, so I decide to take advantage of the library's late hours. As I walk across the dark parking lot, I feel a set of eyes on me from inside a black sedan parked alone in the middle of the lot. Glaring back at the driver, whom I don't recognize, I give him my signature scowl and continue past the car. Weird fuck, just watching students on a Friday night. They really need to increase security around here.

It's quiet in the giant library, but most of the tables are taken by students with headphones and laptops, so I eventually find a lone table in the back where I set up my shit. I have a calculus exam to study for and a bio lab to finish, but there's only one assignment on my mind. Pulling up the shared drive Everly created, I run through the notes we left off on.

There is a shit-ton more in here than I remember. Has

she been working on this since we stopped last week? I know she wasn't doing any of this while we were still together. She would have included me, not to mention we were fucking every spare minute we had together.

Which means she definitely has been working on it this week, which I find interesting, since I know she has to have about two hundred essays to grade in my class alone.

She's found a lot.

Each missing person is organized into folders, labeled by last name and status—missing, found, deceased. Damn, there are a ton now labeled *found*, when I know they had still been missing the last time we worked on this.

There's one folder labeled *Sasha Yates-Missing* with a little lock icon in the corner, and when I try to click on it, it says Access Denied. That's weird. It's possible she locked it by accident, but I can't shake the feeling she did this on purpose. She's hiding something from me.

I have the itch to pick up the phone, but I don't. I could just text her and ask who she is. It could be strictly professional, but once I start that conversation, how do I resist the temptation to go to her house, lie with her in bed, hold her down, fuck her?

I can't. So my phone stays in my pocket.

Instead, I run a Google search of her name. Missing person reports from almost twenty years ago pop up, and I click the image tab to see the girl on the screen. There's a vague recognition, something niggling at me in the back of my mind when I stare at her photo. Why would Everly keep this case locked up? What is it about this one missing person that's worth hiding?

I don't find much else on Yates without Everly's resources, so I move on to writing this paper that's due. I spend the next hour and a half writing the exposé Everly assigned, and it comes together seamlessly. Every detail of this case and every note we took together eases its way onto the page in one superfluous sentence after another. This feeling is rewarding, putting weeks and weeks of work into one document. These are not just facts and claims but a declaration. I don't consider myself a good writer, by any means, but I can suddenly see how Everly commits herself fully to this job.

Five minutes after ten, the librarian has to come over to tell me they're closing, so I pack up my shit and save my progress. Even if I don't get anything else done, I think this is enough to get me a passing grade.

Heading back out to the parking lot, I notice that black sedan is still sitting there. The same stranger's eyes staring at me as I head toward my dorm.

It's probably nothing. But after that attack last week and the growing feeling of unease in my stomach, I'm pretty sure it's not nothing at all.

I only get a few feet past the car when I hear the door open and shoes scrape the pavement. Chills run up my spine as I hear him call my name.

"Cullen," he barks in a commanding tone, one that suddenly transports me to eight years prior, as a little kid sitting on the marble steps of our home as my father called me over to fix my tie.

As I turn slowly to face him, the blood drains from my face.

Chapter 25
Cullen

I CLING to my mother's skirt, the soft fabric clenched in my small fist. Tears stream down my face, and she won't even look at me. There's a drink in her hand, and my father's harsh voice in my ear. He won't stop yelling.

"Sasha, come get him! He won't stop whining."

I don't want to leave my mother, so I clutch her even tighter, trying to attach myself to her body, so I won't be taken away.

When soft hands clasp my sides, lifting me off the ground, I grab anything I can to keep my mother close. The only thing my tiny fingers can reach are the white pearls around her neck. As I'm hoisted away, the necklace snaps, tiny beads scattering across the floor, echoing against the walls and drowning the voices still yelling.

Someone strikes my cheek hard, and I fall silent. The arms around me squeeze tighter.

"You can't hit him like that! He's only a little kid."

"Watch your tone with me. I'm his mother!" my mom snaps, clutching her neck where her necklace once laid.

"Then act like it."

"If you'd like to keep your job as a nanny here, then you better watch your mouth, girl."

"Come on, Cullen," the woman holding me whispers warmly in my ear. Soft lips press against my temple as I'm carried out of the room and into my nursery. I'm no longer reaching for my mother, but nuzzling into the warm embrace of my nanny. It's there I fall asleep.

But when I wake up later, I'm alone in my bed.

And I never see her again.

THE MEMORY IS HAZY, BLURRED AROUND THE EDGES, but it's nagging at me since I found that locked folder on the drive. So many questions swirl around my mind, and it seems I know the right person to ask now.

I'm sitting at a greasy spoon diner on the outskirts of town, rubbing my eyes in case I'm imagining things because my father, the man sentenced to thirty years of prison *eight years ago*, is sitting across from me.

He looks so different, gaunt and gray with heavy bags under his eyes and new wrinkles on his pale face. I can't stop staring at him as he stirs the tiny cups of creamer into his coffee.

"They just let you out early?"

"It's called a pardon. Happens all the time."

"But why?" I ask, leaning back and staring at him.

I have compartmentalized so much anger in the past eight years. Anger at my uncle. Anger at Everly. And anger at the man sitting across from me, the one responsible for knocking the first domino over.

So why am I not raging at him? Shock, maybe?

Or is it because of Everly, because I've already spent so much of this pent-up rage on her that I'm able to sit here with a cool head and feel something other than burning-hot wrath.

"You don't sound very happy to see me," he says, opening his arms and trying to give me that fake charming smile, something I remember he used for the press and clients. Never for me.

"I'm just surprised."

"Well, so was I, to be honest. The lawyers were just working up my case for appeal, when bam—I got the call. I was pardoned."

He goes on and on about getting out, his time in prison, and the entire time I'm seething, biting back my hatred. With a clenched jaw, I stare down at the coffee growing cold in my cup. How is this fair? How is he not serving the time he was supposed to serve? His crimes still exist. Those people are still missing. Some of them died before ever making it back home, and here he sits.

It's not fucking fair.

But what am I going to do about it? Throw my rage at a problem that won't fix anything. Hurting Everly didn't fix shit. It only made things worse because she turned out to be a spitfire who gave me a run for my money. Then things got complicated and now I'm dealing with what feels like a broken heart, and that shit sucks more than anything.

"So, I brought you here for a reason," he says, crossing his arms. I glare up at him, and I search my emotions for anything, but I am coming up empty. The hatred has fizzled, and now I feel nothing for this man who I share blood with. My own father.

"What is it?" I ask.

He lets out a heavy breath and leans forward, speaking in a low whisper so no one hears him. "I'm leaving town for a while. Well, the country, probably. We have some funds tied up in offshore accounts, and I'd eventually like to get the business back up and running. You're my son, Cullen. The business should have been yours anyway. I need you."

My brow furrows. "What?"

"Come with me, Cullen."

"Come with you? Where?" Nothing makes sense, and I feel almost drunk with shock. I find myself suddenly wishing Everly was here.

"I have some contacts in Nassau, a place we can stay until we get the business going again. There's a chance we can work a deal, a merger with—"

"No," I bark, interrupting him. "I'm not going to Nassau. I have to finish the semester."

He laughs, actually fucking laughs, and I have to clench my fists under the table to keep from punching him. "The semester? Cullen, what the fuck do you need college for? I want you to be the new face of our company—once we get you cleaned up a little bit." He gives a wave of his hand, gesturing toward my hair and face, as if cleaning me up will erase the last eight years of my life.

My teeth grind as I lean toward him. "What do you mean we have money? Do you have any fucking clue what I've been through?"

He looks offended, glaring back at me with the same fury-laced expression. "What *you've* been through? Cullen, I've been in prison."

"Yeah, for *your* fucking crimes. I was just a kid."

"Show me some goddamn respect. I'm your father, you little asshole." I can feel the eyes from other patrons at the diner as we argue through seething whispers.

"Yeah, my father who left me without a fucking dime. You think you were in prison? Do you have any idea how Uncle Frank treated me while you were gone? He beat the shit out of me for years, while you were storing offshore funds, and left me to starve. He used to piss on me when he was drunk. He sent me into crack houses for him when I was only twelve, so he didn't have to risk being shot."

"Keep your fucking voice down," he growls at me.

I'm so full of pent-up rage, I have to bite back the urge to hurt him. So instead of pummeling his face with my fist, I jump up from my seat. Pulling out my wallet, I throw a ten on the table to at least cover the coffees and a tip.

"I don't have to listen to you, and I certainly don't owe you shit. Have a nice trip to Nassau. Just leave me the fuck alone."

As I turn to leave, I have so much energy running through my veins. I am already reaching for my phone, ready to call Everly, maybe ask her for a ride. Or maybe I'll just get an Uber to her house, so I can unload all of this anger on her like I know she wants me to.

This shit makes so much sense now. My anger toward Everly was never really anger at all. It was about control. When my life was out of control, she gave me what I needed. Something she *wanted*.

I *almost* make it to the door, free and clear, but his words stop me before I do.

"You've been listening to that bitch reporter, haven't you?"

I freeze. Turning slowly and walking back to the table, I glare at him. "What did you say?"

"Yeah, I heard she was teaching at your school. I even heard you were in her class. I knew she couldn't keep her bitch nose out of our business. Tell me, son," he says, gesturing to the open chair, "what lies has she been spreading now?"

My blood runs cold just from the mention of her.

"You've been spying on me," I mumble, moving toward him. "Spying on *her*."

"You? Yes. You're my son. Of course, I had people watching you. And that bitch created so many waves she has a lot of people on her back who want to shut her up, Cullen. Be smart. Now, sit."

His command feels like a threat, and I still can't shake this eerie feeling that getting rid of my father isn't going to be as easy as I had hoped. So, I take a seat and glare at him.

"You were responsible for that attack at her office," I say without question.

"From prison? Grow up. How could I possibly do that and why the fuck would I care?" He looks so unbothered, so nonchalant about this. "Listen to yourself, Cullen. She's gotten in your head. She's been manipulating you to believe whatever she says, to make you hate me, I'm sure."

"I hated you long before she came along," I seethe through clenched teeth.

"I'm sure you did. Does she have you convinced there's more to the story, Cullen? Has she been asking you questions to get more dirt on me?"

The only sound in my ears is the pounding of my heart in my chest and every single heavy breath I take as I think back to everything Everly and I have been talking about. The missing person reports, the cold cases from eight years ago. Everly never got any of that information from me. She wasn't using me. He's just trying to see something that's not there.

Then I remember the locked folder in the drive and I glare up at him. "Who is Sasha Yates?"

He flinches, his eyes betraying him for only a moment, before he squints at me. Then he forces a cruel laugh. "Oh God, what story is she trying to conjure up there?"

I can't let him know that I know nothing about her, but this feeling that everyone knows something I don't is really starting to piss me the fuck off. Letting my fury bubble to the top, I slam my hand against the table. It rattles the cups and brings the entire room to silence.

"Who is she?"

"Why don't you ask your little girlfriend, Cullen? She's the one keeping secrets, isn't she? I assume if she wasn't, then you would already know that Sasha Yates was your nanny. I'm not guilty of any other crimes that I haven't already been convicted of. Sasha was a brat, your mother hated her, and she got herself fired. Took off when you were only five and I didn't bother going after her."

I feel the eyes on me from everyone in the restaurant as my nostrils flare. Why would Everly keep that from me? Is he right? Is she trying to find a story? Is that all I am to her?

For so long, I've been in control of Everly West, and suddenly, I feel very out of control, almost as if she is the one now holding it all. If she wanted to relive her glory days, dig up more dirt on my family, then she had the perfect weapon to do it—me.

Why would she wait so long anyway? Why was me being in her life suddenly the perfect time to bring all of this back up?

My father snickers again, and I lower my head, hiding my expression. All of a sudden, I'm stuck in the middle again. Just like when I was ten, all of the ash from this fire settles on me.

"You don't want to go to Nassau and get rich, fine. Go live your pathetic little life, Cullen. I don't give a shit. But stay away from that bitch before she tears this family apart again. She will use you for a story and throw you away like trash."

This time, he's the one to stand. He waves to the waitress before he heads to the door, leaving me alone in the diner. And just like that, he disappears into the night, leaving me with more questions than answers and more rage than I've ever felt before.

I still have my backpack from the library, so I quickly open it and pull out my laptop. Then I wave the waitress over, apologize for causing a scene, and order a fresh coffee.

Then, I get to work.

Chapter 26
Everly

Hate doesn't exist. I've come to believe this idea down to my soul. Hate is a cloak we use to hide many other emotions—fear, jealousy, anger, resentment, love. Hate is such an easy escape from facing whatever it is we're trying to avoid.

My fingers trail over the image of a ten-year-old boy I once thought I hated, and I finally come to terms with the real feeling that was coursing through my veins all those years ago. Cullen Ayers represented everything I was meant to overcome. He was born from evil, self-righteousness, and cruelty. I hated him because it made me feel better about myself. It made me feel *better than him.*

And when he walked into my classroom eight years later, I hated him because he had the audacity to overcome when he should have failed. I brought his entire family to its knees, but Cullen did not let that ruin him. He worked even harder, lived through hell, and when the opportunity arose, he brought that hell down on me. And I can't blame him for that.

My life was chaos until Cullen showed up. I never

knew what I was looking for until I met him, someone to quiet the noise. To match my fire with their own. I thought Cullen was my curse, but now I realize, we couldn't have been better matched. He desperately needed an outlet for his anger, and I needed to *be that outlet.*

But it's too late now. We were a fire that fizzled out too fast. And I'm left with the burns to prove it. This heartbreak, this *missing* him is torture. I don't think this was Cullen's plan. If I'm being honest, I don't think his original plan involved *him* getting invested either, but it happened. If he ever wanted to hurt me or make me pay, he did just that. He's ruined me.

"Are you sure you don't want to come?" Thomas asks as he ties his shoes by the front door. As promised, my best friend has sat by my side all week, but when he mentioned meeting up with the twenty-year-old from the dinner party again at the farmers' market, I couldn't possibly keep him from that. Knowing Thomas, he's probably missed out on a lot of sex this week because of me.

"I'm sure, thanks. Have fun."

"Get off your computer for a while. Maybe get out of the house."

"I have so many essays to grade." I'm currently seated on my couch in my pajamas with my laptop and a giant cup of coffee, with no end in sight. "Sadly, this is how I get to spend my weekend."

"Sounds fun. Don't wait up," he adds as he leans down to kiss the top of my head.

"Don't worry about coming back here tonight. Go have fun with your new man."

"Oh, don't worry," he replies with a wicked smile. "I will."

After he leaves, I make it off the couch to shower and

get dressed. My eyes need a break from the computer screen, and my brain needs a break from the train crash that is those poorly written essays.

When I sit back down, this time with a glass of wine instead of coffee, I notice a new email in my inbox. My heart seems to stop in my chest when I notice the name.

Ayers, Cullen.

I couldn't possibly click on an email faster. There's nothing in the email body, but there is an attachment. I don't stop as I open it and start reading. My eyes scan through the essay faster than my brain can read. Tears pool in my eyes as I make my way through the article. *It sounds like him.* It sounds like he is speaking to me, and it makes every wound feel even fresher.

The urge to reach out again is hard to resist. When I try to find my phone, I realize it's not next to me where I thought it was. I must have left it in my bedroom. It's lying silently on my bed, and I pick it up in a rush, eager to call him, but I notice two missed calls and three texts, all from Thomas.

THOMAS: *HAVE YOU SEEN THE NEWS?*
  Thomas: Everly, answer your phone!
  Thomas: I really don't want to tell you this over text.
  Thomas: Ayers is out of prison.

I STARE AT THE LAST ONE FOR SO LONG, I NEARLY DROP the phone. My heartbeat thuds loudly in my ears, but I don't look away from the message, trying to make sense of it.

Ayers is out of prison.

George Ayers, the man sentenced to thirty years for his heinous crimes.

Cullen's father.

Questions swirl around in my head, erratic and disconnected. His lawyers actually pulled it off. I can't believe it. It's only been eight years. Does Cullen know? Am I in danger?

My phone screen pops up with Thomas's picture and begins buzzing, jolting me from my deep thoughts. Quickly, I hit the green button and hold the phone up to my ear.

"Thomas," I say immediately, because I know he's worried and I feel a tinge of guilt for making him worry.

"Sweet Jesus, Ev. Answer your phone next time. You scared the shit out of me!"

"Why are you so freaked out?"

"Why? Maybe because the very powerful criminal you put in prison eight years ago is a free man now, and you just so happen to be fucking his son."

I wince. "Thomas!"

"Now's not the time to tiptoe around this shit, Everly. I'm coming back to the house."

"No, don't. I have to find Cullen."

"Not alone you're not."

"Thomas, please. He has a rugby game today. I'll be in public. I need to be the one to tell him, unless he already knows."

"How could he *not* know? It's his father."

Because if Cullen knew, George Ayers would already be dead, but I don't tell Thomas that part.

"How the fuck did he get out so early?" I ask instead, grabbing my purse and heading out the door with the phone pressed between my ear and shoulder.

"He was pardoned. Some political bullshit for sure. The paper is going nuts."

The journalist in me is usually desperate for a story and would do anything to be in those offices now, putting together a story, but I can't stop thinking about Cullen.

"Keep me updated, Thomas. I want to know everything."

"Stay safe, Everly. I'm serious. Find Cullen, don't go near Ayers, and check in with me."

"I will, I promise."

When I hang up with Thomas, I call Cullen, but it rings six times before going to voicemail, which I don't bother leaving. He wouldn't listen to it anyway, and it's not quite how I want to tell him. His game is on the Florence campus today, so I peel out of my driveway, heading that way.

I have no idea how he's going to take this news. I know he hates his father, so I don't know if he'll see this as an opportunity to tell him how he really feels about him or if he'll be as livid as I feel that the man is not doing the time he really should be doing.

When I get to campus, the game is almost over. Running to the stands, I scan the pitch for that familiar mop of white hair and black tattoos. But he's not on the field, and he's not on the bleachers. Pushing away the frantic fear that is blossoming in my gut, I run over to where the coaches and other players stand.

"Coach!" I yell, grabbing the attention of a man with a Florence U hat staring at the clipboard. He looks annoyed as he glances up at me. "Is Ayers playing today?"

"Never showed up," he mutters, before turning back to the players and making a call toward the field.

Don't panic. Don't panic, I tell myself, but it doesn't work. Cullen doesn't miss games unless he absolutely has to, so this can't be a coincidence. My mind starts racing through scenarios that do not help my mental status. Instead of envisioning the worst, which mostly involves either George or Cullen dead, I imagine that he's just avoiding the press.

As I drive from the game to his dorm, finding it empty, I imagine him somewhere so full of fire and rage, he's boiling over. I imagine him needing *me*. Why, I have no clue. Why I care at this point after everything he's put me through, I really don't know, but I do care, and I can't help it.

The last place I look before going back home is the restaurant, but the girl up front told me he's not on the schedule today, and the last time she saw him was the night before when they cut *him* loose around eight-thirty.

"He was having a bad night," she says, and I nod because I agree. I was here last night, and he wasn't himself. He was a broken version of the Cullen I know.

Leaving the restaurant, I head home, checking my phone and the news as often as I can at red lights. He doesn't respond. *Cullen, where the fuck are you?*

My question is answered as I pull up to my house. Relief hits me like a tidal wave when I spot him sitting on my porch. His backpack is sitting at his side, but when he lifts his head and glares at me, the relief morphs into tension. The look on his face tells me he already knows everything.

Chapter 27
Everly

AFTER I PUT the car into park in the driveway, I step out slowly and approach him like he's a wild animal.

Our eyes meet as I get closer, the connection shrouded with intensity.

"You've heard the news," I say carefully.

"I saw him last night."

My eyes widen. "You did? Are you...okay?" He saw his father, the man he hates more than anyone. This isn't quite the reaction I was expecting, and I just keep watching his expression for some sign that he's okay.

"Can we talk inside?" he asks, without answering my question.

"Of course." Quickly I walk past him and unlock the door. He stalks past me, dropping his backpack on the coffee table next to my laptop. Without a word, he starts unzipping it, and I quickly place a hand on his arm. He's acting so strange, not quite full of the anger I expected. Instead, he's contemplative, and when he glares at me, it's as if he's searching for something, looking at me for the first time ever. He's looking at me like he doesn't know me, and it chills me to the bone.

"Are you okay?"

"I'm fine," he mutters.

"Why weren't you at your game today?"

Without answering me, he turns toward his backpack, pulling out his laptop. "Cullen, look at me," I beg, pulling his arm. Suddenly, he snaps, jerking it away. And I realize that Cullen isn't *not* angry, he's just masking it well. He's keeping it tucked away, holding the storm back until he's ready to let it break.

"Am I just a fucking story to you?" he growls.

My brow furrows. Wait, he's mad at *me*? "What are you talking about?"

"Maybe you started teaching at Florence U just to get to me. Maybe you just wanted another piece of the Ayers story so you figured out how to fuck the son."

My jaw nearly hits the floor it falls so fast. "First of all, *you* forced yourself into *my* life, remember? And you know for a fact, Cullen, that you were never a story to me. Did your father tell you that? Are you really going to believe him?"

"I don't know who to believe anymore!" he shouts.

"Yes, you do," I mumble in response. "Cullen, you know that whatever happened between us was real. It may have started with revenge and hate, but we built trust."

"Then who the fuck is Sasha Yates?" The air stops in my lungs, the room going completely still as I stare at him. I locked him out of that folder for a reason, but even I can admit that the only reason I let him see the locked folder was in hopes that it would bring him back to me. Under different circumstances, it probably would have. But if George got to him first...

Cullen learned the truth from him and not from me, which means he will never trust me again.

"I wanted to be the one to tell you, Cullen..."

"Well, I figured it out on my own," he snaps, and I wince. "Sasha Yates was a fifteen-year-old runaway, expected to be pregnant when she disappeared from Hartford, Connecticut. I found this picture," he says, opening his laptop. It's already open to a photo I found last week. It was taken in one of the Ayers' hotel chains, and I know that it was taken about three weeks before Cullen was born.

In the photo, a young, dark-haired girl trails behind a stoic-looking Mr. and Mrs. Ayers. There is an unmistakable mound under her shirt, while Valerie shows off a flat belly, looking nowhere near close to giving birth. It was a hard image to find because the Ayers kept Cullen's birth discreet and must have paid the photographers a lot of money to have the photo pulled from the papers.

"You've seen this photo, haven't you?" he grinds out. Out of all the times Cullen has lost control or looked so filled with rage he would combust from it, they didn't compare to the way he's staring at me now.

Except I see so much more than anger. I see regret, pain, self-loathing, and fear. Mostly fear. I see the young boy in the courtroom behind the eyes of a man who was never able to grasp at anything good in his life before it was ripped away.

"Yes," I whisper, tears pooling in my eyes. A line has been drawn between Cullen and the rest of the world. Just when I thought I had crossed over to his side, I'm being shoved back.

I hate that he's finding out about it this way, today of all days. All of the rage Cullen has been suppressing lately has just come boiling up to the surface.

"So you know who this woman is?" he asks, and I have to bite down the shards of glass building in my throat.

"She's your biological mother." A single tear falls as I watch his face. He figured this out on his own, sometime during the night, and it breaks my heart to think of him grappling with this truth alone. I didn't want this for him.

"How long did you know?" he seethes.

I want to lie. I really do, but I need to build back his trust. "A couple weeks," I answer, and he reacts as if I've stabbed him in the chest with the truth. I guess in some way, I have. I kept this from him because I knew it would hurt. I knew how much he adored his mother, and learning that she had only taken him from his birth mother seemed like a cruel truth that could wait until he was better prepared to accept it.

Suddenly, the laptop falls with a bang to the floor and his hand is around my throat, shoving me hard against the wall. I'm reminded of the look in his eyes back when this all first started, that lifeless gaze he wore when the rage had taken over.

He wears that same expression now.

But I am not afraid, not like I was then.

I've lost Cullen's trust, and when he has so few people to trust, he needs to know he still has mine. Cullen needs to regain control, and I'm in the position to give it to him.

My hands clasp at his shirt, and I squeeze the fabric in my fists. "Cullen, please," I beg.

With moisture pooling in his eyes, he sneers at me. He's on the edge, ready to lose it. "Why would you keep this from me? Of all people...you."

Pain radiates through my heart at the way he's breaking. Because I betrayed him, kept something from him, and now I regret it all.

"I'm so sorry," I mumble, looking him dead in the eye. With my hands still clutching his shirt, I pull him closer.

"I fucking hate you," he growls, a single tear falling down his cheek. With his hand on my throat, he shakes me, knocking me hard against the wall.

"You don't hate me, Cullen. You want to, but you know I would never hurt you."

"You fucking lied to me." The grasp of his fingers around my neck loosens as this war wages inside his head, and at this moment, I actually don't want him to let me go. I want the opposite.

"So make me pay." His gaze flickers from my mouth to my eyes as my words register. I surrender. I won't fight it. He has all of me, all of my trust, all of my body.

"You don't want me to hurt you, Everly." The fire that burns between us has finally reached a temperature I don't think either of us could survive. But I'm done trying to dull the flames. I'm ready to just have everything out between us, and hopefully, on the other side, he will be able to forgive me and himself.

"Come on, Cullen. You're angry. Give me your anger. I can take it."

His mouth slams against mine so hard, I'm sure it'll bruise. It takes me by surprise, as he owns my mouth in a possessive, harsh kiss. Thrusting his tongue into my mouth, I remind my body to give up the fight, and he dominates me. I have to trust that he won't take it too far. I have absolutely *nothing* to base that on, but I will do this for him.

When he bites my bottom lip, a shock of pain makes me panic, and I let out a whimper.

As his rough hands slide up my body, it's like he owns it. Every inch he claims with his demanding touch: grasping, squeezing, pinching. It's a pain laced with pleasure and anticipation. I realize at this moment, I don't really know what Cullen is capable of, especially when he's so lost in his anger the way he is now.

Adrenaline pumps through my veins as he tears off my shirt, moving his mouth down my neck to my chest, nipping at the flesh of my breasts. It's such a mix of good and bad, it makes my head spin. His touch is brutal, and my body shouldn't be warming up to that, but the moisture in my panties doesn't leave room for lies. I want this. I want it exactly like this. I let out a scream as he takes my nipple into his mouth, biting so hard tears spring to my eyes.

In a frantic motion, he flips me around, and I plant my hands hard against the wall. My body tremors as he tears down my pants until I'm naked in his hands. My heart is beating rapidly in my chest. And when he drops his hand roughly between my legs to palm my sex, I cry out. The feel of him touching me is terrifying. He has me at the most vulnerable spot, but I don't fight back, and he knows it. Right now, I'm his.

"This is all you're worth to me," he says, before plunging his fingers inside me. It's rough and fast before he takes them back out, rubbing the evidence of my arousal across my lips.

"Why are you so turned on by this? You're more fucked up than I am," he growls against my ear.

"I guess I am," I reply, fighting against my heaving lungs to form words. There's a flash of lightning against my ass as his bare palm lands harshly, creating a sting that vibrates through my body.

Grinding his hips against me, I feel the rock-hard erection in his shorts. "This isn't like last time, Everly. It's not for you, it's for me."

Pressing my ass back against him, I'm practically

begging him to fuck me, and I want to tell him, but I don't. He doesn't need to hear how bad I want it. He needs to know he's in control.

His shorts come off quickly, and then I feel him there, pressing against my core. With a harsh grip on my hips, he slams inside me, pounding rough against my flesh. My body flinches from the sudden penetration, but he pulls me back, thrusting again. And he was right. It's nothing like before. We're not connecting on a deeper level or savoring the feel of each other. He's fucking me hard without emotion.

No, there is emotion. It's resentment and rage and dread. He's fucking me in frustration, and like he said, this is for him, not me. Still, my body responds, purring under the almost violent, overwhelming motion of his thrusts.

"Harder," I gasp before I catch myself. He picks up speed, filling the room with the sounds of our bodies slamming together. I don't even cry out when sparks ignite every nerve in my body, throwing me into a silent fit of pleasure. I keep quiet, keeping my orgasm to myself.

Just when I expect to feel him pulsing inside me, he jerks his body away from mine. A warm hand pinches the back of my neck hard, forcing me to my knees and slamming them against the hardwood.

Then his cock is between my lips, forcing my mouth open so he can thrust himself inside. He goes deep, hitting the back of my throat before I can take a breath. Panic flashes through me before he pulls out again.

Holding my head hard, he fucks my face again, pounding against the back of my throat until I choke.

"Do you trust me, Everly? Do you trust me not to suffocate you on my cock?"

My hands grasp his thighs, and I give him a squeeze.

Then I force my gaze upward, just as he shoves his cock hard down my throat again.

I do trust him, and maybe that's stupid. Maybe this is how I die, choking on him because I made the unwise decision to hand myself over to my predator, but these are the only cards in my hand, so I'm playing them. If I win, it will be worth it.

Tears flow down my cheeks without stopping, and saliva drips from my chin as he continues to thrust against my throat. But I don't stop him as he closes my airway again and again. Just as I start to feel lightheaded, he pulls out, and I nearly collapse gasping for air, but he holds me upright, letting his cock spill cum all over my face.

There is agony written all over his face. He stays that way for a while, both of us catching our breaths and letting our heartbeats settle.

Then, he gazes down at me as if he's seeing me for the first time.

"Fuck," he mutters.

Suddenly, he collapses on the floor next to me. It's so unexpected, a cold chill runs up my spine. He's staring at me, his face red from exertion, and I don't know if I should run or fall into his arms.

His shirt comes off in a quick swipe, and then it's running across my face, cleaning up the remnants of what we just did. Once he has my face clean, he slumps down with his back to the brick wall. Neither of us say a word for a while. He doesn't look so angry anymore—he just looks tired, exhausted really.

After a minute, I reach for him, swiping a stray hair away from his sweat-soaked forehead. He flinches, pulling away from my touch.

"You know I was only protecting you," I whisper.

"Why the fuck would you protect me, Everly? After everything. It doesn't make any fucking sense." There are tear tracks across his cheeks, and I itch to pull him closer, but he won't let me touch him.

My bottom lip trembles, moisture pooling against my lashes. "You know why, Cullen."

There's a moment where I'm afraid he's going to run, a fight-or-flight response. He could run from this, from me, or he could face what he needs to.

But he doesn't run. Instead, he gathers me into his arms, and I melt easily into his body, burying my face in his neck. I don't know what this means, but for now, it means he stayed, and that's enough.

Chapter 28
Cullen

EVERYTHING HAS SHIFTED BETWEEN US. We're not the same people we were at the start of the semester. I don't even care about the article she wrote or the case against my dad anymore. Maybe I never did.

I was up all night at that diner, finding more than maybe I was ready to find, but I actually spent most of the night going over every fucking minute with Everly, trying to find the exact moment everything changed. Was it the first time we fucked? The night she stroked my back after a nightmare? The first time I felt her bend, giving me that silent green light I needed.

This shit isn't fucking healthy. If I care about her at all, I can't keep losing my shit like this, taking it out on her, no matter how much she wants it.

"Are you okay?" I whisper against her head.

She nods. "Are you?"

I nod in return. She looks up at me, and her face is a mess. Makeup is smeared down her red cheeks, and her eyes are bloodshot. I did this to her, because I was *mad*. Fuck, what is wrong with me?

I stand up, carrying her naked body toward the bathroom. Setting her on the counter, I turn on the shower. Things feel strange between us. Our fight, the way I yelled and the things I said, is lurking between us as a reminder that we are fucked up. I keep touching her face and her neck, my chest so full of emotion I didn't expect.

As I pull off my pants, I find my phone in my back pocket. Opening it up, I go straight to the settings.

"What are you doing?" she asks.

"Taking off everything I was using to track you. I don't need it anymore."

She doesn't say a word as I remove the apps and every other invasive thing I put on here to keep tabs on her, to control every part of her life. Then I find the photo I took on that first night. She watches as I click the trash icon.

"Stop!" she screams, grabbing my phone from my hand.

"I don't want it anymore," I reply, staring intensely into her eyes.

"I want to keep it," she whispers. Those big brown eyes stare up at me, soft and begging, and there's only a beat of silence, letting her words sink in before I gather her naked body up against mine.

"We can keep it," I whisper back, wanting her to know how I feel, hoping she reads between the lines. Holding her face in my hands, I reach my lips down to hers, kissing her softly, afraid I'll hurt her.

I almost ended things today. Last week, I was so sure I needed to be rid of Everly. Then I almost lost her, for no good fucking reason, and it shook everything I thought I believed.

It rocked the foundation, making me realize I need her more than I need revenge or justice or payback. I just *need her*.

When her lips find mine again, her kiss is hungry. Lifting her in my arms, I carry her into the shower, and the heat of the water barely matches the temperature of the fire burning between us.

"Did I hurt you?" I ask.

She holds my face as she stares up at me. "You didn't do anything I didn't want."

"I always feel like I'm losing control with you."

"But I trust you not to really hurt me, Cullen. I know I lost your trust today, but I needed you to know you have mine."

My lips find hers again, and they taste so good, the warm pulse of her heart against my chest, the steady reminder that I'm not alone. And my new drive to claim her, own her, be her everything is different now. I need her to give herself to me, so I know she is mine and I am hers. Neither of us are alone anymore.

I take my time washing every inch of her body, kissing the parts I know I hurt. My thumb runs over the red spots on her neck that I held too tightly. Then I lean in and press my lips there, trailing them down to her chest. When I reach the pink tips of her breasts, I pull each one into my mouth, sucking until she lets out a soft moan.

Once we are both clean, I carry her into the bedroom, dropping her gently on the bed. We don't bother drying off. There's no point. My cock is already hard again for her.

My heart aches, like it's raw and hurting, and the only cure is her. I need to right my wrongs.

Sliding down her wet body, I kiss a trail from her neck to the apex between her legs. As I slide my tongue ring through her folds, she lets out a sweet moan. Taking her clit into my mouth, I suck until she's writhing. I crave her pleasure like oxygen, and it drives the same need in me as when I used to crave her pain. This hunger is visceral.

While I assault her clit, I slide my index finger in and she nearly levitates off the bed. Her fingers dig into my hair, eliciting a bit of pain, and it only drives me harder.

"God, Cullen. Don't stop."

I'm fucking ravenous between her legs, watching every muscle in her body for a reaction and when she tenses or moans, I do it again. Picking up speed, I take her to the point of ecstasy. When she yells out, her body spasming and her lungs holding in her breath, I memorize it. Sliding a second finger in and hooking it until she's shaking, I let her body ride through the orgasm. It's fucking beautiful.

"I need you," she whispers, pulling me up until I'm lying on top of her again. She draws my face to hers for a kiss, tasting herself on my tongue. I take her hands in mine, pressing them above her head and pinning them to the mattress as I slide inside her.

Her back arches and she cries out. It's a delicious sensation, but I need more. I need everything with her.

Kissing her collarbone, I lick up the water clinging to her skin from her neck to her earlobe. Every moment our bodies are fused makes me feel whole, like she is the piece I was missing.

"I want you to come inside me." She tilts her hips, grinding herself on me. Her arms wrap around my neck, our lips pressed together as our bodies move in one fluid motion.

"Fuck, Everly..." I moan.

One hand clasps the back of my neck, her tongue soft in my mouth. The other hand travels up my body, raking her nails across my abs, and my body breaks out in chills.

"What are you doing to me?" I say. My fingers bury themselves in her hair, loving the momentum of her body.

She keeps it up, and I feel myself breaking, but still, I try to savor this.

She pulls away from the kiss for a moment and stares up at me. "Give it to me, Cullen. Give me your pleasure."

She winds her fingers in mine, clasping our hands firmly together as I thrust harder. When I feel myself shuddering and fighting it, she squeezes my hand even tighter.

With our mouths pressed together, I cry out, "I'm coming." The climax spreads through my body, lasting forever as it clamps down and breaks me, shattering every fragment of who I am until there is nothing left.

Until I am nothing but hers.

When the pleasure finally subsides and I can breathe again, we fall against the sheets together, and she kisses me everywhere, moving from my ear to my jaw, and I steal her lips, piercing her mouth so she knows I need her.

Holding her tight to my body, I kiss her forehead. In the quiet dim light of her bedroom, she whispers, "Does this mean you forgive me?"

I let out a heavy sigh. "You first."

"We have to put everything behind us. Can you do that?"

There are so many words left unspoken on my lips, but I'm not fucking good at expressing them. This shit isn't easy for me, and maybe it's just from the exhaustion or high emotions of the day, but I feel my lips spilling my heart's secrets before I can stop myself.

"My whole life I've leaned on hate to get me through everything that happened to me. I hated my dad, everyone who put him away, my uncle, you..." I add, looking down at her and catching her eyes in the small shred of light leaking through the curtain. "It was easier that way. But this...whatever this is...it feels better. It's just scary for me, Everly.

What if I'm wrong? What if I've been too terrible to you already and you can't find a way to forgive me? What if I fall and you don't? I don't have any more room in my life for pain. I don't want to feel alone anymore."

Leaning up on her elbows, she stares at me, and I remember for a moment that she is older than me. Until this moment, I had forgotten. The reminder doesn't exist in every moment of our lives, so when I do remember that to her I'm just a kid, I search her features for a sign that she sees me like that. But it's never there.

"You're not alone, Cullen, and I do forgive you. And whatever *this* is," she says, gesturing between our bodies, "I think you know what this is, and it's not hate, not anymore."

Pulling her forehead to mine, I hold her close, letting myself enjoy this moment of being so connected to another person. It's scary as fuck, knowing if I end up alone after this, it will hurt that much more, but she is so fucking worth it.

Chapter 29
Cullen

WHEN I OPEN MY EYES, the sunlight is gone, and the space in the bed next to me is empty. I sit up and search the dark room for her. Then I hear the clicking sound of her fingers against the keyboard of her computer coming from the living room, and I let out a sigh of relief. Getting out of bed and throwing on my boxers from earlier, I wander out of the room to find her.

"Ev," I mutter, rubbing the sleep out of my eyes. "What time is it?"

She's at her desk in one of my old T-shirts huddled over a cup of tea. "It's almost ten. I didn't mean to wake you."

Damn, I slept all day.

"What are you doing?"

"Nothing," she replies, quickly closing the screen. She turns back to look at me, a nervous expression on her face.

"What was that?"

"You don't want to see it."

"Bullshit, Everly. What was it?"

Taking a deep breath, she glances back at the screen.

"Well, I found out more about that woman..." Her voice falters as she avoids my gaze.

"My biological mother," I say, finishing her sentence.

"We don't know for certain—"

"Yes, we do. Everly, if you've done the research and that's what you think, then I believe you."

Her chest rises with a heavy breath as her gaze finally settles on mine. The tension between us melts like wax, clearing the air. Grabbing the second chair at the table, I pull it around, so I'm sitting next to her.

There's a screen up with a missing person's photo. It's the same face I stared at last night, my nanny—or I guess, my mother—and as I stare at the photo on the screen, I see a familiarity that makes it hard to breathe. She has crystal blue eyes, dark hair, thick, dark brows, and full lips. Any hope that she could have just been a surrogate is gone now. I look just like her.

"She disappeared from her home at fifteen when I assume she found out she was pregnant. She was hired by your dad, and less than a year later, you were born. Then around the time you were five, she was just...gone. But I don't think she just disappeared, Cullen."

"What? You think he...killed her?"

Without outright answering me, she turns back to her computer. "I still have access to the database at the coroner's office from when I worked at the paper, so I pulled up the unidentified bodies report in that year, and I came up with these twelve women. Most are drug-related, and half of them have been identified since. But then I found this..."

Her hand freezes over the mouse, and I wait for her to move it.

"Everly."

"I want to warn you. There are photos, Cullen."

"Have you looked at them yet?"

"No," she says flatly.

"Are you afraid to see a dead body?"

She glares at me, and I trace my knuckles along her jawline.

"I've seen plenty of dead bodies. I just...I don't know if I want *you* to see it."

Leaning down, I brush my lips against hers. "I can handle it."

With my hand on her leg, she clicks through the case file. It was a woman, guessed to be about nineteen, cause of death: asphyxiation. As Everly opens up the photos tab, I hold my breath.

And as the girl's photo appears on the screen, Everly trembles and looks away.

It's her. Same dark brows and full lips.

"Are you okay?" I ask, glancing at her, and she stares back at me in shock. Jumping from her chair, she crosses the room.

"How can you ask me if I'm okay? That's obviously her."

"I felt the way you reacted seeing that photo." As I approach her, her shoulders melt, and her eyes soften.

"Because it's her, Cullen. It's the girl in the missing person's photo, the girl in the hotel lobby with your parents. That's your mother, Cullen."

"I understand that."

She presses her hands to her face, a shutter in her breath, and I cross the empty space between us to pull her against me.

"This is all my fault," she cries against the bare skin of my chest. "I didn't mean to dig all of this up, and now you have to deal with it. It's not fair."

"Hey," I pull her face away and force her to look me in the eye, "I can handle it."

"No, Cullen. You're not handling it. You're bottling it up, pushing it down, letting it fester and morph into something nuclear that will only detonate later. I can't—"

My arms release her as I step away, suddenly grasping what she's telling me. "You shouldn't have to deal with me again when I snap. I get it."

"No!" She grabs me by the arm, dragging me closer. "If you don't want to lose control later, then don't bottle it up now. Last night...you opened up to me. You were vulnerable. Don't shut down on me again."

"It's not that easy, Everly. I had no one. A dead mom. A dad in prison. A shitty, abusive uncle. I don't know how to open up. I've never done it before."

She places her hands on either side of my face, penetrating me with her warm gaze. "You just found out that you have been lied to your whole life. Your parents aren't your real parents. Your biological mother was a victim of human trafficking and died a violent death. I can see how this would lead you to anger, Cullen."

"I'm tired of being angry."

I can't resist the urge to finally bury my face into her neck, as if I'm trying to let her tiny body absorb me. Our chests are so close, I feel her heartbeat against mine, so that the only sound between us is the cadence of our breaths, and I don't want to leave this space.

But eventually, she pulls away. "So where does that leave us?" she whispers, without looking at me.

"I don't know. I think that's up to you now."

As she finally gazes up at me, I look first at her lips, trailing my eyes to hers.

"If none of this happened, if your father and the case

and the story about your mother was gone, would you still say that? Would you still want me?"

"Why would you ask that?"

"Because, Cullen. It's the thing that binds us, and I understand your anger toward me became passion, but my heart is attached to you, to us, and I want to save myself the pain now if your interest in me is only tied to that passion."

My patience snaps, like the last single thread of a rope. As I snatch her into my arms, I hoist her onto the bed, covering her body with mine. Putting my face directly in front of hers, I speak clearly so there can be no mistake. "I know I'm eighteen, but I'm not a child. I know what I want, and the only thing my interest is tied to is you. Last week, I found you lying on the floor of your office unconscious. And do you know what went through my head when I thought you had died?

"I told myself I never gave you anything good. I was cruel to you because it was the only way to be with you. Every time I forced you to be near me, I did it because I wanted you so bad, I didn't know how else to have you."

My lips crash against hers, and her hand latches around the back of my neck, holding me close. It's not a kiss of heat and passion—it's more like a declaration.

I'm done being angry.

Chapter 30
Everly

I CAN'T TELL if Cullen is taking this news well or if he is bottling it all up again. We're lying in bed, letting the news about Sasha Yates settle on us like a heavy blanket of snow. It's so unfair, it makes me ache for him. Just when he found his real mother, he loses her. He may not be filled with anger, but I am.

"What now?" Cullen asks.

I don't know how to answer that question. There is too much attention around George Ayers's highly unconventional pardon to make a story about Cullen's biological mother, not unless we can pin him for murder. It's too much for just us to handle on our own. I don't think he's going to like this answer.

"You deserve to get back to your normal life, Cullen. Focus on school and rugby."

"And just let him go?"

"What choice do we have?" I ask, touching his face.

We've slept on and off, both of us feeling restless and anxious. I've tried to grade papers, but I'm too consumed with worry for Cullen to do it.

As he clutches my hand, he looks intensely into my eyes. "I understand why you did it now, Everly. I finally get it. But we can't let that asshole get away with this. Do what you do best. Do what you did eight years ago and uncover every filthy fucking secret about him."

Shifting toward him, my heart hammers in my chest. "You realize if we do that, then we'll have to go through it all again. It will be a nightmare dealing with and enduring the court case once again."

"Yes, but this time," he says, kissing my knuckles, "we have each other."

I gaze into his eyes, tears brimming in mine, and I feel more certain than ever that whatever this is, it was meant to be. Leaning forward, I press my lips softly to his. He's come such a long way, and I hate to drag him back down that road, but he's right—we have each other now. And I won't leave him.

"Okay, but you have to help me."

For the rest of the day, we do exactly what Cullen suggested. We compile everything we can, and even though it's not enough to convict his father of murdering Sasha, it's enough to open a case. Bringing Cullen into the process with me feels cathartic for him. Uncovering his birth mother's past, her family, and then of course, the truth about her death.

Tomorrow, I'll call my contacts at the FBI, and maybe Thomas can help me talk the *Florence Times* into letting me write the story.

It feels good, like we're moving in the right direction.

"Let's get out of here for a little bit," he says, taking my hand. "Let's go to dinner. We never go out together."

"What if people see us together?" I say with a laugh. "I'm still your teacher, remember?"

"Not for much longer. We can go somewhere out of town, if you want. I just need to get away from all of this for a while."

He's right. We've been in my house for the whole day and most of yesterday. We need to just get out and enjoy normal life while we still can.

"Okay," I say, "I'll get dressed." I kiss him, loving the easy smile on his face. It's the same as it was before, but the pressure of the past is gone. He doesn't feel the need to hate me anymore.

We're both so desperate to be outside, we end up getting tacos from a food truck and eating in the back of my SUV with the seats folded down and the trunk open. We're just outside some city park, where people walk their dogs and kids play on the playground equipment. It's so completely normal, and I love it. For a few minutes, we're able to forget everything that's happened this weekend and what's about to come because, like I told Cullen, our lives are about to be uprooted again. We'll be pulled into the public eye and who knows where our lives will go from here.

"Why didn't you go into witness protection?" he asks, as he balls up his garbage and throws it into the bag. He's reclining on his side, while his opposite hand softly skims my leg. Sitting cross-legged across from him, wearing his sweatshirt, I can only shrug at his question.

"Would you do that?" I ask.

"Only if I could stay with you."

"Cullen..."

"What?"

I hate this part, where I have to remind him of his age and how different our futures look. Things are good *now*, but he wants to live in fantasy instead of reality. I hate it because I want what he's suggesting, but I can't let myself get lost in the dreams of an eighteen-year-old. Having those dreams ripped away from me would be devastating.

"I know one day you'll move on from me—I can live with that, you're still so young."

His brow furrows at my words and he just stares at me. Warm hands roam my back as he pulls me closer. "What makes you think I would ever want anyone else?"

"I won't lie to myself, Cullen. You're eighteen. I'm thirty-two. You have your whole life ahead of you. I don't expect you to stay with me forever."

Pulling our foreheads together, he says, "You are so stupid, Everly."

A laugh bubbles up from my chest. "When all those college girls throw themselves at you on the rugby field, you're going to be fine coming home to me? I'll be thirty-five by the time you graduate college."

"You're the freakiest woman I've ever been with! We've had more nasty, crazy sex in the last month than I've had in my entire life. Why would I want anyone else?"

I can't deny that. It's true for me too. It's strange the way I like things with Cullen, the imbalance of power between us. After every bully and overbearing man I've dealt with in my career, it seems so wrong to me. But when I submit to Cullen, it's almost a relief. He takes my power, but in return it's like he gives me freedom from my own mind. It's kinky and crazy like he said, but there's nothing inherently wrong with it.

"Your whole life? How long have you been having sex?" I ask with a smile.

"I don't know...since I was fifteen."

"Fifteen?" I shriek.

"I told you. I was six-three by the time I was fifteen, but that didn't mean I knew what I was doing."

I laugh again, covering my cheeks as I'm sure they are growing embarrassingly red. "Well, anyway. That's just sex, Cullen. I'm talking about more than that."

"So am I, Everly. I hated my life before you came along. I was miserable. But you gave me a home, a real home. I don't want to go back to what I had before that."

I think back to that version of Cullen I met just a few months ago, the boy so full of anger and resentment, he was willing to burn the world down, even if he was the only one left standing. But underneath all of that anger was pain.

It tears me up to think about anyone hurting him the way his uncle and his father did. I wish I could erase all the years of torment he endured, but I can't. All I can do is give him the future he deserves.

Biting my lip, I run my hands through his hair. It's growing out fast, the dark roots getting thicker, and I can't decide if I want him to grow it out and go back to jet-black or dye it again so he remains the same. This is *my* version of Cullen. "And what if we could stay together? What would that look like?" I ask, lying down on my back with my head in his lap and my legs kicked out toward the open hatch.

"Fuck this place. I want to go somewhere warmer. Like Florida or Arizona. And we have to have a yard because I'm getting a dog."

"A dog?" I say with a laugh. "What kind of dog?"

"I've never had a dog," he replies with a boyish smile. "I think something small at first, like a Jack Russell Terrier or a bulldog."

"You've been thinking about this, haven't you?" I can't hold back my grin as he talks. His hands are in my hair, stroking his fingers softly through the strands. The air is getting cooler, but it's warm in here. The sun is going down, bathing the park in cool, hazy light.

"I have been thinking about it. I want a girl, and I'd call her Lucy."

I laugh. "Lucy? For a dog?"

"Yeah, I think it's a good name."

I touch his fingers, pulling them to my chest, so I can link them with mine. I don't think I've ever been happier than I am at this moment, talking about a perfect future with the one person I never thought I could see a future with—even if it is a fantasy.

Even if this dream only lasts one month, it's worth it.

He looks down at me, his gaze searching mine. There are words hanging on his lips, and I'm waiting as I stare back up at him, but just when I'm expecting him to say something, he looks away and clears his throat.

"We should get back. I need to be inside you again and I don't think those kids over there need a show like that."

I force a smile. "Yeah, best not to get arrested today."

On the entire drive home, he holds my hand and I think about Cullen with a real, happy home. It's all worth it if he can have that. Another court case, reliving everything, for Cullen to finally be happy, I would do it all in a heartbeat.

Chapter 31
Everly

"I DON'T HAVE any clothes for tomorrow," he says as we pull onto my street.

"I can drive you to campus early, so you can get something before class."

He seems to contemplate this for a moment, but doesn't seem to like that idea. It's really no surprise that this eighteen-year-old boy doesn't like waking up any earlier than he needs to.

"I'll just drive back real quick and grab something."

"Are you sure?" I ask, pulling into the driveway.

"It'll take, like, thirty minutes." He leans across the center console and plants a kiss on my lips. "You better be naked by the time I get back."

"Yes, sir," I reply with a smile. Just as I try to pull away, his hand snatches me by the back of the neck and drags me closer for a rough kiss that has me turning into liquid in my seat. He tastes like minty gum and the metal from his piercings, and I let out a hum as our tongues tangle.

"Are you sure you don't want to wait until morning?" I ask in a breathy gasp.

"Go inside and get yourself ready for me. I want you wet, naked, and kneeling by the door. Understand?" His voice is a husky growl against my mouth. The wet part is already taken care of.

Opening my eyes, I gaze up at him through my lashes. "Yes, sir." This time it comes out with more sincerity, and the lust burns between us like an inferno.

Somehow, I drag myself out of the car. He moves to the driver's seat just as I reach the front door. Sending him one more smile, I unlock my door and disappear into the dark house.

There's a small light coming from the table next to the couch, and I kick myself as I realize we must have left the candle burning when we left. We were both so excited to get out together, and Cullen is so damn obsessed with my apple and cinnamon candles. I should be glad it didn't burn the damn house down.

The candle flickers, and I jump. The tiny flame provides just enough light to cast a shadow moving across the wall. I freeze with my hand on the living room lamp.

"Don't move."

My blood turns to ice in my veins.

"Who's there?" I ask in a shaky whisper.

Before I get an answer, there's a blinding light from a flashlight being shined directly into my eyes. I squint, trying to see beyond it, but it's impossible.

"Have a seat, Miss West."

The flashlight's beam tracks to the chair in the corner, and I shakily move toward it, sitting down with my purse clutched to my side. The gruff and angry voice sounds distantly familiar.

"Toss your purse," he barks at me, and I obey.

Terror has filtered every rational thought out of my

head. All I can think is that I'm going to die, and that I'm glad Cullen isn't here.

Just then, a light flicks on in the kitchen, and there's not an ounce of surprise in my brain when I see the man staring back at me. He looks so much older—I assume prison aged him. He has the same mean scowl and receding hairline.

When he flicks his hand, I see the black pistol aimed directly at me, and I am consumed with cold fear.

"You've been busy," he says, moving toward my laptop sitting on the coffee table. Cullen's is on the couch, half covered by a blanket. "I bet you think you're so smart, Miss West. Finding out everything about Sasha Yates. Then bringing my son into it. You're nothing but a meddling bitch."

I swallow down the fear that has me frozen in my place. "I didn't bring Cullen into it. He found out everything about her himself."

"Because you pushed him to!"

"So I assume the attack in my office was your doing too," I reply.

"I never hired that thug to attack you. I hired him to scare you. He was just supposed to mess up your office a little. You just happened to be there, and I admit, I was pleased to hear he nearly killed you."

"Oh, well, thanks for your mercy," I snap.

"I'm done with mercy, Miss West. You're going to make it very fucking easy to kill you," he sneers, and I have to bite down the whimper that wants to escape my lips.

There's a feeling that sweeps over you when you're facing down death. It's not fear as much as regret. I don't see the past events of my life flash in front of, but I do see the dream Cullen painted in the car tonight. And I *feel* it. I feel his arms around me at the end of every night, coming home with him, kissing him every morning. Shutting my eyes, I fight back tears as I wait for the end.

And sadness washes over me as I realize I'll never see him again. He'll be back here in less than thirty minutes, and I hate that he'll have to find me here like this. I hate that his life will never be spared from tragedy. It's so fucking unfair.

But if I draw this out any more, I risk Cullen getting here before George leaves, and I can't risk that.

"Go ahead then," I say, no longer keeping the tremor of fear out of my tone. "Get it over with."

The smile that stretches across his face draws the bile from my stomach. As he takes aim, and I tense in my seat, a tiny red light from the security camera catches my eye. I forgot the camera is even there, and it's only because of Cullen's recent obsession with tracking me that I even bother to remember it exists and that it's wired to a cloud, which means all of this is being recorded.

Even if Cullen has to move on without me, evidence of my killer exists, and he won't have to fear this man anymore. That's the last thought that crosses my mind as the gunshot goes off.

Cullen is finally free.

Chapter 32
Cullen

I CAN'T SEEM to drive away from her house. Sitting in the driveway, staring at the dark windows, my stupid fucking heart is so caught up in the shit I *should have* said. How fucking dumb is that?

I almost let my guard down. While Everly and I sat in the back of her car, and my big mouth started blabbering on about futures and dogs and picket fucking fences, I almost uttered the three words that I swore to myself I'd never say to a girl. Why? Because that's huge. Saying you love someone is like letting them have the most vulnerable part of you. And I want Everly in my life and in my heart, but it's like there's a mental block keeping me from letting it go.

I regret it. I should have said it.

Maybe after I have her naked and panting beneath me, in post-orgasmic bliss, I'll finally tell her how I really feel. Maybe she already knows.

If I walk in there right now and tell her, she'll think I'm fucking nuts. So I'll wait.

I get as far as putting the car into reverse, rolling just halfway down the driveway, when I change my mind. Fuck it. I haven't ever had anyone in my life I truly fucking loved. My parents were selfish assholes, my biological mother was taken from me before I knew her, and my friends are barely a blip on my radar. But I fucking *love* this woman—like, I'm so goddamn obsessed with her and I used to hate her. Knowing my luck, I'd get in a fatal car crash on my way back from the dorm and I'd never have the opportunity, so fuck it.

Throwing the car into park, I leave it running, and I don't even take the time to slam the door shut. I bound up the two steps of her porch and just as my hand touches the knob of the front door, I hear a voice that stops me in my tracks.

There's a man in her house. Not just any fucking man either...

It's like a block of ice dripping down my spine as I press my ear to the front door. "You're going to make it very fucking easy to kill you."

"Go ahead then. Get it over with." The terror in her voice goes straight to the bones and muscles in my body that push me through the door in a rampage. I don't think, I just act.

The gun goes off, and I see red. I don't register pain as I careen toward the man in Everly's living room. We crash into a tumble over the table next to the couch as I throw his body to the ground. The table flips and Everly screams, but I barely notice any of it because I'm hyperfocused on my fist pummeling the face of the man who keeps trying to fuck up my life.

He tried to take what was mine. And I've spent enough of my life losing people to him, letting him take my mother and now Everly. I'm a burning fire of rage as I pound hit after hit on his face.

When something lands hard against my face, I realize he's still holding the gun. When I tumble over, I feel something hot against my back. Looking back, I see a wall of flames crawling up the dark curtains of the living room.

Everly coughs somewhere across the room, but I'm too worried about the man with a gun. He's disoriented, blood gushing from his nose as he tries to stand, but I'm faster.

When I move to get up, a burning pain in my side stops me, so I jump toward him instead, wrapping my arm around his neck as I use my other hand to force his pistol-holding hand toward the ground.

We struggle for control as the room begins to fill with smoke. The inferno spreads from the curtains to the walls so much faster than I expected it to erupt.

"Cullen!" Everly screams. "We have to get out of here." She coughs again, and I feel her at my back, pulling me toward the door.

But the old man is too strong and won't give up the fight.

"Just go!" I yell, but with every inhale, I lose the ability to breathe and my chest bursts into harsh, aching coughs.

Instead of listening to me, she grabs his gun-holding hand and helps me to disarm him, but he's holding on to it too tight, and we're running out of time.

"Just fucking go, Everly!" I yell, but she won't listen.

I can't drag him out of here like this, and I can't let him go. If we stay like this for much longer, we're all going to pass out and burn.

"Please go," I groan with the little oxygen I have left.

My side burns and my head is getting light.

Suddenly, I'm on my back, tumbling again with George, but I don't let go of his hand. The house doesn't even exist anymore—it's only fire. There's a hard punch against my stomach, and the pain that was already there intensifies, and it's like I'm being split in half. He lands another hit to my stomach and then one to my face.

Once I feel the cold metal of his gun to my face, I know it's over. I stare through the smoke into the bloodshot eyes of the man I once thought was my father, and I try to grab at the gun before he can end me.

Suddenly, Everly is there. She is nothing but a flash as she swings something hard against George's head. He falls with a thud against the ground, and I gasp for air.

"We have to get out of here *now*," she says, pulling my arms to stand, but I am made of lead and pain. I don't have enough strength in my body to even budge from my place on the floor.

"Hurry, get out," I mumble, but I'm not even sure if I'm making sense.

She doesn't leave—of course, she doesn't fucking leave. Instead, she hooks her hands under my arms, and she drags me inch by inch across the floor. We're both going to fucking die here, and I'm so goddamn disoriented I can't tell the ceiling from the floor.

"Please, get up, Cullen. Please," she cries, and she sounds so fucking sad that I try. I do try, but it's so goddamn hard. My feet shove against the floor, and the best I can do is a dizzy crawl on my side.

"That's it, baby. Come on. Stay with me."

When I gaze up at her face, she is framed by smoke and fire. She's so beautiful—big brown eyes and full lips. I know I must be losing it because I want to kiss her at this very moment. Instead, I think about what I was coming in the house to do in the first place.

"Everly, I fucking love you," I whisper as my muscles give out and my body collapses again.

"Dammit, Cullen. I love you, too, so get the *fuck* up."

The next thing I know, I'm being lifted. There are hands and lights and other voices before a cool breeze hits my skin. Then, it's like she can read my mind, because the last thing I remember is Everly's soft lips touching mine and a crystal-clear view of the sky.

Chapter 33
Everly

"MA'AM, PLEASE CALM DOWN."

"I've given my report to the police. I've waited and waited. I've done everything you've asked. I just want to know how he is."

"Are you family?" the nurse asks, looking at her computer. This is just another day at work for her, not the worst day of her life.

"I'm the only family he has," I say, holding back the constant sobs that want to shake through me. "I'm his girlfriend."

I see the way she's scrutinizing me. He's too young for me, I get it, so I just send her an eye roll and plant my hands on the counter again. "Listen. I'll leave you alone if I could just get an update. The ambulance hauled him away almost three hours ago and I don't know if he's dead or alive, and I'm just trying to find out what's going on. Please, I'm begging you." I'm sobbing in earnest now, causing a scene in the waiting room, but I don't care.

Every moment that goes by is torture; the endless waiting, knowing he's in there somewhere, either in pain or dying or looking for me, and I can't stand it.

If he doesn't make it...

No. I refuse to think that. It can't end this way. It was never supposed to be him.

I barely registered what was happening after Cullen burst through the door, but I know that if he hadn't, I would surely be gone. When the firefighters arrived, he was dead-weight, pale and lifeless—a vision I will never get out of my head. I could tell by the bloodstain on his shirt that he had been shot when he surprised George. It didn't stop him from fighting him to the ground, keeping him from killing us both. But by the time I was able to knock George out, Cullen was so weak and tired, I'm afraid it was too late.

Last I heard, they were able to pull George out too, but I haven't even bothered to check on him. If they're not going to give me an update on Cullen, why would I care about George?

"Okay, ma'am. Let me see what I can do." The nurse gives me a sympathetic look with tight lips and soft eyes.

"Thank you," I mumble, wiping my tears on the back of my sweatshirt. No, Cullen's sweatshirt. She disappears behind the wide double doors and I take a seat, trying not to look at anyone else waiting around me.

It feels like an hour goes by before the nurse comes back out. "Miss West," she calls. I jump up and stare at her, wide-eyed and hopeful. "Follow me," she says quietly, and my heart hammers in my chest.

Scrambling behind her, she leads me through the triage corridor and down a long hallway with rooms on either side. "He's asleep and hasn't been moved to his room yet, but the doctor said you could at least see him."

When we reach a room at the end of the hall, she

stands aside and lets me walk in. My hand flies to my mouth when I see him. He is pale white, gaunt, and covered in dirt and soot. Bandages are wrapped around his head from his fight with his father—err, I mean George. There is an IV at his side and blood running through the wires to his body.

Tears pour out of my eyes as I rush toward him. I can't even touch him, afraid I'll hurt him or wake him up, so I settle for standing near him, finding comfort in the beeping of the machine that tells me his heart is beating.

"Is he going to be okay?" I ask the nurse, who is still standing at the door.

"The doctor will come in shortly to talk to you, but for now, he's stable."

A wave of relief floods through me. I softly drift my fingers down his arm, wishing he could open his eyes and look at me, but for now, I'll take what I can get.

A few moments later, the doctor comes in and goes through his injuries and what his recovery will look like. He's already been through surgery to repair the internal bleeding from the gunshot wound. He also suffered a concussion, four broken ribs, and some second-degree burns on his arms and legs.

Not long after she leaves, they come to take him to his room upstairs. I don't leave his side for a second. It's almost three in the morning when I pass out on the small lounge chair in his room. In the morning, they take him in for another procedure, leaving me alone in the room.

"Holy shit, Everly," a familiar male voice calls out. My eyes peel open to find Thomas standing in the doorway. In the next breath, he's rushing toward me, holding me tight in his arms while I sob.

"Are you okay?" he asks. I nod. I know I look terrible,

covered in grime with red eyes and filthy hands. "Did you get checked out by a doctor?"

"I'm fine. I just inhaled a little smoke. The paramedics cleared me."

"Where is he?" he asks, looking around.

"Back in the burn unit for a procedure."

"But they said he'll be okay?" The genuine look of worry on my best friend's face is heartwarming. I'm sure he never truly approved of me and Cullen, but he's supporting me regardless. Like friends are supposed to.

"Yeah, this one won't be long."

"Come to my place and shower. I'll get some food, okay?"

"That sounds like a perfect idea," the nurse says from the doorway. "I will call you if anything changes."

Thomas drives me to his house and pushes me directly toward the shower. Once I get out, there is a stack of his clothes on the counter that I climb into, and then I settle on his couch. The people at the hospital gave me Cullen's phone before I left, which they had found in his pocket. I stare down at it, feeling a hit of emotion when I see the image on the lock screen.

It's our first kiss.

We've come so far since that day, both of us. We came from such a place of toxicity and pain. But deep down, I think we were both trying to fill a void left from that court case eight years ago. He wanted to find a family and I wanted to find purpose. If anyone had told me back then how it would end, I would have laughed, but here we are.

When I get back to the hospital, I hear his voice as I get off the elevator. Rushing toward his room, I hear him mumbling, "Can you just call her, please?" When I round the corner, our eyes meet, and the tears start to well up again.

Gasping, I drop my purse on the table and run to his side. There aren't as many wires or tubes anymore, and his right arm and leg are both bandaged. But he's awake. Before I can stop myself, I lean down and press my lips to his. He hums against the contact.

"Are you happy now?" the nurse behind me says, "I told you she'd come back."

"Are you giving your nurse a hard time?" I ask, my face only inches from his.

"He woke up an hour ago and has been begging me to call you ever since," she says, her voice laced with humor.

"I just wanted to see you," he mumbles.

"He's on a lot of pain meds, so he's being a little feisty."

I let out a quiet laugh. "He's always feisty."

Cullen's pupils are dilated and his skin is still a little paler than normal, but he can't seem to tear his eyes away from me.

"Well, I'll leave you two alone. He's got another two hours before his next dose, but buzz me if you need anything."

As soon as she leaves, I sit on the side of his bed, clutching the fingers of his good hand in mine.

"Nurses said he survived," he says without hesitation, and it takes me a moment to realize he's talking about George Ayers. He feels miles away from us already.

"It doesn't matter, Cullen." Reaching down, I wish I could run my fingers through his hair, but it's still hidden in the bandages. "There is enough evidence against him now. He's going back to prison."

His eyes search mine for a long time, and I'm sure the

drugs are making it hard to process this news. Finally, he mutters, "It's over?"

"It's over," I reply, kissing him again.

A heavy exhale leaves his body as he lets his eyes close. His fingers squeeze mine, and I can't help the smile that tugs on my lips. The dread and the fear dissolve into thin air just like that. Cullen still has a long road left in his recovery, but we can finally focus on the future. The past can't hurt us anymore.

Chapter 34
Everly

A couple months later

"What are you working on?" I ask, crawling carefully onto the bed next to Cullen. He's lying against the headboard with his laptop open. I notice the way he winces as he scoots over. He's still so sore and he had physical therapy today which I know tires him out quickly.

"The email again," he replies grimly, putting his arm around me to pull me close to his body.

I rest my head against his chest and read the words on the screen.

Mrs. Yates,

I hope this email finds you well. By now, you have heard the news and know that your daughter gave birth to a son eighteen years ago...

"Too formal?" he asks.

"A little," I reply, looking up into his eyes.

"Fuck it." He selects the text and hits *Delete*. Then he quickly types out:

Hi Mrs. Yates, I'm your grandson. Sorry.

"Cullen..." A laugh bubbles up from my chest.

"I hate this," he mutters, resting his chin on the top of my head. It's been a lot; I know that. Finding out your biological parents aren't who you thought and then having to reach out to a family you don't know, who tragically lost their teenage daughter almost twenty years ago. It's heavy, and I wish he didn't have to deal with this.

"Do you want me to do it?"

"No," he groans. "I'll figure it out."

"There's no rush, you know." My arms wrap around his middle, being careful around the sore spots. All of the stitches have come out and his burns are still covered but are healing nicely. "I'm sure she's trying to figure out how to write that email too."

The article about Sasha Yates and her baby just came out, and as predicted, it was huge. The story went viral, and we've been trying to lay low since. Along with George's second impending trial, Cullen and I don't even want to leave the house. Luckily, Cullen has been able to take his classes online, and I've been able to keep my teaching job at the university.

He closes his laptop and sets it on the bed next to him. We're still staying in the rental while my house is under construction. It was almost completely demolished, but with the insurance money, we chose to rebuild. I have too many good memories in that house, and I like the idea of building a new life in the ashes of the old one. A new life with him.

My parents came out for the holidays, and although I know Cullen was uncomfortable with that at first, I think it was good for him to have his first real family holiday experience. They were a little uncomfortable with his age at first, and of course were more than shocked by his appearance, but then they were amazing, treating him like any other boyfriend of mine.

But now the holidays are over, the new semester has begun, and it's time to move on. I can tell we're both ready to get back to regular life.

"So...what did the doctor say?" I ask, letting my fingers cascade down his chest.

Cullen waggles his eyebrows at me with a sly smile. "He said when I'm feeling up to it, I'm cleared."

"And are you?" I ask, pressing my lips to his neck, tracing the black designs crawling out of the collar of his T-shirt. It's been so long since we've been able to do *anything*, and it's been literal torture.

He grabs his shirt in his fists and tears it off in a quick swipe. "Does this answer your question?"

Grabbing the back of my neck, he pulls our faces close in a rough kiss. But when I lean against his body, he winces in pain, and I pull away in a rush. Guess he spoke a little too soon.

"Motherfucker," he grunts, grabbing his side. Placing my hand over his, I kiss him a little softer.

"I think I have an idea," I whisper, letting my lips trail down from his mouth and chest to the scar on his abdomen. Lifting his hand, I kiss the stitch marks, and he hums in response. Moving my mouth a little lower, I reach the hard bulge in his sweatpants.

"Think you can handle this?" I ask, pressing my lips against his cock through the fabric.

"Fuck, I hope so," he whispers, running his fingers through my hair.

"Tell me what you want, Cullen," I mumble darkly. Ever since the fire, I can feel Cullen holding back, and I know a lot of that was from his injuries and the dramatic change in the course of his life, but little by little, he's coming back to me.

So my body lights up in excitement as he gathers my hair in a harsh grasp, a biting pain in my scalp as he pulls me to his face. "I want you to choke on my cock, Miss West."

"Yes, sir," I breathe. He yanks my head back, and my lips part as he kisses me again. I make sure not to rest my weight on his body, and when he shoves my face back to his crotch, I drag down the waistband of his pants and find his cock already leaking at the tip.

When I swallow him down, he lets out a room-shaking groan. And while I move my mouth to the rhythm of his gentle thrusts, the hold on my head changes from harsh to gentle. By the time he comes, warm jets of cum hitting the back of my throat, he's caressing my scalp and covering me with praise.

"You're so fucking perfect," he mumbles. "I love you so much."

I quickly use his discarded shirt to clean myself up, and crawl up to rest beside him as he recovers.

"I hate this," he groans, pulling me tight against him. "I just want to fuck you already."

Holding him close, I smile against his chest as I hear his

breathing change as he begins to relax from his orgasm. I do wish he could fuck me already too, but he doesn't see it the same way I do. I thought I lost him that day in the fire, and every day together is another day he heals and returns to the same Cullen I fell in love with. I know we have so much ahead of us, so I can be patient.

Leaning up on my elbows, I kiss him again, moaning into his mouth as he strokes my jaw. Pulling away, I smile down at him. I'm struck for a moment by the intensity in my chest that I feel when I sometimes look at him. It still amazes me that we ended up here, especially when I look back at where we started.

For so long, I kept chasing this dream in my work, trying to find the excitement that I felt when I wrote that article about George Ayers. I had no idea I'd find it in someone like Cullen. We work so well together but in the strangest way. I love him for the way he dominates me and for the way he softens. I love him for the fierceness and the tenderness.

Cullen lit a fire in me when we met, and for the first time in a very long time, I am excited for our future. I will always burn for him, now and forever.

Epilogue
Cullen

A LITTLE OVER a year later

PEEKING THROUGH THE WINDOW IN THE DOOR, I notice the room is dim as the PowerPoint presentation is projected along the big wall at the front of the room. Quietly opening the door, I sneak into the lecture hall and take a seat in the back row. No matter how discreet I try to be, her eyes still find me mid-sentence. It'd be hard to miss me. My hair is still stark white, and there are a whole new batch of tattoos up my neck.

A subtle smirk pulls at her lips as she continues her lecture. Biting my lip, I watch her teach the same lesson I've listened to about twenty times already. My class ended twenty minutes ago, and I'd rather wait here in her class than go to the library or drive the car home.

After she dismisses her class, I stay in my seat, waiting for the room to clear out. She packs up her things and turns back toward me with a sly smile on her face. Without a word, I walk down the steps and close in behind her as she's sliding her laptop into the case. My lips find her neck and kiss a line up to her earlobe.

"I should report you to campus security for this," she whispers.

My fingers find my way into her hair, pulling back until she lets out a moan of pain. "Do it and you'll get punished."

"Is that a promise?" she asks with a dirty smile.

"I love it when you wear this skirt," I mumble against her skin. My fingers pull the skirt up until I see the round peaks of her ass pressing against my pants.

"Someone could walk in, Cullen." She gasps as my hands slide along the thin line of her thong, tracing it to the front and dipping my fingers underneath the soft fabric.

"That's the fun part," I joke as I pull her face back, so I can kiss her. She melts in my arms, especially when I slide a finger inside her.

"Lock the door," she pants.

"No chance. We're just going to have to risk it."

When she grinds her ass against my cock again, I know she's not stopping me. She won't outright tell me to fuck her, but that's part of the game we're playing. She's the dirty professor, and I'm her student, talking her into something she knows she shouldn't be doing.

I make quick work of my belt, tearing open my zipper until my cock is out and touching her soft warmth. After pulling her thong aside, I slide in easily, and we both fill the silent room with our moans. Her hands clutch at the hard wood of the desk as I pound into her. The tight grip I have on her shoulders gives her leverage to rock herself back toward me.

"We'll get caught," she moans.

"I know you want this," I reply, pushing her down, so her hips are high and I can fuck her even deeper. She can't keep in her cries now, but she tries, moaning into the top of the desk. I reach into my back pocket and pull out my phone, quickly opening the camera and swiping it to the video option before clicking the red button. I have a perfect view of her ass slamming against me, and I pan the camera to her face. She stares back at the screen, biting her lip, and it's so fucking hot I almost blow right there.

"Keep quiet, Miss West."

Her body shudders, and her cries reach a pitch so high, I know she's about to come.

"Yes, yes!" she cries as quietly as she can.

I can't stop my climax either, and suddenly, I'm spilling myself into her. Jerking my hips hard with her hips in my hands. Sweat beads on my forehead as I pull her back up, so I can kiss her again. I slide out of her, and she turns so she can wrap her arms around me.

"I love it when you come to my classes."

"I love coming to your classes too."

After she cleans up and we stop by her office to get her stuff, we head toward the car. "What do you want for dinner?" she asks as we climb in.

"Tacos?"

"That sounds good," she replies, and I watch her as she starts the car, pulling out of the parking lot and heading to our favorite taco truck. We have settled into the same rhythm we were in a year ago before the fire. This was the life I wanted, the one I nearly died for. This life is safe and easy after nearly a decade of hard.

It's been a long road to this point. The house took almost six months to rebuild, but it was worth it to finally be able to move back in together. There was no talk of me staying in the dorms. She wanted me close, and I wasn't about to argue.

Once I found out George was arrested and the whole ordeal was behind us, I finally felt free to move on. With Ev's help, I finally sent the email. Miranda Yates responded immediately, sending pictures of her and her husband, their other two children and seven grandkids. We had a video call over the summer, and it was strange, but I felt the familiarity in all of them immediately. I'm not ready to see them in person yet—it's still too much to process—but I know when I am, Everly will be there.

The case against George for Sasha's murder is still ongoing, but I'm not carrying that weight anymore. I'm done with other people's burdens.

After picking up our order, we go home, and as we pull into the driveway, I spot a very happy face peering at us from the window. Lucy starts barking before we even get out of the car.

"I think she missed you," Everly says with a laugh.

Heading into the house through the garage, I greet the barking black-and-white pup by hoisting her into my arms and letting her lick the shit out of my face. We picked up Lucy a few months ago after we moved back into the house. I'm clearly her favorite, but I also give her everything she wants.

"If you let her kiss you like that you can forget about kisses from me," Everly says with a face full of disgust.

Letting out a laugh, I set the dog down and gather Everly up in my arms. "What makes you think you get to call the shots?" She lets out a squeal as I force a harsh kiss on her face, but when she manages to force me off of her, she slaps me.

We settle on the couch with our dinner and watch the football game on TV. It makes me miss rugby. The physical therapist says I should be good to start playing again next season, but I'm not getting my hopes up. It was a small price to pay for this life. I would have jumped in front of a hundred bullets to save Everly, so it's hard to miss rugby too much. I lost my scholarship, but Ev helped me apply for more, so with that and financial aid, I'm able to keep working on my degree at Florence U, even though I still have no fucking clue what that will be.

The game is turning out to be a landslide win, so I get bored with it, pulling out my phone. My finger goes straight for the videos and I open up the one I filmed today. When Everly's moans of pleasure blare from the speakers, her head snaps in my direction.

"Cullen!"

"What? You didn't think I'd want to watch it?" I ask with a lopsided smile. She tries to swipe the phone out of my hand, but I hold it out of her reach, bringing her almost entirely on my lap. My mouth finds hers and I kiss her to the sound of her being fucked over the desk in the lecture hall.

Dropping the phone, I pull her legs on either side, so she's straddling me. "You have to delete that," she says with a warning glare.

"I can't do that."

"Cullen, if someone finds that... What if you lose your phone?"

"Then I guess you better do what I say then. I need something to hold over your head."

Her eyes wrinkle with a hesitant smile as she glares at me. I rock her hips over me, seeking the friction over my hardening dick. She's just about to come on the video—I can tell by the sounds she's making.

"So, what do you want me to do?" she asks.

"Get on your knees and find out." Running my hand

through her hair, I pull her down so I can nibble on her ear, and she hums in response. Slowly, she slinks to the floor, sitting on her knees between my legs.

"Now what?" she asks in a silky, sweet tone.

"Damn, that was easy. I'll just have to hang on to this video so you can never leave me. You'll have to stay with me forever."

She stares into my eyes. "If that's what you want."

With that, I lean down and press my lips to hers while I mumble, "It is."

Acknowledgments

Thank you for reading *Burn for Me*. I know there were difficult moments in this book, and it's not always something you see in my writing, so I appreciate you making it through.

This was a cathartic process for me, writing Cullen Ayers, putting him through what he went through, and then the same for Everly. I put all of my pain and grief into these characters, but I also wrote all of my hope into them too.

I couldn't have done any of this without my amazing team who I owe more than you know.

My editors, Amy Briggs, Rebecca's Fairest Reviews, and Rumi Khan.

Wander Aguiar and his amazing team for the beautiful cover photo.

My beta readers: Lacey, Adrian, and Amanda - Thanks for talking me through this.

My publicist: Amanda Anderson of Wildfire Marketing Solutions - I'm so glad I found you.

My assistant/rock: Lori Alexander. You work so hard behind the scenes, you keep me afloat, and I couldn't do anything without you. Did someone say spreadsheet?

My Sinners—the best street team in the business.

My soulmate, Tits, for hyping me up when I needed it and keeping me going when I doubted myself.

My husband and kids for giving me room to grow and lots of hugs.

And Rachel. I said you're the best because you are. You showed up when others didn't. You support me, encourage me, make me laugh, and keep me sane. I know we joke that neither of us could make a decision without the other, but it's true. Thanks for being my best friend. I love you. Wolah.

Also by Sara Cate

Wicked Hearts Series

Delicate

Dangerous

Defiant

Age-gap romance

Beautiful Monster

Beautiful Sinner

Wilde Boys duet

Gravity

Freefall

Reverse Harem

Four

Cocky Hero Club

Handsome Devil

About the Author

Sara Cate writes forbidden romance with lots of angst, a little age gap, and heaps of steam. Living in Arizona with her husband and kids, Sara spends most of her time reading, writing, or baking.

You can find more information about her at
www.saracatebooks.com